MYSTERY AT MURRIEMUIR

IAN SKAIR INVESTIGATES

HILARY PUGH

Housemouse Press

Copyright © 2022 by Hilary Pugh

All rights reserved.

No part of this book may be reproduced in any form or by any electronic or mechanical means, including information storage and retrieval systems, without written permission from the author, except for the use of brief quotations in a book review.

❦ Created with Vellum

1

With her tail wagging, Lottie jumped onto a chair, pushed her nose through the partially opened window and sniffed the salty morning air blowing in from the estuary. Dogs had enjoyed lockdown; extra walks, twenty-four-hour company and, in Lottie's case, twice the usual number of delivery men to bark at. She began to growl softly and Ian, not sharing the same enthusiasm for lockdown, glanced through the window hoping that the van that had pulled up at the end of his garden was a sign that it was over at last. He could see from the logo painted on its side that this was not a delivery van but one that, after a wait of many weeks, might contain builders. He'd been waiting for them to start for what seemed like months, although when he counted on his calendar it was only eight weeks. Time passes slowly in lockdown but still, eight weeks was long enough. The builder had sent in his estimate promptly after a quick, heavily masked, socially distanced visit to see what Ian wanted doing. Just putting in a bathroom, doing a bit of decorating, converting his current bathroom into a laundry and decorating the room – once a junk room – that would now be his bedroom. They'd agreed a price and Ian paid a deposit. Prices were rising alarmingly and if he was to keep to his estimate, the builder would need to order supplies *now*. Why were prices rising? Ian had wondered. Brexit, the builder had muttered, and the fact that everyone was working from home and needed extra rooms and loft extensions. Ian was no economist, so he took the builder's word for it and handed over the money. They agreed a date for the work to start. The second Monday in June. So, the weekend before this Ian cleared out the rooms. He carried boxes of all the stuff he'd not known what to do with since he'd moved into the house and stacked it up in his bedroom. The room he planned to turn into extra office space once he'd moved his sleeping quarters to the newly decorated room upstairs. It had been a long, exhausting day but at least he was ready for the builder to move in and start work. Which the builder failed to do. Not that Monday and not the following Monday. He also failed to respond to calls and Ian was about to write off his deposit and start looking for someone else when he got a text from the builder. His wife had been in hospital and he was getting behind but promised to be there the week after next. He wasn't. By mid-August he'd been ill himself and had lost his grandmother. He was either extraordinarily unlucky or taking Ian for a ride. But it was a difficult time for everyone. And people had been in hospital, caught covid and lost elderly relations. Or perhaps the man was a consummate liar and had never intended to do the work. But if that was the case, why was he stringing Ian along like this? Ian had just drafted a mildly threatening letter when the van pulled up at the end of his garden and the builder strode up the path, whistling and blaming lockdown for messing up his schedule. Ian directed him to the back of the house where he unloaded toolboxes and a spotty-faced lad called Dennis, whose job, the builder explained, was to prepare the room for the plumber who would move in next week and install the new bathroom suite. This had been sitting in Ian's garden shed for the last eight weeks while with each day that passed Ian had become more and more convinced that he might just as well cancel the whole project and sell the bathroom suite for whatever he could get on eBay. He'd lived here for two and a half years now and had managed perfectly well without the two upstairs rooms. The only thing that kept him from cancelling was the prospect of moving all his stuff back up there again.

His next-door neighbour Lainie was sympathetic but pointed out that everything had changed since the start of the pandemic, and he should be patient. *She was probably right,* he thought, reflecting on the different ways it had affected people. Builders, it seemed, were making a mint. And for Ian himself lockdown hadn't been too bad. He felt guilty about that. He knew it had been hell for a lot of people. Families suddenly thrown together day after day, trying to work in their kitchens or lofts *and* home-educate their children while worrying about jobs and money and wondering how to make ends meet. All while the threat of a possibly deadly disease hung over them like a dark cloud. He'd escaped all of that. He had always worked from home and his work hadn't dried up. Slowed down a bit perhaps, but there were still people who wanted him.

Eighteen months since the first lockdown. During that time, he'd been busy. Apart from his own clients, he had been working with the police again. Only two days a week, but it was enough. Patrolling parks in Dundee for youngsters breaking lockdown rules wasn't so different from rounding up truants in Leith. He'd been partnered with a young constable just setting out on his career when the pandemic hit, and they both got on well with teenagers. They'd devised a fun social distancing game and by the time the first lockdown was coming to an end the youngsters they had met seemed quite disappointed that they were now allowed to roam free once again.

He and Caroline had formed a bubble. That was not nearly as much fun as it sounded. Caroline was exhausted. She'd not had the luxury of working from home. Her workload had doubled – teaching face-to-face classes of kids of key workers as well as running online sessions and trying to extract work from teenagers who were shut up at home fighting over internet connections. All while battling with advice from the government that was either contradictory or impossible. And Ian didn't dare mention the chaos of exams, or rather their lack. But things eased over that first summer. They'd managed to go away for a week to a cottage in the Highlands, where they slept a lot and occasionally ventured out with the dogs to explore bits of Scotland that were new to them, visiting interesting pubs that were cautiously serving meals in their gardens regardless of the weather.

Christmas that year was the best he'd ever had. His parents had locked themselves away and forbidden any visits from their nearest and dearest until everyone had been vaccinated. Ian and Lainie had spent Christmas Day in the garden, where they wrapped themselves in sweaters and blankets – products of Lainie's passion for knitting – and shared a dinner of roast pheasant and Christmas pudding, which they passed to each other over the fence. As this involved a number of spills, it was probably Lottie's most memorable Christmas as well.

The biggest surprise of the whole eighteen months had been Ian's new best friend. Nigel Burrows, a man who lived on the other side of Greyport and who had pestered Ian, and presumably everyone else in the village, with petitions. Until lockdown Ian had thought of him as an annoying little man who was obsessed with traffic in the village and who regularly held him up when he needed to leave for somewhere with endlessly boring facts and figures about speed bumps and parking restrictions. But people like Nigel Burrows are just what every village needs in times of crisis. Within days of the first lockdown Nigel had mustered a team of volunteers to deliver food parcels to the vulnerable, collect prescriptions and check up on the lonely. It was thanks to Nigel that no one in the village was left worried, scared about where their next meal was coming from or going insane with loneliness. Nigel made sure that everyone had someone to chat to even if it had to be over a garden gate or through a window. He rode round the village every Thursday evening on his bike, cheering as people emerged from their houses to applaud the NHS. All of this he coordinated through weekly Zoom meetings and Ian found himself unwittingly appointed as his right-hand man.

When things began to ease up, Ian and Nigel started meeting at the pub for a chat over a pint. Nigel had lived in the village since starting his first, and as it happened, only job. He had worked all his life for a company in Dundee where, by the time he retired, he had managed an office of twenty-seven employees. His wife had died more than ten years ago, and Ian suspected his frenzied interference in village life was probably the result of loneliness. 'But,' Nigel said, 'life has to go on. I keep myself busy. And I love my little house, and the garden.'

Ian had never been inside Nigel's house, although he had caught glimpses of a tidy, rather dated dining room at Zoom meetings. He imagined a house furnished by his wife when they first married, and probably unchanged in the last forty years. The garden was immaculate; a lawn groomed to perfection, borders where no weed dared show its face, and a regularly trimmed hedge probably free of any kind of wildlife. Nigel was old school when it came to gardens. Nature was there to be tamed.

Ian was surprised to discover that Nigel had a daughter and a grandson, although why that should surprise him, he didn't know. They had moved in with him last spring and the grandson, five-year-old Ryan, now attended Greyport Primary School. Ian asked where they had moved from. Glasgow, he was told and then Nigel changed the subject. He'd not mentioned Ryan's father, so Ian guessed there was history that Nigel didn't wish to discuss. Ian thought it best not to ask any more. He did wonder what effect a five-year-old boy would have on the immaculate garden. Small children liked to ride bikes and play football, didn't they?

Now it was late August. Children had gone back to school and life was cautiously getting back to normal. People were still catching the disease, but far fewer were dying from it. Ian and Caroline had decided not to go away this year. They'd spent the summer in each other's gardens and going for long walks. But now the school term had started again for Caroline, and it was time for him to get back to work as well. There had been a sudden rush of enquiries to his email inbox, and he needed to sift through them. He also had to find a new assistant. He'd meant to do it the autumn before last, when Nick had returned to New Zealand, but he'd put it off during the autumn and by the time he got around to thinking about it the pandemic had started to take hold. But now his paperwork was stacking up again.

Quite literally stacking up, in an untidy heap of cardboard boxes in the office. Well, currently in the office but threatening to encroach into the rest of the house within days. He needed help. Possibly not full time, but after checking his accounts he thought he could afford to pay for twenty-five hours a week.

Today was the day to get on with things. The builder had started work at last and Ian was thankful for that, but he'd left Dennis to get on with it and whatever *it* was, he was making a great deal of noise doing it. It was a lovely day and Ian moved into the garden where he sat enjoying the later summer sun, although the enjoyment was slightly tempered by the worry that the noise would disturb the neighbours, and the thought that the work might not be finished before the weather cooled down and he would need to move back inside to work. But for now, he could relax. Most of the neighbours were also out working or enjoying the sun. And how much noise could there be after the initial search for pipes? He pulled out his notebook and started making a list of what he needed in an assistant. He tried not to think too hard about how good Nick had been and how difficult it was going to be to replace her.

What did he need?

1. *Someone trustworthy and discreet. He couldn't have anyone who would gossip about his cases. Client confidentiality was essential.*
2. *A car owner. He didn't want to confine his assistant to the office. A lot of the work was about going out and watching people.*
3. *Local. It had been useful having Nick in Edinburgh because that was where their client had lived at the time. But he'd had to pay her train fare and although she rode a bike, she'd not been able to go out and about as much as he would have liked.*
4. *Must have IT skills. The information he needed to dig up was more and more online.*
5. *Dog lover. He didn't think he could sit in an office all day with someone who didn't like Lottie.*

So where was he going to find this dog-loving paragon of discretion and efficiency? He thought about posting it to his Facebook page, but so few people ever read it that it wouldn't be worth the effort. He had an idea that he could pay Facebook to target suitable people but wasn't sure how to do it. In any case, he didn't know what he was looking for. He didn't want an advert to go out to thousands of people and he didn't think there was a way of narrowing it down to *people who might want to work for a private investigator*. He had often been oddly targeted himself. It was probably better to leave Facebook to search out people who wanted to know about kitchen cleaning equipment or medication for painful legs or, and this one had really puzzled him, upmarket homes for the retired.

After a little local searching, he uploaded some details to a job search site in Dundee. Then remembering local was good, typed a card to put in the village shop. He also emailed his friend Duncan Clyde. As a police inspector working in Fife, Duncan might know the type he was looking for. Someone like Ian himself, who had retired from the police, could be a possibility.

Dennis had stopped hammering. He was sitting on the ledge of the open window eating a pork pie and swinging his feet in time to loud music on his phone, which he was playing through some speakers that looked like skulls. The music was blaring out not only into Ian's garden, but those of his immediate, and probably not so immediate, neighbours. Ian wondered if it would disturb Lainie and glanced over the fence. He needn't have worried. She was hanging out her washing and dancing in time to *Believer*.

He decided to take advantage of the comparative quiet of the house and went inside to read through his emails. Then, his mouth watering at the thought of Dennis' pork pie, he closed them down, deciding it was time for fresh air and some lunch. He and Lottie would walk to the village, put his card in the shop window and buy his own pie, which he would eat sitting on the harbour wall. After that he would come back and get down to work. Definitely.

2

'I've got some work for you.'

A phone call from Stewart. That was a surprise. Ian didn't see his brother very often and he couldn't remember when they'd last spoken to each other. Well before lockdown, he was sure. Family Christmas was usually the only occasion they met and that hadn't happened last year. He wasn't sure if it had happened the year before either and tried to cast his mind back. That would have been the year of his two most spectacular cases so far. The search for the Drumlychtoun ring in the spring and the mystery of the Lansman murder in the summer. Then he remembered. He'd stayed at home for Christmas that year, excusing himself from family celebrations for reasons he didn't remember. He and Caroline had been at Drumlychtoun for Hogmanay, and he'd driven up to his parents' house in Aberdeen from there the day before New Year's Eve. He went alone, not wanting to inflict his family on Caroline, who was quite happy to stay behind at the castle with the dogs. He remembered sitting down to a tea of overly rich Christmas cake, which had given him indigestion. On that occasion he'd been the only visitor and he was glad about that because it meant he didn't have to stay for very long.

He didn't dislike Stewart. As a small boy Ian had been in awe of his brother. Stewart had been a brave and adventurous child with Ian trying, usually unsuccessfully, to out-dare him. He recalled an incident, a vivid memory of his own failure to measure up to his brother. He must have been seven, Stewart eleven. They had been visiting the home of some distant relative, a farmer who lived in a rambling house with barns and outhouses. Someone had carelessly left a ladder leaning against the wall of one of the barns, a tall building with a hayloft and a steeply pitched roof from which Stewart promised they would be able to see the sea. The coast was several miles away, but Ian was young and gullible, and Stewart had promised a view of pirate ships. He followed his brother up the ladder and they sat on the ridge of the roof until the farmer spotted them and yelled at them to come down. Stewart slid effortlessly down the ladder. Ian remained where he was, paralysed with fear, until one of the young men working on the farm climbed up and carried him down unceremoniously tucked under one arm. It had left Ian with a lifelong fear of heights, roofs in particular.

Ian wasn't sure if Stewart disliked *him*. He suspected that what his brother felt for him was mostly indifference. Stewart was always the ambitious, go-getting member of the family. In that way he was like their mother. Ian had never been very ambitious. And even if he had been, Stewart would have been an impossible act to follow. As soon as he left school – the very same day, if Ian remembered correctly, Stewart had talked his way into an apprenticeship with an oil company, where after a short training he had been dispatched at intervals, by helicopter, out to the oil rigs where Ian had never really understood what he did. Only that he was eye-wateringly well paid for it. His sessions on the rigs ran for six months, after which he would be home for six months. Again, Ian had no idea what he did. In his late twenties and mostly, Ian suspected, to stop their mother's nagging and to give him an excuse to leave home, Stewart married Freya. They moved into an expensively restored period cottage in Stonehaven, a small town south of Aberdeen that had a ruined castle on a rocky promontory and a small harbour where Stewart kept a boat. When not stuck out in the North Sea on oil platforms, Stewart liked to chug up and down the North Sea coast catching mackerel and sea trout.

Ian liked Freya. At first this was because his mother obviously *didn't* like her, but once he got to know her better, he liked her because she was likeable. She was a willowy, arty type with long hair, which she usually wore in an untidy bun on top of her head. She dressed in loose dungarees and tie-dyed t-shirts adorned with mystical symbols. She drove around in a van buying up old furniture, which she then repaired, painted it in fashionable colours and sold as *shabby chic*. They had two children; Lyra and Will. One of them, Ian suspected it was Stewart, was obviously a Philip Pullman fan.

Seeing Stewart's number flash up on his phone was the last thing he expected. It was, however, an excuse to put off work for a little longer. In any case Stewart said he had a job for him, so in a way it was work. Did Stewart even know what kind of work Ian did? The last time Ian remembered talking to his brother about work was when he was recovering from being shot in the leg and the only prospect of a long-term career was as a carer for their grandfather. Ian hoped there wasn't a problem with their parents and prepared to be firm. He'd never begrudged his family-appointed role as Grandad's carer, but he was damned if he was going to do it again. Grandad was lovely. Ian's soulmate. His parents were not at all lovely. If they needed help with their care, they had the financial resources to pay someone to do it for them. But they were not old. There had never been any hint of them needing care. They had ridden out the pandemic with determination. Any virus would probably take one look at his mother and head rapidly for a victim in the opposite direction.

'What kind of work?' Ian asked, wondering if he could claim to be busy right now and unable to take on anything new. But he was a dreadful liar. Stewart would see right through that.

'How are you doing?' Stewart ignored the question. He sounded upbeat and jovial. If he'd been in the same room, he'd probably have slapped Ian heartily on the back.

'I'm fine,' said Ian. 'You? And the family?'

'We're well,' he said. 'But things are changing big time.'

'Oh,' said Ian, wondering why he was being privileged with this information and suspecting the change would be some kind of upward move that would impress their mother and show Ian up, in her eyes, as even more of a loser than he already was.

'Yeah,' said Stewart. 'Got a new job.'

Presumably one with double the salary leading to a bigger house, even more foreign holidays, and expensive private schools for the children. Not that Ian was jealous. 'Leaving the oil industry?' he asked, trying to sound pleasant and interested.

'Got to move with the times,' said Stewart. 'Fossil fuels are ruining the planet so oil's on the way out. Haven't you heard? They're contributing to global warming. I'm moving into offshore windfarms.'

'Still out at sea then?'

'No, working for a company in Edinburgh. Mostly research and admin, occasional trips out to the turbines to see what's going on.'

'You're commuting to Edinburgh?' That was a round trip of nearly three hundred miles. Stewart may be doing well but he doubted that he was doing well enough for his own helicopter.

'We've moved,' said Stewart. 'Bought a house in Fife. Not far from you actually. That's why I'm calling. Freya and I would like you to visit. Come for a meal. Try and behave like brothers.'

How did brothers behave? Were they about to collapse into each other's arms and declare a lasting fraternal love? He doubted it. More likely Freya's idea. 'You said you had work for me?'

'We can talk about that when you come over.'

'Is this a social visit or am I going as an employee?' He could hear Stewart sighing impatiently.

'Come on, Ian. I'm trying to extend an olive branch here. Stop trying to bite my hand off. All I'm doing is offering a nice, friendly evening with the family and the possibility of a bit of work.'

'Sorry,' Ian muttered. He really did need to drop his poor little injured brother act and grow up. 'So where's this house of yours?'

'I'm just sending you the address.'

Ian clicked on the message that arrived with a ping. Murriemuir

House. It sounded rather grand. 'Is Freya moving her business there?' he asked as Stewart suggested a date and Ian typed it into his calendar. It sounded like somewhere that was big enough for a good deal of shabby chic furniture production. Knowing Fife well, Ian thought it was probably an old farmhouse. There'd been quite a few of them on the market recently as land was bought up by big farming conglomerates who didn't need the housing.

'No,' said Stewart. 'She retrained during lockdown as a yoga teacher. She's opening a wellness centre.'

What the hell was a wellness centre? 'Doing what?' Ian asked.

'Oh, you know,' said Stewart vaguely and Ian suspected he knew about as much as he did himself. 'Yoga classes, forest bathing, reiki, that kind of thing.'

'What's reiki?' Ian asked.

Stewart sighed. 'I think it's a kind of hands-off massage thing. Look, just ask Freya.'

He would need to ask her what forest bathing was as well. But he could imagine her doing yoga. She already had the t-shirts. She just needed to exchange the dungarees for some stretchy leggings, and she'd be good to go. Caroline went to a yoga class in Cupar, so he was familiar with the look. She'd tried to persuade him to go with her, but so far he'd managed to resist it on the grounds that he didn't bend easily. He was fond of Caroline but there were limits to a friendship, and spending an evening lying on a rubber mat trying to get his legs round the back of his neck wasn't something that appealed. He'd stick to dog walking and occasional Scottish dancing.

'And,' Stewart added. 'We can talk about the work we need you to do for us.'

'What kind of work is it?' Was wellness anything like caring? He really hoped not.

'Freya's employing a few people. We're going to need background checks. You do that kind of thing, don't you?'

'Oh,' he said with relief. 'I can do that. Just give me some details and I'll check them out for you.'

'Great,' said Stewart. 'We're trying out a Punjabi chef that evening.

He'll have stuff for us to sample. You okay with spicy vegetarian food?'

Sampling spicy food was more than okay. Perhaps the evening would turn out to be better than he expected. He'd enjoy Freya's company and they'd be paying him to do their background checks for them.

Ian typed the address into Google Maps. Stewart was right; they were almost neighbours. Murriemuir House was just outside a village of the same name and was fifteen miles south of Greyport. Thinking about it, he decided he quite liked the idea of living closer to his brother. He could become a regular kind of uncle. The sort that turned up at family gatherings and made the children laugh with dreadful jokes.

Murriemuir House was even larger than Ian expected. It stood on a small hill and was visible from half a mile away as he turned into the road to the village. Even Lottie seemed impressed as she stood on her hind legs and sniffed out of the window. It was perfect dog walking territory. Ian was right about it being a farmhouse, but it was one with pretensions. He suspected the farmer who had built it had ambitions to live in a castle. The house was a double-fronted, three-storey sandstone building with stone steps leading up to a very large front door. He knew there was money to be made on the rigs. It seemed there was even more money in offshore wind farming. He drove in between two stone gateposts and up a long drive, which ended in a turning circle with a lily pond in the middle, where a small boy was sailing a model boat, pushing it between lily pads with a stick. He looked up when Ian and Lottie climbed out of the car, decided they were not interesting and turned back to his boat.

'Will?' said Ian, restraining Lottie from joining the boy's boat in the pond, and wondering how long it was since he had last seen his nephew, who he remembered as a dribbling toddler. 'Do you want to tell your mum and dad I'm here?'

The child shrugged. 'They're in the kitchen,' he said, pointing to a path at the side of the house. It looked like the child had as much time for him as the rest of the family.

Ian walked round the house until he found a door he assumed would lead him into the kitchen. He tapped and opened it, peered cautiously into the room and, relieved to find that it was indeed the kitchen, went inside. His sister-in-law was sitting at an enormous pine table with a laptop surrounded by dozens of small bowls. Several saucepans were bubbling on a huge cooking stove, catering size, Ian assumed. A young man was dipping a spoon into the pans, taking sips of the food, and looking thoughtfully at the ceiling. Then he added pinches of what Ian took to be spices from the small bowls on the table. Ian enjoyed a good curry and this all smelt wonderful.

Freya looked up from her laptop and smiled at him. 'Ian,' she said. 'Lovely to see you. It's been too long. Grab a seat.'

He sat down at the table. 'It's good to see you too, Freya. It *has* been a long time. I hardly recognised Will. He's grown.' *Typical uncle remark*, he thought. But honestly, what does one say about a nephew one barely recognises?

'He has grown,' said Freya. 'Children do that, as long as you remember to feed them.' She turned to the young man at the stove. 'This is Arkash. He's trying out some of his dishes for us this evening to see if we want to employ him. And, of course, if he can stand to work for us.'

Ian nodded at him and smiled. Arkash, wearing a striped apron and cotton hat, smiled back at him. 'Come to taste my cooking?' he asked.

'Looking forward to it,' said Ian, his mouth already watering. 'It smells lovely.'

'Arkash comes from a family of chefs,' said Freya. 'His grandfather owns an Indian restaurant in Glasgow.'

'It goes back further than that,' said Arkash. 'My great-grandfather worked in the viceroy's kitchens in New Delhi before partition. His father before him, if you believe my grandfather's stories.'

'So you're following in the family tradition?' Ian asked.

'Looks like it,' said Arkash, with a shrug that made Ian wonder if it was perhaps a family decision rather than Arkash's. But the food smelt great. He was going to enjoy this evening's meal even if Arkash decided not to take the job and go off and do, well, he'd no idea what Arkash wanted to do, and if he didn't take this job they'd probably never know.

The door opened and a girl breezed in. She was dressed in what Ian thought of as posh school gear. A purple blazer with a crest on the pocket, a kilt of unknown tartan, dark yellow socks with black patent shoes and a purple beret with a gold tassel. She tossed her backpack onto the floor, pulled off her beret and unclipped a ponytail, letting her auburn hair fall around her shoulders. His niece, Lyra, twelve years old and with the confidence of a polished twenty-five-year-old. She reminded Ian unsettlingly of his mother.

'Hi, Mum, Uncle Ian,' she said. 'Come to see the family pile?'

'Lyra,' he said, nodding at her, not really sure what to say.

'Is that your dog?' she asked. 'It's not very big, is it?'

Ian agreed that Lottie was quite small.

'I'd get a German shepherd,' she said. 'Or an Afghan.'

How about a Rottweiler? Ian wondered.

'Had a good day?' asked Freya, tactfully breaking into the conversation. 'What did you do?'

Lyra sighed. 'You know, school stuff. Anything to eat?'

'Arkash has cooked us all this lovely Indian food,' said Freya. 'We'll be eating that very soon.'

'But I'm hungry now. School lunch is really stingy.'

'Then have an apple.' Freya pointed to a bowl of fruit on the table and turned back to Ian. 'Lyra's just started at St Maghread's in Glenrothes. It's a longer day than she's used to.'

'How do you like it?' Ian asked, watching as Lyra picked out the largest apple and wondering what twelve-year-old girls were interested in.

'It's school, isn't it?' She gave him a look that made him feel he should have known better than to ask such a stupid question. He obviously wasn't going down as a fun uncle type; dog too small, boring questions...

'Have you got homework?' asked Freya.

'Did it on the bus,' said Lyra, dipping her finger into a bowl of chutney, gasping and flapping her hands as she licked it. She rushed to the sink, filled a glass with water and gulped it down.

Serves her right, Ian thought. She'd probably gone for a lime and chilli chutney that even he would have approached with caution.

'Go and change out of your uniform,' said Freya. 'It's your turn to clean out the rabbits.'

'No, it's not,' Lyra said, turning as her father came in. 'Hi, Dad,' she said. 'The rabbits stink and it's Will's turn to do them.'

'Will did them last week,' said Stewart, ruffling her hair. 'And they stink when they've not been cleaned out properly. Now get on and do it or I'll be asking Arkash if he has any rabbit curry recipes.'

Lyra sighed loudly and flounced out of the room. Ian felt a fleeting moment of respect for his brother.

'Don't leave your bag there,' Freya called after her, too late as the door slammed behind her.

'She gets more like Mother every day,' said Stewart, grinning at Ian. 'So, you found us okay?'

'I do know how to use a satnav,' said Ian, grumpily.

'Ouch,' said Stewart. 'You need to be a bit less prickly, young brother.'

He was probably right. He'd have to join one of their mindfulness classes and learn how to put his feelings towards his family in a box at the back of his mind.

'Don't be horrid to Ian,' said Freya. 'Why don't you take him on a tour of the estate? We won't be eating for half an hour or so.'

'Okay,' said Stewart. 'We'll start with the grounds. Got any wellies? We've probably got some you can borrow.'

'I've got my own in the car, thanks.'

They walked out to Ian's car. Stewart watched as he changed into his boots. Then he led him around to the back of the house and down a hill towards a small, wooded area, Lottie scampering ahead of them. Ian followed Stewart through the trees to a small clearing with a rustic bench. 'This will be our forest bathing area,' said Stewart.

Ian had googled that. 'Sitting around under trees thinking of nothing?'

Stewart laughed. 'That's about right,' he said. 'It's Freya that's into all of this mystical hoo-ha. But it seems popular. We've already got bookings.'

'When do you open?' Ian asked.

'Won't happen all at once. The yoga studio's ready. Freya's got her first classes next week. Then we'll add things gradually over the next month or so. By October we hope to be open for residential courses.'

'You want me to do some background checks?' Ian asked.

'Yeah, I'll give you the details before you leave. I assume you'll do that from your own office.'

Ian nodded. 'How many are there?' he asked.

'At the moment there are four. Another yoga teacher and someone who does mindfulness classes. They'll be living in. Then there's a Chinese herbalist who will visit at weekends, and Arkash. He'll be living in and might be working with clients on their diets as well as catering for the dining room. There are other domestic employees, but they're local and only working during the day. We can check out their references ourselves.'

'Shouldn't take long, then,' said Ian.

Will bounded towards them, his boat tucked under one arm. He crouched down to stroke Lottie. 'Can we get a dog?' he asked.

'You've got rabbits,' said Stewart. 'And most of the time you ignore them. Dogs are a lot more work. And they'd probably bark and disturb the meditation sessions.'

'Are you showing Uncle Ian the graves?' Will asked.

'Graves?' asked Ian. People were buried here?

'Might as well,' said Stewart. 'As we're down here anyway.' He led Ian to the back of the clearing, to a line of small gravestones. 'Pet cemetery,' he said.

Ian stooped down and looked at the stones. The first one was inscribed *Rex* and someone had carved a dog's head onto it. There were several more, each one with a name and a carving of either a dog or a cat. The final one simply said *Clover*. It was a larger stone, but with the name only. No picture of either dog or cat.

'We don't know what Clover was,' said Will. 'I think it might be a donkey. We're going to dig them up, then we'll know.'

'Dig them up?' Ian asked. 'Why?'

'Freya thinks being surrounded by animal corpses might upset the forest bathers,' said Stewart. 'We're going to move them over there.' He pointed to a fence at the end of the garden, which Ian assumed was the boundary. Beyond it was well-tended farmland.

'We're going to have a digging-up party,' said Will. 'And cook potatoes on a bonfire.'

'Why don't you join us?' said Stewart. 'Now we're more or less neighbours, we should spend some time together.'

'Really?' said Ian. 'Why?'

Stewart put an arm around his shoulder. 'Look,' he said. 'I know you had a raw deal from the family over Grandad's house.'

Yeah, you could say that. Being taken to court by one's own parents over the validity of a will wasn't a load of fun. Particularly while grieving for the grandfather he had loved and still suffering the after-effects of a bullet in the leg and an unfaithful wife.

'I was stuck out in the North Sea while it was all going on, but Freya gave me a right bollocking when I got back. And she was right. So how about trying to be brothers again? Come along on Saturday. Bring someone with you if you like. Don't tell me you've not got some lovely woman hovering in the background somewhere.'

'Well...'

'What's bollocking?' asked Will.

'It's a very rude word for a ticking off,' said Stewart, laughing. 'And you must absolutely never use it when your mother's around. Do you understand?'

Will nodded.

'Perhaps not when your grandmother's around, either,' Ian suggested.

'Oh, definitely,' said Stewart, grinning at him. 'Come on, let's go and see what Arkash has cooked up for us.'

3

That was Saturday sorted. Maybe even something to look forward to, and looking forward to family meetings was not a familiar feeling. Ian wasn't sure if playing happy families with his brother was how he wanted to spend his weekend. On the other hand, Stewart had presented him with an olive branch, and it was probably time Ian himself put in a bit of effort where family was concerned. And his parents wouldn't be there. At least he hoped they wouldn't. That would be a step too far and he wasn't ready for it. But Stewart was right. They were now almost neighbours, and they were definitely still brothers. He'd also like to know about Clover. Someone had gone to a lot of trouble to carve animal portraits onto the gravestones. So why not Clover's? He wondered what kind of animal was too difficult to carve. It was a large stone, so could it be a donkey, as Will suggested, or a goat? But were they any harder to carve than dogs and cats? Or perhaps it was simply that the carver had left the area and whoever took on the job found animals too difficult. But that wasn't likely. Clover's lettering was beautifully done; if anything it looked more skilful than the lettering on the animal stones – an elaborately carved capital C and a scattering of flowers wound in and out of the other letters. It was not a problem of huge importance, but it still intrigued him. And Murriemuir was a great place for dogs – even small ones. Will had taken to Lottie. And Lyra? Well, Lottie didn't appear to have taken offence at Lyra's dismissive remarks. She was admittedly a small dog, but she was feisty.

Bring a friend, Stewart had said, possibly still thinking that Ian was a friendless loser. He'd invite Caroline, and of course her dog, Angus, who was also small, was in fact remarkably like Lottie to look at. He'd tell Will the story of Lottie's kidnap, the result of having been mistaken for Angus. He liked his nephew. He could sympathise with him, having himself grown up in the shadow of a strong-willed older sibling.

~

Ian always looked forward to a day with Caroline, and she was waiting for him when he pulled up in front of her house on Saturday. Like himself, she was dressed for an afternoon in the garden in jeans, wellies and a bright red parka. Well, hers was red. His own was a shade of muddy brown. Caroline picked Angus up and stowed him in the back of Ian's car with Lottie and then climbed in next to him, clipping on her seatbelt.

'So,' she said as she kissed him on the cheek. 'Let me get this right. You've invited me to go and spend an afternoon digging up dead animals. You really know how to show a girl a good time, don't you?'

Ian grinned at her. 'And to meet my brother and his family, and sit around a bonfire eating baked potatoes. It won't be all fun.'

'Why does your brother want to dig up animals?'

'It's a pet cemetery. Freya, his wife's opening a wellness centre and there's this grove of trees in the garden that she wants to use for forest bathing. She thinks animal graves might put off the bathers.'

'I don't know why they would. I find cemeteries quite restful. How many graves are there?'

'Seven. With artistic headstones. Three dogs, three cats and one unknown. My nephew thinks the last one might be a donkey, but my money is on a goat, or perhaps an alpaca or a pig.'

'And what happens when we've dug them all up? A call to the council animal disposal team?'

Really? The local council disposed of animal corpses? But someone had to do it. Most people didn't have a garden the size of Stewart's and dead animals piling up in the streets didn't sound like a good idea. 'I think the plan is to rebury them, although we're not sure how old they are and it's possible there's nothing left except the headstones. They'll be moved to the end of the garden along with any remains we find.'

'The remains being bones?'

'Probably. I don't think there'll be any actual corpses. My brother bought the house as a failed hotel a few months ago, and before that they think it was let out as student flats. It must be a while since it was a family home, and it's unlikely that students or hotel guests had pets. The animals were probably buried years ago. There might not be much left of them.'

It was only a few miles from Caroline's house in Cupar to Murriemuir. 'Do you know the village?' Ian asked.

'I've driven through it. I don't think I know anyone who lives there.'

'It's a very ordinary village. Just a shop and a few houses, farm labourers' cottages once, now gentrified commuter homes, I suppose. For people who work in Dundee or at the whisky distillery in Glenrothes.'

'The church looks rather dour,' said Caroline as they drove past a gloomy granite building. Ian agreed. On the whole Scots didn't go to church for fun. He couldn't see Stewart or Freya becoming pillars of village life. Stewart probably worked long hours in Edinburgh and would barely have time to notice local villages as he sped through them in his top of the range Mercedes. Freya's clients would most likely be four-by-four drivers from Cupar or St Andrews, fitting in yoga classes in between dropping their children off at school, picking them up again and driving them to ballet or horse-riding lessons.

'Looks like your brother's doing well for himself,' said Caroline as Ian pulled into the drive at Murriemuir and she had her first glimpse of the house.

'Yeah, he's the family success.'

'What does he do?'

'He started off in oil, now it's offshore wind. He earns big money working for a company in Edinburgh. When he's not there he flits around in the company helicopter overseeing the maintenance teams out at sea.'

'Very timely, going into sustainable energy.'

'He's giving a seminar at the COP conference in November. I guess he's hoping to save the planet, single-handed,' said Ian, trying not to sound cynical.

'You don't get on?'

He needed to think about that. 'We did as kids, but I guess my parents didn't help. He was always the one they were proud of. And to be fair we didn't see a lot of each other once I left home.'

'Well, now you live so close to each other it's probably as well not to be at each other's throats.'

She was right, of course. 'We're patching things up. And I do like his wife, Freya.'

He drove up the drive and parked in front of the house where a group of welly-clad people was mustering. Stewart, Freya and the children, Arkash, whose Indian meal had impressed everyone and who now seemed to have taken up residence to prepare for the paying customers. And a brawny man in overalls who was standing by a flatbed truck and appeared to be in charge.

'This is Guy McCulloch,' said Stewart, as Ian and Caroline climbed out of the car. 'He's our head groundsman.'

Head groundsman? How many were there? Ian shook Guy's hand and decided this was not someone to get on the wrong side of. He towered over everyone on the drive. Probably spent his time caber tossing at Highland games or taking part in Tough Mudders.

Ian introduced Caroline to the family. 'It's lovely to meet you,' said Freya, with a wink in Ian's direction. 'Ian's a dark horse, isn't he?

We knew nothing about you. Come with me,' she said in a *let's be best friends* kind of way. 'I'll find you some gardening gloves.'

'Right,' said Guy, sounding impatient and clapping his hands loudly. 'We'll work in teams. You and you are helping me,' he said, pointing to Ian and Arkash. He reached into his truck and handed them each a spade. Arkash took his cautiously and stared at it as if it was a lethal weapon. Rather larger than his kitchen implements, Ian supposed. Being slight in build, he didn't look designed for digging. He was going to need help. 'We'll move each stone in turn,' Guy continued. 'Dig gently around them and put any remains we find into the wheelbarrow together with the stone.'

Ian took pity on Arkash. 'Grab a trowel,' he suggested. 'I'll do the heavy digging and you can scrape the loose earth away from anything we find.'

'What's a trowel?' Arkash asked.

Ian sighed and found him one from the selection of tools in Guy's truck. 'Spent all your life in the city?'

'Aye, most of it in the kitchen.'

'Sorry you decided to leave?'

'You ever lived and worked with a family of seven? Even digging's got to be better than that.'

Ian laughed. 'I found a family of four was bad enough,' he said. 'And heaven forbid we ever try to work together.'

'Stewart,' said Guy, trying to reassert a degree of control, Ian assumed. 'You're in charge of the barrow.'

Just as well Guy's put him in charge of something. Ian didn't think his brother would take well to being given orders.

'We keep each stone and its remains together, and separate from the rest. So once each grave is empty you wheel it down to its new position and lift out the stone. You ladies,' he said, looking at Freya and Caroline. 'You need to place each stone up against the fence, assess the remains and dig a suitable hole for them.'

Caroline, now kitted out with a pair of elbow-length leather gauntlets, saluted. Freya giggled.

'Kids, your job is to place the bones in the new holes and cover them with earth.' Lyra stared at him with an expression that suggested she'd rather be sticking pins in her eyes, but Will nodded with enthusiasm.

'Do you all understand?' Guy asked. They all nodded. Ian doubted that any of them were brave enough to admit any degree of doubt about what they were to do.

'Right,' said Guy. 'Onwards and upwards.' He marched off down the garden, brandishing his spade over his head.

Caroline nudged Ian in the ribs. 'I think he's done this before,' she said.

'Nah,' said Ian. 'He was probably just a boy scout.'

The gravestones stood in a curve on the edge of the clearing. They started with Rex the dog, who was closest to the group of trees. Ian was worried their own dogs would want to join in with the digging and was afraid they might show a bit too much interest in any bones that were dug up. But they seemed happy enough chasing each other through the first autumn leaves. Will was having fun scooping up armfuls of leaves and hurling them at the dogs, who jumped up and down trying to catch them. Guy looked on disapprovingly and Ian suggested that Will should take the dogs and join Caroline and Freya at the far end of the garden, where they stood waiting for Stewart with his first barrow load.

There was quite a lot of Rex left. An almost intact skeleton, Ian guessed. He must have been a large dog. Possibly the kind of German shepherd that Lyra wanted.

'It's the soil here,' Guy explained. 'Damp and peaty. Good for preserving remains.'

The carving on the stone had suggested something small and sweet. A poodle perhaps. Poor old Rex had probably spent the last however many years turning in his grave in disgust at the way he had been portrayed.

They placed the bones carefully in the barrow and Stewart set off wheeling them, along with Rex's gravestone, down towards end of the garden where Will and Lyra were waiting with ghoulish anticipation to arrange Rex in his final resting place. At least Ian hoped it would be his final resting place. He really didn't fancy having to do this all over again any time soon, or ever. He hoped Stewart wouldn't find any more graveyards in his garden. Or if he did, that it wouldn't be somewhere Freya had earmarked for any mind-emptying, trance-inducing type activities.

The two other dogs were smaller with less well-preserved sets of bones. 'Spaniels,' Guy said, with the authority of one who knew all there was to know about dog skeletons. The carvings on the gravestones were identical to Rex's, which suggested to Ian that the artist only knew how to carve one kind of dog. Perhaps his (or her) creativity had been scarred for life by the death of their own pet poodle at an impressionable age. But unless Ian began extensive research into local stone carvers who specialised in pet memorials, this was something he was never likely to know. And if, perish the thought, Lottie ever met with an untimely end, Ian didn't think he could bear to have her buried in his garden with a headstone that suggested she had been a poodle.

There was nothing at all left of the cats. They lifted the three headstones into the barrow together and Stewart set off down the garden with them. Guy and Ian leant on their spades and watched him. Arkash sank down onto the bench. 'In my family,' he said, 'we have never kept pets. Animals are for eating.' He added, 'When my grandfather lived in India, some animals were sacred. Cows mostly, I think. We still don't eat beef.' He seemed vague about his heritage.

'What happens to sacred animals when they die?' Ian asked.

'No idea,' said Arkash. 'We don't have any sacred cows in Glasgow.'

Stewart returned with his barrow and wiped the sweat from his forehead with his sleeve. 'One more barrow load and we'll light the bonfire,' he said. 'Time to start heating up those baked potatoes, I think.' He rubbed his hands together. 'Only Clover to go now, then we'll crack open some beers. It's thirsty work, all this barrowing.'

'Not to mention digging,' muttered Ian, easing his spade into the ground behind Clover's headstone for what he hoped was going to be last time. Although if Clover turned out to be something large like a donkey, there could be a lot more digging. He sank his spade into the ground and hefted the stone out of the way as Arkash moved in with his trowel and carefully scraped away the surface soil. Ian stood back and watched. Then he heard the sound of the metal trowel clink against something hard, and Arkash jumped back with a shriek. 'Oh, my God,' he said, kneeling down again to scrape away more of the soil, gazing at what he had found, the colour draining from his face. Ian peered over his shoulder and stared in disbelief. Then his police training took over. 'Stand back,' he said, gently nudging Arkash out of the way. 'Stewart, call the police,' he shouted to his brother. 'And we need to cordon off the area.'

Stewart patted his pockets in search of his phone, eventually finding it in the back pocket of his trousers. Ian could hear him describing what they had found and giving directions. 'They said to keep the area clear,' Stewart said as he ended the call.

'There're some hurdles in the shed,' said Guy, recovering from the shock. 'I'll run and get them.'

'What is it?' Freya shouted, running towards them.

'Keep the kids away, and put the dogs on their leads,' he said, as Caroline joined them. 'It's a human skull.'

Freya gasped and then skilfully headed off Lyra and Will as they ran to see what was happening. 'Come on, kids,' she said, wrapping an arm around each of them. 'Let's go and get those spuds heated up.'

Caroline rounded up the dogs and joined them, letting Will hold Lottie's lead to distract him.

Ian watched them as they made their way back to the house. Then he turned to see Arkash throwing up into some bushes.

∽

'That was interesting,' said Caroline, as they climbed into Ian's car a couple of hours later and set off down the drive. 'Just like on the telly.'

Ian laughed. She was right. The police had arrived as Ian, Stewart and Guy stood guard over Clover's grave. Everyone else having been hustled back into the house, where Freya tried to pretend it was still a party and that eating baked potatoes in the kitchen was just as much fun as sitting around a bonfire. A team of police had cordoned off the glade with blue crime scene tape and a white tent was erected over the skull. A scene of crime team turned up with a pathologist who, after a quick glance at the skull, declared the death to have been 'not recent' and ordered further digging, which revealed more bones.

Photographs were taken and a team arrived with equipment that could tell them if there were more bodies to be found. Neither stayed for long and Ian was relieved when Duncan appeared and told them he had been appointed chief examining officer.

'Looks like a complete skeleton,' he said, lifting a flap of the tent and peering into the hole in the ground.

The bones were removed, zipped into a bag and driven away in an unmarked van to a lab in Dundee where they would be cleaned, examined and a cause of death established.

'The lab will tell us more, but it doesn't look like a recent death,' said Duncan.

'So where does that leave us?' Stewart asked.

'We'll do a fingertip search of the immediate area, and a geo-scan of the whole garden, but I don't expect to find anything. All being well we'll be done here in a couple of days.' He took Ian aside. 'I'll get back to you as soon as we have the report,' he said. 'Your brother will need to be kept informed since it's his land. Perhaps you could act as liaison?'

'Sure,' said Ian. 'What happens next?'

'It'll depend on the date of death and if foul play is suspected. But it obviously dates to well before your brother came here. Hopefully we'll discover who the deceased is and if they have any family. If not, your brother might need to make some decisions about the future of the body. But to be honest, this doesn't happen very often. I'll need to check the procedures myself.'

'How long will it take?' Ian asked, thinking of Freya's plans to open the centre.

'We'll know more in a day or two when the age of the bones is established. It's perfectly legal to bury a corpse in your own garden. Hopefully it will all be in the local records, although that should have come up in the conveyancing searches. It would have been listed on the deeds but those are all online these days. I'm not sure lawyers study them as closely as they ought to.'

'And if it's not on the deeds?'

'It will be up to the Procurator Fiscal to decide on how to proceed. There might need to be an enquiry.'

'So he could open up a murder investigation?'

'He could but let's not get ahead of ourselves. With funding the way it is he'll only do that if it's a recent death.'

'Recent meaning?'

'Not sure. Presumably within the possible lifetime of a murderer, so around fifty or sixty years?'

Caroline was gazing out of the car window as they drove back to her house in Cupar. 'A bit of a shock for your family, finding they'd bought a house with a body in the garden.'

'I can see Stewart giving whoever did the conveyancing a hard time.'

'It might not have been their fault, not if there was no permission recorded for the burial.'

'There must be a register of where bodies are buried,' said Ian. 'You can't just lose one and leave it unaccounted for.'

'Unless it was buried a very long time ago.'

'Scottish records are excellent,' said Ian. 'It's bound to turn up filed away somewhere.'

'What if it was a murder?'

'Then there will be a matching missing person. I just hope it won't give the children nightmares.'

'They didn't seem like the kind of children who have nightmares.'

She was right. It had made Lyra's day. She'd have plenty to talk about at school on Monday. Even Will was more intrigued than upset.

Although he was disappointed at the lack of a bonfire. Stewart had promised something on Guy Fawkes Night to make up for it.

'Freya and Stewart are probably more concerned about whether or not they'll be able to open as planned,' he said. 'And if it will put people off booking for their weekends of pampering and mediation.'

'The only one who seemed upset by it was Arkash,' said Caroline. 'But he's quite young. It's probably the first time he's seen a dead body.'

'Seeing a body is upsetting, but this was a skull. It doesn't usually have that effect on people, but he was standing quite close.'

'What happens next?' she asked.

'We wait to hear from the lab. It depends what information they get from the bones.'

Caroline shivered. 'That will be Monday at the earliest?'

Ian nodded. 'Probably longer.' Unless it was a more recent death than they thought, he couldn't see them treating it urgently.

4

Finding bones in his brother's garden had distracted him but now Ian really needed to concentrate on the hunt for an assistant. Duncan had hinted about him helping the police and if that happened there would be a lot of paperwork, which he had no intention of doing himself. Not having paperwork was one of the upsides of his foreshortened career. But the search for an assistant wasn't going as well as he had hoped it would. Where were the hundreds of people who had been made redundant during lockdown? Why weren't they queueing up to work for him? He'd had a couple of responses to his online advert, but one didn't drive and lived the other side of Dundee. The other was just looking for a job to fill a gap of a few months before moving to something more permanent. He politely declined both and now wondered if that had been a mistake. Perhaps no one else was going to apply and he'd have to struggle along on his own. He'd not heard back from Duncan who was now very busy. The tourist season was winding down and this was a time of year when he expected to be less busy. But the discovery of a body on his patch would have put a stop to that. However, he'd probably be glad of a relaxed evening in the pub before the students returned and life became even more hectic.

Duncan's wife Jeanie's line dancing sessions in the village would be starting again soon. Line dancing evenings were great for all of them. He and Duncan could enjoy a proper drink in the pub, which was a short step from the village hall. Jeanie could join them for a glass of lemonade after her class and then drive Duncan home. He got out his phone and sent Duncan a text suggesting a drink in Greyport on the next line dancing evening. He then had to send another text to apologise because he'd forgotten which evening the line dancers met. His brain must have gone soggy during lockdown. He suspected it was not only *his* brain that had done that.

He'd just pressed send when another text arrived. *Fancy a pint this evening? Something I want to discuss with you. Nigel.*

Seemed like a good idea. Nigel was better experienced in small doses, but Ian hadn't seen him for a while. Surprisingly, he had missed the chats about speed bumps, which hadn't seemed to bother anyone much during lockdown since there were far more serious things to worry about. He'd nothing on this evening and he could go the long way to the pub giving Lottie a walk at the same time. It would be good for both of them. All three of them if Nigel also walked rather than drove there.

Nigel had neither walked nor driven to the pub. He'd taken advantage of the remaining light evenings and cycled there. Still wearing his cycle clips, he had a pint waiting for Ian when he arrived. Nigel was normally a strictly 'pay your own way' man. *He must want something,* Ian thought. And then he felt guilty. The guy was just trying to be friendly. It always surprised him how someone as obviously good and well-meaning as Nigel could also be quite so irritating. He'd done a marvellous job of motivating the village during lockdown while at the same time getting under everyone's skin. Ian pulled up a chair and sat down next to him. Nigel pulled his face mask down so that he could take a swig of beer then pulled it up over his nose and mouth again. Regulations said that masks should be worn in bars unless eating or drinking. Nigel was taking that very seriously. Ian, and everyone else in the pub, took a more relaxed view. Having a pint of beer or a plate of food in front of you counted as eating or drinking. Replacing one's mask after every mouthful was a step too far. But Ian didn't want Nigel feeling uncomfortable on his account, so he placed his own mask on the table next to his glass, ready for when he'd finished his drink. 'How are you, Nigel?' he asked.

'Not so bad,' said Nigel.

He always said that. He'd probably say the same if he'd just broken both legs and was in bed with a temperature of a hundred and two. 'I haven't seen you for a while. Been busy?'

'As ever,' said Nigel. 'But I just wanted a quick chat with you.'

'I'm all ears,' said Ian. 'Chat away.'

Nigel downed half of his pint and then took a deep breath. 'I see you're looking for an assistant,' he said. 'Saw your card in the shop window.'

Ian nodded cautiously. Was Nigel about to offer himself? He'd undoubtedly be a hard-working, not to say dogged assistant. But could Ian stand sharing office space with him five days a week? He thought it would probably drive him mad, but how on earth was he going to refuse? He ran through a list of excuses in his head, hoping to alight on one that might allow him to refuse Nigel's offer without causing offence. Could he say he was looking for someone similar to his last assistant who had been a young woman? But he didn't want to be ageist or sexist. He didn't want to be accused of any kind of discrimination but was having trouble not being biased against men of a certain age with clipboards and fixed ideas about traffic regulation.

'It's not for me,' Nigel explained, and Ian hoped his expression wasn't giving away the huge wave of relief he was experiencing. 'I've quite enough to do keeping the village on its toes and I don't need the money.'

'But you know someone who'd like the job?' He was quite happy to consider one of Nigel's acquaintances. It would be easier to turn down an unsuitable applicant if it was someone he didn't know.

'My daughter, Molly,' said Nigel.

'She's seen my advert?' Why hadn't she just called the number he had written clearly at the bottom of the card? He'd prefer to employ someone who was able to speak for themselves rather than get their father to do it for them.

'I'm not sure,' said Nigel. 'She's not said anything to me about it. I'd point it out to her, but I thought it might be good to chat to you first. I wouldn't want her to apply if you think she's quite unsuitable.'

The only unsuitability that Ian could see right now was that she was either not in the least interested in his job or she was too scared to contact him about it. Neither boded well for her.

Nigel hadn't finished. 'She's had a tough time recently and she's already had the confidence knocked out of her.' He looked across the table at Ian. 'And I mean that literally,' he said, banging his glass down and splashing some beer across the polished tabletop.

Nigel had spent the last year organising often unwilling village residents, pestering them for help, often being refused and not always politely. And all through this he had been upbeat and cheerful. He had a skin like a rhinoceros. Nothing from irritable comments to blatant insults ruffled him. He'd smiled benignly through it all. Never once had Ian seen him display even marginal grumpiness. And yet the man sitting next to him, red-faced and spilling his beer, was suddenly speechless with anger.

'Do you want to talk about it?' he asked, not wishing to pry into Nigel's personal life, or Molly's. But clearly something was wrong, and Nigel probably had no one else to talk to about it.

'She's a qualified librarian,' he said slowly, taking a calming sip of his drink. 'She worked in the university library in Glasgow until she was pregnant with Ryan. She was damn good at the job. But she took maternity leave and never returned.'

Some women wanted to be stay-at-home mums. Nothing wrong with that. But Nigel, it seemed, disapproved. That surprised Ian. He'd have expected Nigel to be quite the opposite. He'd always assumed that the late Mrs Burrows was the traditional 'I'm just a housewife' type.

'That worried me at the time,' he said. 'But one doesn't like to interfere.'

Interfering, Ian had always thought, was exactly what Nigel liked doing. It was, in fact, what he was doing right now. But did it matter? He took a gulp of his beer and thought about it. As an assistant a librarian would be ideal, however she had come by the job. She'd be organised, good at searching online and used to dealing with people. So why wouldn't Nigel just point out his advert to her and let her decide? 'She's living with you permanently?' he asked, remembering that he'd also hoped for someone local.

'At least until she's back on her feet again. It seems to suit all three of us.'

'You said she'd had her confidence knocked. Can you talk about that or would you rather not?'

Nigel hesitated as if considering this. 'I want to be strong for Molly,' he said. 'But it would be good to share what happened with, well, someone not directly involved. But she'd probably be furious if she thought I'd been talking behind her back. She may have seen your card at the shop and just felt too nervous to do anything about it. I didn't want to point it out to her until I knew there was a chance you might consider her.'

'I don't want to pry,' said Ian. 'But perhaps it would help if you could tell me a little more about her... situation?'

Nigel stared into his beer for a moment and sighed. 'I thought she'd married well,' he said. 'He seemed a nice enough type. Guy called Tel, worked for a finance company and made good money. Bought a nice little flat in a new block in Glasgow. I thought she was happy. She seemed to have everything she wanted. She didn't visit much after Ryan was born, but that happens, doesn't it? No time for elderly parents.'

Ian certainly didn't have a lot of time for his, but that was quite different. Glasgow wasn't so far. Why would Molly suddenly stop visiting her father? It sounded as if they were quite close now. What could have changed?

'Then there was lockdown,' Nigel continued, 'and no one visited anyone any more. I called her of course, but she was always busy. Said she had to keep Ryan entertained. Tel was working from home and needed quiet.'

'So when did you seen her again?'

'I hoped she'd visit after the first lockdown, but she didn't. She was always too busy, she said. I offered to go over there. Take them out. Take the little one to the zoo, or something. But she didn't want that even though I told her it was all open air and numbers were restricted, everyone wearing masks. And then we were all back in lockdown again.'

Ian was trying to remember the dates of the lockdowns. First one from March until the summer. And then again through the next winter. 'She's been living with you since March, you said?'

'That's right. That's when the schools started up again. Ryan was five in January and should have started then but that was delayed until March. Anyway, he's a sociable little fellow, and a brave one as things turned out. He couldn't wait to start school, and what's more, to start chatting to people. At the end of the first week the teacher got them to draw pictures of their families – a get-to-know-you thing for them. Well, the teacher was concerned because Ryan drew Molly with two black eyes. Okay, five-year-olds aren't the most accurate artists. But she asked him about it, and he said Mummy's eyes *were* black sometimes and that alerted the teacher. She and the head had a chat to Ryan in the lunch break and he told them his mum's eyes were black because his dad hit her.'

Poor little scrap, Ian was thinking. *And poor Molly.*

'At the end of school that day they kept Ryan back and the teacher went to meet Molly at the school gate. Most of the mums waited in the playground, but Molly stayed at the gate. They thought she was just shy and that she'd come in and get to know more of the parents when she was more used to it. She didn't have a black eye that day, but they took her into the head's office to talk about Ryan's drawing and offered her a cup of tea. That was when they noticed she couldn't move her left arm. She told them she'd fallen, but they were suspicious and kept her there chatting while the secretary called social services, who came at once and took Ryan aside to ask him some questions. He told them she'd fallen because his dad pushed her and then jumped on her arm.'

By this time Nigel was shaking. Ian went to the bar and bought them a couple of whiskies. 'Take your time,' he said, as he put the glass down in front of Nigel. 'Had he hurt Ryan as well?'

'Ryan didn't say he had and there was no sign of bruises. But social services weren't prepared to risk it.' He tossed back his whisky in a single gulp. 'You can probably guess the rest,' he said. 'Molly was taken to hospital with a broken arm which needed setting under a general anaesthetic. She had to be kept in for a few days. Ryan was put into foster care at an undisclosed location until she was ready to be discharged. They offered to find them a place in a refuge, but she called me and asked me to take them in, which of course I did. I drove to the hospital straight away and brought her back here before Tel even noticed she was missing. I found a good lawyer and had a restraining order taken out against him.' He drained his glass and signalled the barman for a refill. 'He didn't take it well. Turned up outside the house, drunk and brandishing a hatchet. You've seen my house,' he said, smiling at Ian. 'It's like a fortress, even more so since Molly moved in. Anyway, I called the police and Tel was arrested. It seems Molly wasn't his only victim. A couple of women he worked with came forward and accused him of rape with violence. So now,' Nigel said with a satisfied look, 'he's on remand and looking at a longish stretch in Barlinnie.'

'And how are Molly and Ryan?' Ian asked, feeling nauseous.

'Ryan's a resilient little fellow. Bounced back in days and settled in happily at the primary school here in Greyport. Molly's stronger than I thought. But like I said, she's lost confidence. So have I. I should have realised what was going on and done something about it.' He pulled out a handkerchief and blew his nose noisily.

'You can't blame yourself,' said Ian. 'You couldn't have known what was going on but as soon as you found out, you rescued them.'

Nigel shrugged. 'We're getting there, both of us. I bought Molly a little car so she's getting out and about now. She's signed up to help the kiddies with their reading at the school. And she's made some friends with a group of women in Dundee who've suffered something similar.'

From what he knew of Dundee there were probably quite a few women with Molly's experiences. 'And she's looking for work,' he said. 'That must be a good sign.' Nigel fiddled with his empty glass. 'I'm not sure I should have told you all that. I hope you don't think I'm asking you to employ her out of pity.'

'Ask her to call me,' said Ian, thinking that if she was brave enough to do that and to come to an interview, she'd be worth thinking about. 'I promise she'll be considered on her own merits alongside all the other applicants.' Although right now it didn't look as if she'd have much competition.

'I'd better be getting back,' said Nigel, having apparently regained his usual composure. He stood up, put his coat on, straightened his mask and slipped his bicycle clips on. 'Thank you,' he said, offering Ian his hand to shake, and then withdrawing it. 'Sorry, I forget whether shaking hands is allowed now.'

'No worries,' said Ian, thinking it was probably the first time in Nigel's life that he'd not remembered a regulation. He watched as Nigel made his way out of the pub. It was a five-minute bike ride to his house and with any luck that would be enough to clear his head. They'd both knocked back a few whiskies, but they'd needed them. They'd been medicinal and he wasn't sure he could have stomached what Nigel told him without their help.

He gathered up Lottie and started to make his own way up the hill to his house, still shaken by what Nigel had told him. He was flattered that Nigel had felt able to talk to him and hoped that it might have helped him to come to terms with a horrible situation. He knew that things like that happened and had been made worse by lockdown. But this was as close as he had come to anyone who had experienced domestic violence first hand. He hoped Molly would call him and that she'd be what he was looking for. But he would need to be careful. Nigel was right. He shouldn't employ her out of pity.

Lottie trotted up the garden path ahead of him and he pulled out his key to unlock the door and let them in. He sank onto the sofa and Lottie jumped into his lap.

5

The next morning Ian booted up his computer and found another application from the job search site. Trevor Smith had worked at a camera repair shop until the first lockdown. His furlough was about to end, and he'd been given notice. He would not be employed by them again. In any case, he wrote, he was nearing retirement age and was looking for something part-time. He sounded promising; computer-literate, well organised, motivated... all the qualities everyone probably put on job applications. At least he didn't claim being a perfectionist as one of his faults. Plus, he said he was a dog lover and could start immediately. Ian eyed the piles of unsorted papers on the floor of his office. Immediate was good, not to say vital. But should he wait and see if Molly called him? He decided against it. If she phoned in the next few days, he could still interview both of them, forget what he knew of Molly's background and assess them on their ability to do the job. If he waited too long, he might lose his one and only applicant. He typed a reply to camera repair man and invited him to come for a chat about the job the following afternoon.

He had just clicked send when his phone rang. It was Molly asking about the job she'd seen advertised in the shop. She didn't mention her father and Ian could understand why. It wouldn't look good having one's father soliciting for jobs as if she was still a teenager. He asked her to come round the next morning and discuss it. With any luck he could have it all sorted by tomorrow evening. No need to trouble Duncan, although Ian would still enjoy meeting him for a drink. This might even be a drink to celebrate the start of a new assistant.

Molly was exactly what Ian expected a librarian to look like. *Rather shy*, he thought. But that could just be interview nerves. She was wearing plain black trousers and a baggy grey cardigan, which she wrapped around herself like armour. She had long hair that curtained her face, and from which she peered out at him through heavy-rimmed glasses. Was she trying to hide? Was her nervousness fear of him as a possible employer, or fear of men in general? Either would be understandable. And whichever it was, she was crying out for someone to make her feel comfortable and safe.

'We'll sit in the garden,' he said, hoping he sounded relaxed and friendly, and not as if he was suggesting that he didn't trust her in the house. He really wished Nigel hadn't told him so much about Molly. Knowing what she had been through, it was difficult not to treat her like an injured bird. He hoped Lainie would pop her head over the fence and offer them coffee and cake. It might reassure Molly. No one would find Lainie anything but motherly and safe. But it must be her day for knitting, or shopping. There was no sign of her. No laundry flapping on the line. No cheerful, inquisitive face peering over the fence. He left Molly in the garden and went inside to make coffee, which he carried out with a tray of biscuits, Lottie trailing after him. He cleared some plant cuttings off the table and pulled up a chair for Molly. Then he sat down and lifted Lottie onto his lap, hoping that a man with a lapful of small dog might look kind and gentle. He offered Molly a biscuit and Lottie strained in her direction.

Molly pushed the hair back from her face and smiled timidly. 'Can I give her some of my biscuit?' she asked.

That was encouraging. He'd forgotten Lottie's excellent ice-breaking skills. 'She'll love you forever if you do,' he said. Lottie jumped off his lap and edged closer to Molly's legs, nudging her gently. Molly reached down and stroked her ears. That was a good start. He could tick off the dog-loving part of his job description. 'Tell me about your work at the university,' he said. 'Librarian, wasn't it?' Had he just put his foot in it? He couldn't remember if she'd told him that herself when she called or if he was remembering what Nigel had said. If he had slipped up, she hadn't noticed and started chatting about her work.

'It sounds as if you enjoyed it,' he said.

'Oh, I did, I loved it. I was sorry to give it up,' she said, looking down at her hands, which were fidgeting in her lap. She was silent for a moment. 'Ryan needed me,' she added after a pause.

It was probably more than that. Why hadn't she returned after her maternity leave? Had she been forced to give up work that she loved? Nigel had hinted that she had, that her life had been manipulated by her husband. But it was a sensitive topic. Better to keep to practicalities. 'And now Ryan's at school, you're looking forward to getting back to work again?'

She nodded. 'He's settled in and, well, I need to get out of the house and earn my keep. Not that Dad isn't happy for us to be there but... well, you know. Anyway,' she said, 'what will I be doing if I work for you? If you offer me the job.'

'There'd be quite a lot of desk work here; record keeping, internet searches, sending out invoices, keeping the office organised, that type of thing.'

'Would I be... would any of it be actual detective work?' She looked at him hopefully.

'I'm sure that would be possible,' he said. It was good that she was interested in his work rather than just looking for a job to pass the time. 'I could train you if that's the direction you would like to take. And if you feel it's something you want to develop, we could think about sending you on a course.'

'Can you tell me about some of the work you've done?'

'Of course,' said Ian, leading her inside. He upended a couple of boxes and shuffled through an assortment of letters and postcards, emails and lists of websites. All the evidence they'd kept pinned to his incident board. Why on earth had he kept all that once the case had finished? He had the whole lot stored on his computer.

Molly flicked through the postcards. 'It's fascinating,' she said. 'I read about the case in the papers but it's amazing to actually see it all.'

'It was important evidence at the trial,' he said modestly. 'We cleared an innocent man, and the murderer was given a life sentence.' Molly looked impressed. 'But it's not usually that exciting,' he told her. 'Most of what you would be doing would involve background internet searches to start off with. Then perhaps a little surveillance.'

She put the papers carefully back in the box and looked around the room. 'You definitely need someone to tidy the office,' she said. 'If you don't mind me saying...'

'Not at all. You're absolutely right.'

They talked about the hours she could work. She wanted to fit it around the school day, which was fine with him. Twenty-five hours a week would suit them both nicely.

'But I can be quite flexible,' she told him. 'It's one of the advantages of living with my father. He's offered to take on some of the childcare.'

There can't be a lot of advantages, Ian thought, not able to imagine having Nigel as a housemate. But he shouldn't make assumptions. Ian himself hadn't proved particularly easy to live with even without the stress of having to arrange childcare. At least not when he'd been married. He and Grandad had got on well enough though, so it probably wasn't all his fault. 'Do you have any more questions?' he asked.

'How well do you know my dad?'

Not a usual question for a job interview, but fair enough that she should ask. She probably knew they had spent an evening together in the pub. Fathers talked about their daughters, didn't they? She would have guessed that Nigel had told him at least a little about what she had been through.

'I got to know him quite well during lockdown,' he said, skilfully sidestepping details of their conversation in the pub.

'You helped him with all the volunteer stuff, didn't you? He told me you were his right-hand man.' She giggled. 'Sorry, that's the way Dad talks. He said you were very kind, the way you looked after all the people who needed shopping and a bit of company.'

'Most of the chatting was through windows.' Ian shrugged. 'But the village would have been in a sorry state without your father. It was all thanks to him that no one was left on their own without food or a bit of company. He's probably the most organised person I've ever met.'

'I'm very organised too.' She fiddled with her hair, pulling it back to hide part of her face.

'He talked a bit about you the other night when we met for a drink.'

'I don't like to talk about what happened to me,' she said.

'That's fine,' he said. 'You don't need to tell me anything if you don't want to. I'm only interested in your work and whether we'd work well together.' He smiled. 'And being organised is an excellent thing.'

'I don't want anyone being sorry for me. I want a job that I can do well because I'm good at it, not in spite of anything.'

Ian could understand that. He'd felt the same after his leg injury. People were kind to him, but he often felt patronised. They thought he did a good job regardless of what had happened to him, not because he was actually good at it.

They talked a little more about the work and then he walked with her to the gate. 'Thank you for coming,' he said. 'I've someone else to see this afternoon. Can I let you know about the job one way or the other this evening?'

'Of course, and thank you for seeing me,' she said, bending down to give Lottie a goodbye pat on the head.

He watched as she walked down the hill towards the waterfront. They had a lot in common; both of them trying to cope with violent pasts. He liked her ambition. This wouldn't just be a stopgap for her.

She could see a future in it, and so could he. They'd work well together. One day she could be more than an assistant. Skair Cases might have two detectives. He could change the name to Skair and Partner, or even Skair and Burrows. But he mustn't get ahead of himself. He still had another candidate to interview. He almost hoped the man he was seeing this afternoon would not be too good.

He needn't have worried. Camera repair man Trevor got on his nerves from the moment Ian opened the door to him. He spent a lot of time droning on about spreadsheets and then looked around the office and started demanding a special chair for his bad back and regular breaks when he could lie on the floor to ease the pain. Ian was treated to a long account of camera problems Trevor had overcome. How he had come to the rescue on many occasions and saved countless weddings and christenings from the potential disaster of photographers with faulty cameras. He would, he told Ian, be able to take on all the camera surveillance work, his skills being far superior to those of a mere investigator.

After half an hour of being told how to run his business, Ian had had enough. Special chairs were one thing — he'd had his own mobility problems in the past. But as the boss, *he* would be the one to say who did what. The final straw was the man's blatant lie about his fondness for dogs. Well, to be fair he may have been a dog lover. But Lottie was definitely not a Trevor fan. She took one look at him and spent the entire interview huddled in a corner growling. Even if it hadn't been the interview from hell, Ian would have trusted Lottie's judgement. An easy, unanimous decision then. Lottie liked Molly and hated Trevor.

After Trevor left, Ian sent him a polite email saying that he had been impressed with Trevor's knowledge but that he was not quite what Ian was looking for right now. Then he called Molly and offered her the job. He'd expected her to jump at it and she did sound pleased. But then she asked if she could take a day or two to think about it. He was disappointed and hoped this didn't mean he would have to start searching all over again. He'd given Trevor no indication that he was a second choice. Under no circumstances was he going to offer him the job, however desperate he felt. He'd rather carry on alone. And then he had a thought. *Molly wants to check up on me.* Very sensible of her after what she'd been through, although he did wonder how she would do it. She had given her Glasgow employer as a reference. Should he have given her the name of someone who would vouch for *him*? He was sure Duncan would put in a good word if necessary. But he'd wait and see. Maybe she really did want to think about it. Barging in and suggesting references of his own would just seem desperate and might put her off altogether. Was there, he wondered, a 'how to be a good employer' handbook? Or perhaps a 'self-help for the inexperienced boss' website he could consult. Oh well, it wouldn't hurt him to wait a day or two for her decision. He had other work he could be getting on with. That reminded him that in all the fuss over finding the skeleton in his brother's garden, he'd forgotten to pick up the file containing details of Freya's prospective employees on whom he'd promised to run background checks. He sent off an email to Freya and said he'd drop by to pick them up later that day. He could also give Lottie a good walk somewhere between Greyport and Murriemuir and he would be driving right past his favourite farm shop, where he could pick up some delicacies for tonight's meal. He'd put assistants out of his mind for the rest of the day.

6

Molly hadn't kept him waiting long before calling back and, to his relief, accepting the job. And she was well into her second week of working for Ian before there was any news about the skeleton. They were, in fact, just talking about the find at Murriemuir when Duncan called him. Molly had a load of questions that Ian was unable to answer. 'How do they know how old the bones are? Can they tell if it was male or female? What will happen to it now?' It was great that she was interested. He just wished he could give her some of the answers. 'It will probably turn out to be a member of the family who died from natural causes,' he told her, wishing he felt surer about it. Murder cases were all very well. They made for excellent crime fiction and Scandi Noir would be lost without them. But when it was right on your doorstep? And involved a member of the family. Well... not so much fun.

'But,' Molly argued, 'they'd have had to get permission to bury a body in the garden. There'd be paperwork. I've been checking online. There's all kinds of forms to fill in.'

It was true that Stewart had known nothing about it, but it was probably something that was missed during the conveyancer's searches. Murriemuir had changed hands several times in the last fifteen years. Things like that could get overlooked but there'd be records somewhere. He clicked to accept Duncan's call. 'Any news of the Murriemuir skeleton?' Ian asked.

'We've had a report from the lab so we do know a bit more, but there's something I'd like to discuss with you. Fancy meeting at the Pigeon this evening?'

'Line dancing night?' Ian asked.

'Well remembered,' said Duncan. 'They've had a longish break because of lockdown but now Jeanie's dusting down her cowboy boots and raring to go.'

'And you're up for a pint or two?'

'Aye, maybe even a whisky chaser. We can take a look at the lab report at the same time.'

'I'll look forward to it,' said Ian. 'Lottie too.'

'So what's on the agenda for today?' Molly asked as Ian ended the call.

She'd been working hard in the office since she'd joined him. *Time to get out and about,* he thought. She'd done a great job tidying up and getting his paperwork up to date. Now she needed something more interesting. A bit more investigator related. Not that the case he had in mind was one of his more exciting ones. But she had to start somewhere. She could practise the basics on this case and move on to better things as she became more experienced. 'Bit of field work,' he said.

'We're going out?' She looked excited.

'I'll show you the basics of surveillance. It's not a difficult case but you'll get some hands-on practice and then learn how to document it all for the client.'

'Where are we going?'

'To a housing estate in Dundee to sit outside the house of a woman who thinks the neighbours are stealing from her wheelie bins.'

'Why would they do that?' Molly asked. 'If it's stuff that's been thrown out, wouldn't she be pleased that someone can use it?'

'Technically it's still theft,' said Ian. 'But the area she lives in is part of a council trial to get people to recycle more. They use a system that weighs the recycling bins, and the householders get tokens when their recycling reaches a certain weight.'

'People steal rubbish to make their own bins heavier?'

'Apparently. Or that's what our client thinks.'

'Not major crime, is it?'

He laughed. 'I like your enthusiasm,' he told her. 'But actual crime is usually best left to the police.'

'But you help out sometimes? Like with the Lansman murder.'

That was true. She had done her homework and he *had* worked with a detective inspector in Arbroath tracking down a historic murderer. 'Yes, but that was unusual. Most of what we do is rather more down to earth. But not necessarily dull,' he added, noticing her look of disappointment.

'So how's it going to work this morning?'

He opened a small rucksack and showed her its contents. 'This is my basic in-car surveillance kit; zoom lens camera – ever used one of those?' She shook her head. 'It's not hard. You can try it out this morning.' He pulled out a notebook and pen along with his phone. 'I use the voice recorder on the phone and occasionally the video camera. It's more discreet.'

'What about this?' she asked, holding up a thermos flask.

'I fill it with strong black coffee. When I'm on my own I sometimes find it difficult not to nod off. With two of us chatting we should be able to stay awake, but we'll take coffee if you like.'

He pulled out a pair of trainers. 'I wear these if I'm likely to be following someone. They're quieter and more comfortable than normal shoes.'

'I've got some at home,' she said. 'Will I run and fetch them before we leave?'

'No need. We'll just observe from the car today.'

'Why the mints?' she asked, holding up a bag of extra strong peppermints.

'I like them,' he said. 'But I'm happy to share.'

'I like sherbet lemons,' she said. 'I'll bring some next time. But mints are fine for now. Does Lottie come with us?'

'No, not this time. We won't be long. She'll be fine here for a wee while.'

Ian repacked the rucksack and they set off down the garden to his car. Lottie gazed at them sadly from the window. 'She'll be curled up asleep on a chair the second we're out of sight,' he said.

'How do you know? She might still be there looking sad when we get back.'

'She'll be sound asleep until she hears my key in the lock. Trust me.'

They drove to a street of granite two-up-two-downs on the outskirts of Dundee and sat there watching the row of bins lined up along the pavement. It was a quiet street. Most residents, Ian guessed, would be out at work. There would be some working at kitchen tables or holed up in attic rooms working from home. But they wouldn't have time to gaze out at bins. His client had been vague about the time of the bin collections, and they sat in the car chewing mints. 'Told you it might be dull,' he said, glancing anxiously at Molly.

'It's not dull at all,' she said. 'I love watching people's houses.'

She did actually sound as if she meant this. He stared glumly out at the street.

'There's someone.' She nudged him excitedly.

They watched as a young lad strolled along the street eating from a McDonald's red cardboard pouch of fries. He glanced around furtively, and then slid his wrappers into the client's recycling bin. Molly took a photo of him just as he let the wrappers slip out of his hand.

She showed Ian the screen. 'Very good,' he said. 'You can add it to the client's folder when we get back.'

'My first photo as an investigator,' she said proudly. 'What happens now?'

'We wait for the bins to be emptied, then go back and update the file. At the end of the week, I'll send her all the evidence and invoice her for the work.'

Molly looked at him in surprise. 'She pays you for sitting outside her house for a couple of hours?'

'Yes, but on this occasion, not very much. A lot of my work with new clients is trying to persuade them, in the politest way, that they really don't have much of a case.' He watched through his rear-view mirror as the bin lorry clanked round the corner and headed slowly in their direction. 'There's no more to do now,' he said. 'If the client does want us to keep watch again next week, I thought it might be a good chance for you to try a bit of surveillance on your own.' He didn't expect that. Not many people would pay good money to have someone watch teenagers throwing their rubbish into bins. But if the client did want to try again next week, it would be a nice easy job for Molly. It was mid-morning. There were a few people about but not too many. He'd already pointed out parking places that gave them a good view of the bins, but were easy to leave in a hurry if necessary. He was fairly certain it wouldn't be, but he didn't plan to take any risks over Molly's safety. They'd kept the doors locked and he'd shown her how to take photos discreetly.

He drove them back to the office and after a quick sandwich lunch Molly spent the rest of the day updating the client's file. By three o'clock she'd finished and tidied up. She picked up her bag and put her coat on. Ian knew her routine now. A dash down to the shop to buy food and then she'd spend what was left of the afternoon at the school listening to children practise their reading. Sometimes after school she'd take Ryan to the park or to swimming lessons. 'I can't leave it all to Dad,' she explained. 'He wouldn't mind shopping and cooking, but he's done such a lot for us already.'

She was, as she had said, organised. It was all work and childcare, but she seemed happy enough and was coming out of her shell since she'd started work, even becoming quite chatty. She'd thrown herself into the job and asked an encouraging number of questions, but he wondered how long it would be before she had any kind of social life. He should have mentioned line dancing at the village hall this evening — she might enjoy that, and she had a resident babysitter in the form of Nigel. She might even join the crowd of after-class dancers for a drink at the pub. It wasn't much of a life for her if a five-year-old and an elderly father were her only company. But he was only her employer and couldn't push it. His concern for her should be restricted to office hours. Anyway, it was a friendly village with plenty going on. No doubt she'd soon make friends with other mums at the school.

He spent the early evening catching up on correspondence and then took Lottie for a run in the park before heading down to the Pigeon to meet Duncan. He bought himself a pint and sat at the bar, which after so many months of the pub being closed felt quite exciting. It was nice to see that life was starting to get back to normal again. It was the small things he'd missed. He hadn't been all that bothered about the inability to travel abroad or to go to the theatre, but he had missed evenings in the pub.

Duncan arrived and they performed an elbow bump. Was that still necessary? Perhaps handshaking and hugs would never make a return. Not that he and Duncan hugged. Jeanie was a big hugger so that could be something to look forward to once she'd finished her class.

'Let's grab a table,' said Duncan, clutching his pint. 'I've things to show you and a spot of work you might be interested in.'

They sat down and Duncan pushed a folder in his direction. 'The lab report on the skeleton you found,' he said.

Ian sipped his beer and opened it.

The skeleton, the report said, *was likely to be that of a young girl. There was a long footnote explaining processes and accuracy of determining the age and sex of bones. Current techniques were believed to produce 90% accuracy. Dating suggested she was eleven or twelve although she was smaller than average height for that age and probably of slight build. Soil analysis showed that the body had been in the ground for between fifteen and twenty years. It was in good condition (apart from being dead, Ian thought). There was no obvious cause of death — no broken or damaged bones, no evidence of bone disease or poisoning and nothing to suggest ill health.* Amazing what an expert in bones could deduce. *However, there was nothing to give any idea of who she was. Samples were also taken from the sites of the animal bones and again there was no suggestion of anything other than natural death. From soil samples it was thought that the animals had been in the ground for around the same amount of time. The only other items of interest were a number of broken plastic doll parts — a head, arms and legs. The torso was likely to have been fabric and therefore could have disintegrated along with any clothing and other cloth items such as bedding.*

Duncan took gulp of his beer. 'We've done some searching of records. Any young girls reported missing in Fife fifteen to twenty years ago have been accounted for. There was no record of a burial at Murriemuir, and no permit was issued for burial elsewhere. There's no death certificate for anyone of that age called Clover. It's a complete mystery.' He sighed.

'Is that what you wanted to discuss?' Ian asked.

'Partly. It doesn't look like an unlawful killing so the Fiscal will probably decide not to take it any further. There'll be an inquiry at some stage but they'll need a lot more facts first.' He took a swig of his beer. 'I can't help thinking there must be someone out there who is missing a daughter or a sister. It'll be entered on the missing person's database, but after so long it's likely that whoever missed her will have stopped looking.'

'And you'd like me to look into it?'

'I've had a word with the super and he's agreed to release some funding. He doesn't want to take up police time, but he agreed with me that we need to find out more.'

Ian nodded. 'It has to be something to do with the house, doesn't it?'

Duncan nodded. 'That's certainly the place to start. Bodies are occasionally dumped on private land but it's unusual to find one with a named headstone. Whoever buried her body there knew who she was and probably had a connection to the area, if not to the house itself.'

It would be interesting to know more. He'd be happy to work on that and find out what he could. 'There'll be plenty of records to check,' he said. 'And I'm sure Stewart will be interested to know a bit about who lived there before he bought the house.'

'Stewart's your older brother?'

'Yes. He moved down here a few months ago for a new job.'

'I didn't even know you had a brother,' said Duncan. 'You've never mentioned him.'

'We move in very different worlds.' *But possibly not quite so different right now.*

'And Jeanie tells me you've a new assistant.'

Nothing gets past Jeanie, Ian thought with a smile. 'Molly Burrows,' he said. 'Nice young woman. Lives in the village with her father. She's a little boy, Ryan, who goes to the village school.'

'Not Nigel's daughter?'

'You know him?'

'Oh, yes, we know Nigel. Well-meaning busybody type. He's always calling in with some gripe about cars parking on pavements or dogs crapping in people's front gardens. Can't imagine he'd be easy to live with.'

Ian laughed. 'He did a great job during lockdown.'

'I'm sure he did. Like I said, a well-meaning bloke with too much time on his hands.'

'Molly's recently divorced from a miserable marriage. That's why she's using her father's name again. I don't want to interfere in her life, but I don't think she has a lot of fun. It's just work, school pick-ups and cooking for her dad.'

'Can't be easy getting back into the swing again after a divorce...'

'It isn't,' said Ian. He knew all about that. 'I was wondering if Jeanie might help. Maybe get her to join her dancing class. Molly's probably a bit nervous about trying things like that on her own.'

'I can't think of anything Jeanie would like better than taking Molly under her wing. You know what she's like.'

'I'm just not sure how to bring it up. Molly's working for me. I don't want it to look like I'm taking over her social life as well.'

'Hmm,' said Duncan, tapping his fingers on the table. 'You said her kiddie was at the village school?'

'That's right. Primary one, I think. Molly helps out with reading sometimes.'

'Perfect,' said Duncan. 'Jeanie's working on a safety project we've got going with local school kids. The village school's bound to be on her list. I'll get her to look out for Molly.'

That was a good evening, Ian thought as he walked back up the hill with Lottie. Some interesting work for him and a bit more fun for Molly. And not a mention of himself and Caroline. Had Jeanie given up her mission to pair them off?

7

The next morning the electricians arrived. Two of them to rewire the upstairs rooms and ask difficult questions about how many power sockets he wanted and where to put them. And where they could find his consumer unit. Ian had no idea what a consumer unit was until they explained that he might know it better as a fuse box. Ah yes, that was in the cupboard under the stairs. He cleared out a vacuum cleaner, brooms, some old coats and boots, a box of empty jam jars and two mousetraps that he'd never used. One of the electricians peered in and tutted. His fuse box was obsolete, not to say dangerous. Ian was quite glad he hadn't known that. He'd have had nightmares about leaping from upstairs windows while his house burnt to ashes.

'Not a big job,' he was told. 'We'll get that one out in a jiffy.'

It had to be done, he supposed, wondering how long exactly a jiffy was and how he'd be able to work with no electricity for... how long?

'A couple of hours, three tops.'

Not too bad, he supposed, although his recent experience of workmen suggested he should at least treble that. A whole day of not being able to use his computer or make a cup of coffee. He wasn't sure which of those he minded most. But it wasn't going to happen today. They'd strip out the old wiring from the upstairs rooms and come back tomorrow to install his new consumer unit. *Today at least will be quiet*, he thought. Wrongly, as it turned out. It was a two-man job. He understood that. What he hadn't realised was that one man would be up on the first floor while the other would be installed in the under stairs cupboard. There would be a lot of shouting at each other while they identified what connected to where.

He joined Molly in the office and downloaded emails. He'd answer as many as he could today before he had to rely on his phone to do it. He should go and get his eyes tested and start using reading glasses; a thought he found depressing, but needs must if he was going to be regularly deprived of his desktop with its twenty-four-inch screen.

The first email he opened was from the woman he thought of as wheelie bin lady. She'd had a letter from the council. Notification that the recycling voucher scheme was ending because there had been too much cheating and not enough genuine recycling. She thanked him for the photo Molly had sent but didn't want to proceed any further. She was quite pleased to know that at least some young people were litter conscious even if it did mean using her bin.

Ian turned his screen so that Molly could read the email.

'Oh,' she said. 'That means I don't get my stint at surveillance. I was looking forward to it.'

'There'll be other opportunities,' he told her. 'This morning you can finish off the report and send it to the client. You'll need the computer, so we must get it done today while we still have electricity. And when you've done that, I've something much more interesting for you.' He showed her the notes he had made last night, explaining that Duncan wanted them to find out more about Murriemuir House and its previous owners. 'What do you think?' he asked. 'Ready to do a bit of research?'

She read the lab report excitedly. 'That's the body they found there last week?'

'A skeleton rather than a body, but yes. How did you hear about it?'

'Everyone was talking about it at school pick-up yesterday.'

It was bound to get out, he supposed. He hoped Stewart and Freya weren't being bothered by journalists looking for a juicy bit of news. He wondered if it would be good or bad for Freya's business. Stewart had once said there was no such thing as bad publicity. This could put that theory to the test for him. 'What do you think?' he asked Molly. 'Can you handle that?'

She was already making notes. 'I can do a lot online,' she said.

'Any chance you can work from home tomorrow?' he asked, explaining about the lack of electricity.

'No problem.' She laughed. 'I'd better send Dad to do a big Tesco shop, or he'll be looking over my shoulder all day wanting to interfere.'

Ian hadn't thought of that, but he could imagine that Tesco would keep Nigel busy for quite a while. He'd be in there with a calculator working out things like value for money offset against carbon footprints. He'd probably also got a food storage system that involved spreadsheets and lists of *best before* dates. Good thinking on Molly's part. An excellent way to keep her father happily occupied and out of her hair for at least the morning.

'Not all local records are digitised yet,' she continued. 'Can I go and visit the Fife archive?'

'Of course.' He was pleased that she felt confident enough. There was more than an afternoon's work there. Then a day or two to get a report together. In the meantime, he would get on with Freya's background searches. Best to get started today because he wasn't sure how he could do it with no electricity. It would probably involve a visit to the library in Dundee. With his library card he could get an hour of free internet use. And if the library was quiet and he smiled nicely at the librarian, he could get a lot more. But he still had today. He could make a start and draw up a list of essentials to follow up in the library if necessary.

He reached for the folders Freya had given him; four different coloured cardboard wallets containing copies of various adverts, application forms, reference details and covering letters. He opened an orange folder labelled 'Arkash Panchuli' and skimmed through his details. Twenty-six years old and, at the time of the application, working as a chef with his father, Hunar Panchuli and two brothers. Arkash was born in Glasgow and attended a grammar school there, where he picked up a fistful of exam results and had done particularly well in his Highers. Clearly a bright lad, Ian wondered why he'd not gone to university. Instead, he'd trained on a catering course, also in Glasgow and then worked in the family's Indian restaurant. Freya had noted at the interview that he was keen to gain experience away from the family business. Ian remembered him saying something about living and working in a family of seven and imagined that working for Freya might give him a way out. However much he wanted to get away from the family, they had taught him to be an excellent cook. The meal he produced the evening Ian was there was spectacular. Ian fancied himself as a connoisseur of Indian food and he'd never tasted anything better than he had that night. Freya also noted that Arkash was a third-generation immigrant with a British passport, so there would be no problem with his right to work in the UK. *You need to see his passport and take a copy,* he pencilled into the margin.

Ian logged into various databases but there was no record that Arkash had ever been in trouble with the police. He also checked social media pages. All open and as they should be with photographs of family weddings. Many, many photos — they were a large family. Arkash had been to India three years ago to visit cousins. He kept in touch with old school friends and went to a gym in Glasgow once a week. He was also interested in electronic music and created sound effects for local youth drama projects as well as a side-line as a conjuror for children's parties. Ian found his website with a photograph of him wearing a purple robe covered with stars and half-moons and wearing a gold turban with a feather. *An ideal employee,* Ian thought. He was qualified, experienced and was obviously who he claimed to be. Just as well, since Arkash already seemed to have started working at Murriemuir and had even moved into a room in an annexe attached to the kitchen. It would have been embarrassing for Freya if Ian had uncovered something unfortunate in his past and she'd had to turf him out. Ian noted all of this down and returned all the paperwork to its orange folder, ready for its return to Freya.

Arkash was the only one of the four he had met. He opened the next folder and found a photograph of Shining Lotus, aka Sharon Lofts from Luton. Sharon (or should he call her Shining?) had left school with five GCSEs and studied hairdressing at a local college. She'd worked for a while at a salon in Leighton Buzzard before getting involved with an environmental group who protested about a third runway at Heathrow and the proposed high-speed railway that would cut the journey from London to Birmingham by twenty minutes. Ian checked Google Maps and discovered that HS2, as it was known, would run right through some glorious countryside very close to Leighton Buzzard. Sharon didn't appear to have a personal connection to Heathrow but that didn't mean she couldn't be passionate about it. He wondered if she'd be prepared to lie down, Boris style, in front of bulldozers to prevent it. Although that had all gone a bit quiet recently. The pandemic had already had an effect on long haul flying and the Prime Minister had no doubt had other things on his mind during the last eighteen months. But that was nothing to do with Shining Lotus and her suitability to work for his sister-in-law. He turned back to the file and read more about Sharon. Why, for instance, had she changed her name? Was it just to attract clients with a more yoga-type pseudonym? Probably. She wasn't trying to disguise anything about her two names.

Having spent time with the group, Sharon turned vegan and decided that hairdressing was not an environmentally friendly way to earn a living. She retrained as a meditation and yoga teacher with a side-line in singing bowls. Ian had to look up singing bowls. He discovered that they were an ancient and respected tradition from Tibet, a means of healing through sound (although not recommended when pregnant). At that moment there was a yell from one or other of the electricians. *Some* sounds might be healing. But not things like fingernails on blackboards, or people tearing one's house apart.

Freya had noted that Sharon was keen to move to the pure air of Scotland. She'd suffered from asthma as a child, apparently. Freya also found her *refreshingly unposh*. She hadn't given her age – *quite right*, Ian thought. Age shouldn't be an issue. Looking at her photo — a petite woman with cropped hair — he guessed she was in her mid-thirties. As with Arkash, he couldn't find any record of her being in trouble. Even as a protester, she had kept the rules. She didn't have a website of her own although she was listed as a qualified yoga teacher on a site for tradespeople in Hertfordshire. A bit out of the way if she was moving to Scotland, but not keeping online details up to date wasn't a sin. She had a Facebook page but kept it private and didn't use it to advertise herself. Again, nothing wrong with that. He jotted down some notes for Freya, but as with Arkash she seemed to be who she said she was, even with two names.

He put the folder aside and turned to the next one. At this rate he'd be done today and would have no need to drive to the library in Dundee. He would be able to take the morning off and sleep late. Although, perhaps not. The shouting would continue tomorrow as the two electricians reconnected everything to the new board thingy under his stairs. He sighed and turned to the next folder.

Sonia Greenlow hadn't responded to an advert. She'd read an article about Murriemuir in a magazine and contacted Freya through her website to offer her services. She was qualified in reiki and mediation. She had attached copies of her certificates along with her birth certificate and a letter from HMRC as proof of her right to work in the UK. Since qualifying she'd worked as a private consultant and taken short contract work for a long list of organisations, which she had attached.

During lockdown she had run online sessions. That intrigued Ian. He supposed meditation was possible remotely. There was probably a range of suitable Zoom backgrounds for it, but how was reiki possible? Palms resting on computer screens? Seemed unlikely, but what did he know? He checked Sonia's website and found several reviews, all of which said she was excellent both face-to-face and online. So obviously it was possible.

According to her birth certificate she was in her late forties. He wondered what she had done before she took up reiki. Her early employment history was vague, saying only that she had done casual domestic work. Her references were all recent; from organisations she'd worked for and a couple from private clients. Gaps in employment history usually flagged up warnings. There could be a perfectly simple explanation; she might have been a stay-at-home mum bringing up children, although most people would have mentioned that. She could have been ill; struggling with her mental health perhaps. Or she could have been in prison. He couldn't find a criminal record. That didn't mean she'd never had one; all but the most serious offences were considered spent after a number of years. She could also have been sectioned, which again would be hard to trace after eight years. He put in a note drawing Freya's attention to this but supposed that the glowing praise for work over the last fifteen years was enough.

Finally, he came to Zhang Ming. And this time he hadn't found Freya, she had found him. A friend she had made on her yoga course suggested that yoga worked well alongside alternative therapies such as homeopathy and oriental medicine. Freya had checked out local alternative practices and had found the Zhang Centre for Chinese Medicine in Dundee, a small building in a narrow shopping street near the city centre. He'd been surprised, it said in Freya's notes, to be invited to work with her, but the moment she mentioned Murriemuir he'd jumped at it.

Mr Zhang gave his age as sixty-five and had been running the Chinese medicine surgery in Dundee for more than thirty years. Freya had noted that at interview he told her he was ready to hand over the business to his son and the opportunity to continue his practice part-time was timely. Freya had discussed hours with him, and they agreed that he would visit Murriemuir once a month, staying from Saturday morning until Tuesday evening. He would offer acupuncture and consultations in herbal remedies. Ian checked out

Zhang's Dundee surgery. He'd opened it after arriving in the country from Hong Kong with his wife and young son. He'd enclosed a copy of his British passport as evidence of his right to work in the UK. Ian couldn't remember the exact status of Hong Kong citizens at the time of the handover to China, but holding a British passport was enough. Freya should ask to see the original rather than accept a copy and ask for a document showing his National Insurance number. Apart from that everything was in order.

Ian shut down his computer as the electricians were packing up and leaving. He'd done a good day's work and there was no need for a library visit the next day. But there would probably be a lot more shouting as they installed the new box, so he decided to drive to Murriemuir in person and deliver Freya's folders. With any luck she would be brewing up coffee and Arkash might be in need of someone to taste his latest dishes.

8

Molly had spent three days on her research. One day working from home and two more in the Fife archive, where she told Ian they'd been extremely helpful and she'd made friends with a young man called Alan, who made cups of tea for her and did all her photocopying. She'd arrived back in the office between the departure of the electricians and the arrival of more plumbers. This time they would be installing things rather than ripping them out.

'Do plumbers make a lot of noise?' she asked.

'Almost certainly,' said Ian. 'And we need to fill the kettle and coffee machine. The water's going to be off for a couple of hours.'

'I'll make coffee now, shall I? And I've made some shortbread. I thought I'd bring you some before Dad and Ryan ate it all.' She was carrying a large shoulder bag, which she hung on the back of a chair, and pulled out a red tin decorated with a dog wearing a tartan ribbon around its neck. She put the tin on Ian's desk. 'Don't eat it all before I've made the coffee,' she said, heading towards the kitchen to fill the kettle and a water jug.

This wasn't the timid little person Ian had interviewed just a few weeks ago. She was like a butterfly emerging from a long spell as a chrysalis, or should that be caterpillar? He should mug up on his natural history. Molly was getting out and making friends. This was thanks to Jeanie, but he hoped her work had helped her as well.

She handed him his coffee and opened the tin of shortbread. Then she opened her bag again and took out a bright green folder. 'My report on Murriemuir House,' she said, putting it down on the desk in front of him. 'I bought the folder because I wanted it to look nice.'

'You must pay yourself back from the petty cash,' he said, slowly turning the pages. He was impressed. It was a beautifully presented report with a list of contents and footnotes. She'd also printed out records and photographs from the archive. He'd opened an account at the various Scottish records offices, and he was probably about to receive a hefty bill. But he'd not placed a limit on what Molly could spend and it looked as if it would be worth it. Duncan would be impressed as well. 'Talk me through it,' he said.

'I know you told me to check out the house's recent history, but I went right back to when it was built. I think you'll be glad I did.'

'That sounds intriguing,' he said, taking a bite of shortbread.

'Right,' said Molly, turning to the first page. 'Murriemuir was built in 1860 by Andrew Buckland-Kerr, who is described in the records as a gentleman farmer. On every census up to 1911, that's the last one available, there were a number of servants recorded. I found the census records online and made copies of them. They're all at the back here.' She flicked to the last pages of her report. 'I've highlighted people who lived at Murriemuir and were listed as servants. None of the names seem relevant at the moment, but I thought it would be useful to have them. It could save a trip back to the archive.' Then she pointed to some of the family names. 'I've highlighted Buckland-Kerrs in a different colour so it's easy to trace the family. Andrew's wife was called Hilda and they had two children; Malcolm was born in 1895 and died in 1962, and Janet, who was born in 1898 and died in 1906.'

A daughter who died at the age of eight. That was sad, but probably not uncommon in those days. He sighed.

Molly turned back to the beginning of the report. 'Don't look so impatient,' she said. 'You need to know all of that.'

Had he been looking impatient? He hoped not. He wanted to encourage Molly, not put her off. 'Sorry, I was thinking about the daughter who died so young,' he said. 'Carry on.'

'Janet. Her death was recorded as an infection, but while Malcolm appeared on the 1901 census as a scholar, Janet was missing, although she didn't die until 1906. That's odd, don't you think?'

He nodded. 'Perhaps she was at boarding school or staying with friends.'

'Anyway,' Molly continued, 'I found out from local records that Andrew and Hilda died in the 1920s. Their son Malcolm appears as head of the household and was married to Beattie. I checked birth records and found they had two children; Clover and Charles.'

Ian looked up suddenly. 'Clover?'

'That's interesting, isn't it?'

'Very, but it can't be our Clover.'

'No. This one died in 1945. It's in the records and she's buried in Murriemuir churchyard.'

Ian checked the timeline Molly had made. 'It says here she was born 1938, so if she died in 1945 she was only seven.'

'It's really sad how many children died young. Beattie, that's Malcolm's wife, died in 1940 giving birth to Charles. Malcolm continued to run the farm until his death in 1962. Charles never married and died in 2005. At the time of his death, he seems to have been living on his own, although according to the local paper account of his death, there may have been a housekeeper. There's no record of one on the voter rolls though. The farm was failing, and Charles died in debt. The house and land were sold separately; all the land that hadn't already been sold was taken over by a big farming company. The house was sold to St Andrews University and used as rented accommodation for PhD students until 2009, when it was sold again and reopened as a hotel. Not a very successful one, but it struggled on in spite of poor reviews on sites like TripAdvisor until your brother bought it at the end of last year.' She closed the folder and grinned at him.

'Brilliant job, Molly.'

She smiled. 'I enjoyed doing it. But it's not going to help, is it? We still don't know who the Clover who was dug up is and why she died.'

She had a point. All they had to go on was the coincidence of the name. Clover was an unusual name. There had to be a family connection of some kind, didn't there? He typed Buckland-Kerr into Google. Plenty of both Bucklands and Kerrs but no entries for the two together. 'Did you check birth records for Clover Buckland-Kerr?' he asked.

'Of course, first thing I thought of. But there was nothing. Charles is the last recorded birth with that name. Same with deaths.'

'I'll pass this on to Duncan,' he said. 'You kept an online copy, didn't you?'

She nodded. 'Shall I print another one?'

He shook his head. 'Not at the moment. Just print out the timeline and pin it up on the board. It might be helpful to have it as a quick reference.' He found a large envelope and wrote Duncan's address on it. He could have emailed it all to him from Molly's backup copy, but she'd gone to so much trouble to make it look professional. It would be wasted in one of his office drawers.

'Shall I post that?' Molly asked. 'I'm going to the shop on my way home.'

'Yes, thanks,' he said, passing it to her. He'd planned a walk down to the village himself with Lottie, but she'd probably prefer a run in the park.

Molly read the address on the envelope. 'Duncan Clyde? Is he related to Jeanie Clyde?'

'He's married to her,' he said, smiling. Looked like Jeanie was a fast worker.

'I met her at school,' said Molly. 'She's really nice. I'm going to help with her safety project and we're going shopping together tomorrow. Dad's taking Ryan to the wildlife park.'

'Sounds like a nice way to spend a Saturday,' he said. 'For all of you,' he added. Shopping wouldn't be his idea of a fun day out, but he guessed Jeanie and Molly didn't see it like that.

'Dad's looking forward to it,' said Molly. 'And Ryan loves animals. I suppose all five-year-olds do. Dad's been so good to me, buying my car and giving me some money for new clothes. I just wish there was a way to pay him back.'

'I think seeing you happy will probably do that.'

'I'll cook him something delicious for dinner tonight. That's why I'm going to the shop.'

'Well,' said Ian. 'Enjoy your weekend. You deserve it.'

'I'm doing okay then, at the job?'

'More than okay.' He smiled at her. 'I can honestly say I've never had a better assistant.' Nick had been great and a lot of fun. But she didn't have Molly's organisation and presentation skills. And he'd always been a bit on edge over her enthusiasm for hacking.

He watched as Molly put her coat on and stowed the folder away in her bag. He'd made a good decision to employ her. As he didn't need to walk to the village, Lottie could wait for an evening walk. He'd spend the afternoon checking out private investigator training opportunities. He was sure he had heard of day release courses. If not in Dundee, then probably in Edinburgh.

9

On a Friday morning in early October, Ian was at his desk early. This morning a plasterer was arriving, and he needed to be there to let him in. Lottie had to make do with a quick run round the garden and was now snoozing next to a radiator, Ian having decided that autumn had progressed far enough to keep the heating on during the day. Best of all, the upstairs plumbing was now complete. He had a lovely new bathroom and a bedroom almost ready to sleep in. All it needed now was plastering, tiling and painting. And someone strong to help him move his furniture upstairs. But today was a plastering day and plastering was quiet, wasn't it?

The doorbell rang. Lottie leapt up and scuttled towards it, barking. Ian picked her up and opened the door. The man standing on the doorstep was tiny, barely five feet, Ian thought. Somehow, he had staggered up the garden path with bags of plaster, a box of tools and a couple of objects that looked like instruments of torture. The kind of things he'd seen in the hospital rehab department being attached to people who had lost the use of their legs.

'Morning,' said the man, grinning at him. 'Pete, the plasterer.' He held out his hand and grasped Ian's in a grip that seemed way beyond the strength of a man his size.

'Let me help with those,' said Ian, grabbing a bag of plaster in each hand and heading for the stairs, trying not to laugh because Pete the plasterer sound like a character from a kids' cartoon and Pete's appearance didn't do much to dispel the image. He showed Pete the two rooms that needed plastering and wondered how he was going to reach the top of the walls. Should he offer to lend him a ladder?

Pete must have read his thoughts. He waved the two metal objects at Ian. 'Stilts,' he explained. 'Plasterers' best friends. Good job you've had the plumbing done,' he added. 'No need to keep popping downstairs for water.'

Ian left him to get on with it and went back down to his desk just as Molly arrived. She was usually at work before him. She now had her own key and could let herself in while he was walking Lottie. She bustled in, blowing on her hands. 'Mornings are getting cold,' she said. 'Dad's already bringing his tender plants inside. Says there could be frost any day.' She took off her coat and hung it on a hook behind the door. 'Not late, am I?'

'Punctual as ever,' said Ian. 'I needed to be here to let the plasterer in.'

'A quiet day then,' she said. 'Plastering doesn't make a lot of noise, does it?'

'Can't imagine why it should,' he said, settling down to read his latest crop of emails.

'I'll make coffee,' she said, disappearing into the kitchen, an ever-hopeful Lottie in her wake.

Molly had changed in the weeks she had been working for him. She'd cut her hair and no longer hid behind it. She also had some new clothes, colourful jumpers and a pair of cowboy boots. Jeanie's influence, he thought. But that wasn't all. She'd come out of her shell. She no longer crept into the office like a timid mouse but strode in confidently and got down to work before he'd barely had a chance to pass the time of day. Palling her up with Jeanie had been a great idea. He and Duncan could feel pleased with themselves. He wondered if the cowboy boots meant she'd taken up line dancing. She hadn't mentioned it and in any case what she did outside working hours was none of his business.

Ian sent his emails and clicked open his calendar. He noticed that he'd marked in the following two weeks as the school autumn holiday.

Molly returned with coffee and placed a cup on the desk beside him. 'Are we busy today?' she asked.

'Not particularly. A few files to catch up with.'

'I'll get going on them, shall I?'

He stood up and let her sit at the computer. He really should buy another one. A laptop perhaps, for working away from the office when he had workmen in. 'I've just been looking at the calendar. I meant to ask if you need time off during the autumn break, with Ryan off school.'

She shook her head. 'I've booked him in for an activity club. And he's got a sleepover next week for a friend's birthday. The rest of the time Dad's happy to step in.'

'What about taking some days off? You've earned it.'

She laughed. 'I've only been here a few weeks. I can't have earned any leave yet.'

'Well,' he said, making a sudden decision. 'I'm going to take a couple of days off next week. No reason why you shouldn't as well.'

'Doing something nice?'

'I haven't decided yet.' He'd only just decided to take time off. And he'd only done that because he didn't know how else to make sure Molly did the same.

'You could spend time with Caroline. Teachers will be off for the next couple of weeks.'

'You've met Caroline?'

She looked down at her work for a moment and then nodded. Jeanie, he supposed. She and Caroline were long-term friends and Jeanie was all for connecting people. Perhaps Molly's friendship with Jeanie wasn't such a good idea after all. Not if they'd been gossiping about him behind his back.

'Jeanie says you and Caroline are made for each other.'

That didn't surprise him at all. Jeanie would have had them married off months ago if it had been up to her. 'You need to watch Jeanie,' he said. 'It's her mission in life to see everyone paired off. She'll be finding no end of nice young men for you if you let her.'

'She's already started,' said Molly, with a grin. 'We had a harvest sale at school yesterday to raise money for her safety campaign and she introduced me to a very charming young constable from St. Andrews. He was there giving out high vis sleeve bands to the kids who have bikes.'

'Hot date coming up?' Ian asked, wondering if he didn't sound as bad as Jeanie.

She shook her head. 'Not ready yet,' she said. 'I think I'll do what Caroline does and just stay friends.'

'Excellent idea. Caroline and I have agreed to stay uncommitted friends.'

'Oh yeah?' said Molly with a grin.

This conversation was going in a direction he didn't feel entirely comfortable with, and it was a relief when they were greeted by the sound of footsteps overhead. The clonking of metal feet on the wooden floorboards. Molly looked up at the ceiling. 'Whatever's that?' she said. 'It sounds really sinister. Like a ghost. Is there someone trapped up there?'

'That'll be Pete on his stilts,' Ian explained.

'Stilts like they have in circuses?'

'Something like that. Pete is very small. It's the only way he can reach the ceiling.'

She sighed. 'And we thought it was going to be a quiet day.'

'It's better than the hammering and shouting though, don't you think?'

'Yes, and once the plaster's dry there'll just be decorators and then it's done.'

'Thank goodness, yes.'

'Have you decided what to do with all the extra space?'

'I'm moving my sleeping quarters upstairs and I'll use the downstairs bedroom as extra office space. I'm not sure how exactly. Any ideas?'

Molly looked around. 'It would be good to have more whiteboard space. You could use two walls in the new room. And move the printer in there. And the filing cabinet.'

'You don't fancy your own office?'

She shook her head. 'Not really. It's nice to be able to chat while we're working.'

She was right, it was nice. He'd discovered that when Nick was working for him. 'Are you done with those reports?' he asked. 'I need to order a laptop. We can't keep up this musical chairs over the computer. We need one each.'

'Can I just check something?'

'Sure.'

'Can I look at the Clover photos? The ones you took at Murriemuir.'

He clicked on the folder. 'Any in particular?'

'The doll remains.'

He found the photo of the dismembered doll; a bald plastic head, two arms and two legs. He found those way more gruesome and disturbing than the actual skeleton. 'Why did you want to see them?'

'I found something at that sale we had at school yesterday.'

'Where you met the dishy young constable?'

'Yes, that one,' she sighed and frowned at him. 'I told you…'

'Sorry, just teasing.' And possibly getting back at her for the banter about Caroline.

'Anyway, people brought lots of home-made stuff; jam, chutney, cakes and craft stuff.'

'Craft stuff?'

'Quilted bags, knitted hats, crocheted loo roll holders, macramé plant holders, that sort of thing.'

He should have taken Lainie. She could probably raise a small fortune for the school in knitted products.

'I bought this.' Molly opened her bag, pulled out a doll and passed it to him. 'I think it's the same as the one they dug up,' she said.

Ian looked at it and then at the photo on the computer screen. She could be right, although the one she was holding was wearing clothes and had hair. She sat the doll on his desk, and it stared at him with a cross-eyed, sombre expression. Did kids actually like things like this?

Molly picked up the doll and stripped off its clothes. An action he found even more alarming than the blank stare. She had revealed a padded torso. 'I talked to Viv, the woman who makes them. The bodies are made of jute and the hair is wool. She said that was unusual. Most factory-produced dolls have synthetic bodies and hair. These are only made by a few people. It's a local tradition that dates back to when Dundee was the centre of the jute industry. There's a museum about it in Henderson's Wynd.'

'What are you thinking?'

'I googled it and jute and wool are both biodegradable. They'd disintegrate in damp ground. A synthetic mass-produced doll would have been complete for years and years. I think Clover's doll might have been one of these locally made ones.'

'Good thinking,' he said. 'If we can find out who was making them twenty years ago, we might be able to trace people who bought them. But if Clover was eleven or twelve when she died, wouldn't she have been a bit old for dolls?' He couldn't imagine his niece, twelve-year-old Lyra, being attached to anything like this. But it was likely that she was more sophisticated and worldly than the average twelve-year-old.

'It could have been something she was given as a child and kept because she was fond of it. Lots of teenagers still have their dolls and teddies.'

It was their first real lead and was something they should check out. It could give them a clue about who Clover was and, more importantly, who the adults in her life might have been. They needed to know not only who she was but why she had never been reported missing. 'Can you get back to this woman and see if she knows other people who make them? Then find out if anyone's selling them online. Have a look at eBay.'

Molly wrote it all down in her notebook. 'Viv, the woman who makes them, is Ellie's mum and Ellie's quite friendly with Ryan. I can easily talk to her when I pick him up this afternoon.'

'Excellent,' said Ian, thinking that the village school was a good source of local information. 'I might call round local schools and see if any of them had a Clover on the roll.' He did a quick calculation. If Clover died at the age of eleven or twelve, she would have been in primary school around twenty years ago. He assumed schools kept records going back twenty years. Whether they would be prepared to give him the information, he wasn't sure. They wouldn't want to risk breaching the Data Protection Act. But presumably he could call on Duncan for a warrant if necessary. He'd mention it to him. It could well be something he'd already looked into, although he'd probably have let him know if he'd found anything.

'I could try local craft shops as well,' said Molly. 'Some of them must have been there twenty years ago.'

'Good thinking. Make a list and we'll follow them up next week.'

They were just tidying up for the day when there was loud crash from upstairs, followed by the shouting of some unrepeatable curses. Ian and Molly rushed up the stairs and found Pete sitting on the floor rubbing his leg, a splintered floorboard and water flowing out of an underfloor pipe.

'Turn the bleedin' water off,' Pete shouted as he staggered to his feet. Ian looked at him blankly then remembered the stopcock by the back door. He ran downstairs and turned it as far as he could. When he returned, he found Pete wrapping the fractured pipe in a dust sheet. 'Better call a plumber,' he said, pulling out his phone. 'Some stupid blighter forgot to nail that floorboard down, got caught in me stilt and tripped me up. Broke the pipe when I fell.'

The good news was that a plumber arrived within the hour. He made a temporary repair to the broken pipe, turned the water back on and then delivered the not so good news. 'It's good for a day or two,' he said. 'But your piping's knackered. We'll need to replace all the pipes that run under these floorboards. I can fit you in after the weekend, but you'll be without water for two days.'

10

Ian would have to close the office for two days. They weren't too swamped with work and both he and Molly would benefit from a break.

'Shouldn't I work from home again?' Molly asked.

'No, take a couple of days off.'

'I can't take two days off,' she told him.

'Why not?' he asked. 'Everyone needs a break. You'll get holiday pay,' he reassured her.

'It doesn't seem right,' she said. 'Not when I've only just started. Although...'

'Although?'

'A couple of the girls I used to work with asked me if I'd like to go for a night out in Glasgow. I said no because I'd need to stay overnight, and I wasn't sure if I could ask Dad to babysit for a whole two days.'

From what Ian knew of Nigel, he'd be only too glad of a couple of days on his own with Ryan. Was it more than that? Was she nervous about returning to Glasgow? She'd be in no danger as her ex was securely banged up for the foreseeable. 'Look,' he said. 'We're closing the office for a couple of days. It's a great chance for you to get out and have some fun.'

'Maybe,' she said. 'But what will you do?'

A good question. Suddenly he had the answer. 'I'll call Caroline and ask if I can stay with her for a couple of days.'

'It would be nice for you to have time off together.'

'And if I'm having a nice time, you should as well.'

Molly agreed to think about it.

Just to drive his point home, he mentioned it to Nigel that evening in the pub, pointing out that he'd have Molly home again for two days. He also managed to drop in the fact that Molly had been invited for a night out with friends in Glasgow but had turned them down. 'Silly girl,' Nigel said. 'Why didn't she tell me? A night out with the girls would do her good.'

'She doesn't want to take you for granted as a babysitter,' said Ian.

'Pretend this conversation never happened,' said Nigel. 'I'll suggest it myself. I'll tell her Ryan and I want to go on an adventure together. A strictly boys only thing.'

'What kind of adventure?' Ian asked, wondering if that might make Molly more determined not to go away.

'The kind of thing we did together when she was Ryan's age. Setting up camp in the attic was always popular.'

It was hard to imagine Nigel scrabbling round on all fours making camps, but it sounded like fun.

He walked home and called Caroline.

∼

Ian was relieved, if surprised, when the plumber turned up exactly when he had said he would. This was not the original plumber but the one called out by Pete the plasterer. Ian waited until he had turned off the water and then loaded a small backpack, walking boots, Lottie, her bed and several towels into the back of his car.

'I'll be back around midday tomorrow,' he said. 'Mrs Crombie next door will lock up after you when you leave and let you in again tomorrow morning. You've got my number. I won't be far away if you need anything.'

~

A long walk, they decided. They drove to Crail and walked the four and a half miles along the coast path to Anstruther, where they lunched at what was generally considered to be the best fish and chip shop in Scotland, if not the UK. They took a bus back to Crail and returned to Caroline's house with windswept hair and with two tired dogs, and collapsed into comfortable chairs by a log burning stove.

'A perfect day,' said Caroline. 'And after that lunch, I'll just heat up some soup for supper. Is that okay?'

'Sounds good,' Ian said, yawning and reaching for the beer she had just poured him.

'Netflix or a book?' Caroline asked.

A book, he thought. It was easier to pick up again if, as seemed very likely, he fell asleep. He looked along her shelves of books and picked out one that he'd read before *The Puppet Show*.

'Do you know Cumbria?' she asked.

'A little,' he said. 'It's a great setting for a crime story. I enjoyed this one the first time I read it and there are always things worth revisiting in a complicated crime novel.'

'A professional interest?'

'I suppose so, although Poe is in the police and his cases are way more grisly than mine.'

'And is your Molly anything like Tilly?'

Had he told her about that? He didn't think so. She knew he had been looking for a new assistant. He didn't remember telling her he'd found one.

'How do you know about that?' he asked.

'Molly told me herself.'

Of course, he'd forgotten that they knew each other. Brought together by Jeanie, who liked to make sure everyone knew everyone else.

'She told me she'd been offered a job. She said she really wanted to do it but was nervous about working with you, just the two of you alone in your house.'

He understood that. 'I know she's not very confident, but she's nothing to worry about. I'll take good care of her.'

Caroline held his hand. 'I know,' she said. 'And it's what I told Molly. I said you were one of the nicest, gentlest people I'd ever known and that she needed to start trusting men again.'

He could almost feel himself blushing.

Wait a minute. Molly and Jeanie hadn't met until after she started to work for him, so she and Caroline must have known each other before that. 'Where did you meet Molly?' he asked.

She stared at the fire for a few minutes. 'I've never told you about my marriage, have I?'

'Only that it was unhappy, and you moved back to Scotland to be as far away from your ex as you could.'

'I married a man with a high-powered career in banking. He wasn't home a lot but when he was, he had no way of unwinding except to treat me as a punchbag. I ended up in hospital having a miscarriage, brought on by a blow to the stomach. I was discharged after a couple of days and took the first train to my sister in Perth. I had some spectacular bruises, which were photographed by the hospital. I filed for divorce on the grounds of unreasonable behaviour. I had to leave my job without giving notice and my solicitor insisted on him paying a month's salary. Apart from that I refused to take a penny from him. He tried to go for a financial settlement as a bribe to stop me going to the police. I declined that and reported him.'

'He was arrested?'

'No, they decided not to press charges. Lack of evidence, apparently.'

He was speechless. 'I didn't know,' was all he was able to mutter.

She reached for his hand.

'It's not something I talk about much. It's all in the past. I've moved on.'

'But you always seem so... tough and sure of yourself.'

She shrugged. 'And how do you think I got to be like that?'

'And Molly went through it as well.'

'It was worse for Molly. She'd been forced to give up work and had a small child.'

'I can't begin to imagine what it must be like living with an abusive partner.'

'You can't?' she said, giving him what he thought was a quizzical look. 'I suppose one of the hardest things is to admit that one is a victim.'

'Is that how you met Molly?'

'Kind of. Once I'd settled into a new job, I started a support group with four other women. Not the kind where we sat around feeling sorry for ourselves and hating all men forever. It was enough to be with people that you knew would understand. The first thing we did was enlist a brilliant ex-army woman called Big Brenda who taught us self-defence. Not that we liked the idea of matching violence with more violence, but it gave us the confidence to get out of dangerous situations. After that we started going on 'reclaim the night' pub crawls.'

'In Dundee?'

She nodded. 'Groups of us in pink bobble hats buying pints for ourselves.'

'Blimey, that was brave.' *He'd* think twice about going to a Dundee pub at night. 'Did you get a lot of hassle?'

'There was a bit of jeering but mostly it was good-natured. We collected a lot of support.'

'And Molly joined you?'

'We've quietened down since those first events. We do still have evenings out, but now it's more about being there for each other and meeting for a quiet coffee when we're needed. Molly joined us in the spring. Her social worker gave her my name. Her father had just bought her a car, but she wasn't brave enough to drive to Dundee, so she came here for a cup of tea. I think she sees me as a kind of older sister.'

She topped up his beer and he tried to return to Poe and Tilly but found his mind wandering. 'What are *you* reading?' he asked.

'It's called *The Room,*' she said. 'It's about a woman who was kept a prisoner in this man's cellar and how she escapes with her young son.'

11

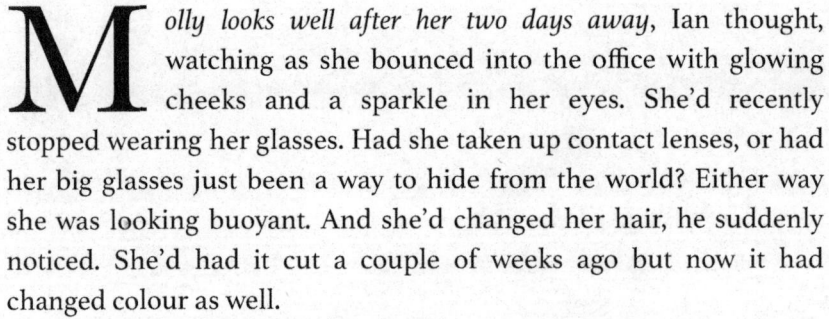

Molly *looks well after her two days away*, Ian thought, watching as she bounced into the office with glowing cheeks and a sparkle in her eyes. She'd recently stopped wearing her glasses. Had she taken up contact lenses, or had her big glasses just been a way to hide from the world? Either way she was looking buoyant. And she'd changed her hair, he suddenly noticed. She'd had it cut a couple of weeks ago but now it had changed colour as well.

'Enjoyed Glasgow?' he asked.

'It was great,' she said. 'I'd been nervous about it. I don't know why. It was silly, wasn't it?'

'It's perfectly understandable,' he said. 'I remember how scared I was when I first came out of hospital, limping around wondering why the world had sped up without me.'

'How long were you in for?'

'Three months.' And no real transition. One minute he'd been confined to his bed apart from therapy sessions. The next he was cast out into the world again. He'd been discharged to a messy divorce and nowhere to live. Recovery was way more than simply being patched up and helped to start walking again. But all that was behind him now. 'So you had a good time?'

'Lovely. A proper girly time. We went out and had our hair and nails done.' She flashed her sparkly nails at him. 'Then we hit the town.'

'Is that why your hair's different?'

'Just some coloured highlights for a night out. They'll wash out in a bit.'

He recalled Stephanie doing something similar with her hair. He hadn't liked it, but then Stephanie had never learnt how to be subtle about that kind of thing. With Molly it was different. Molly had a kind of elfin look since she'd had her hair cut. Never in a million years could anyone have described Stephanie as elfin. She went for more of a pouty-lipped soap star look. But it was none of his business what Molly chose to do with her hair as long as she didn't put clients off. He decided his antipathy was Stephanie rather than hair colour related. Time to let that go. He really was better off without her. It was what Stephanie had done to him that rankled, rather than the woman herself. She had a new life in America. He had a new life right here. And he had Lottie. An excellent exchange. Unfaithful wife swapped for faithful and adoring dog.

'The girls took me shopping,' Molly continued. 'They persuaded me to buy a new dress. Bright red with sparkles. I'd not worn anything like that since... well, since I was a student probably.'

'And Ryan was okay without you?'

'He was fine. And Dad looks years younger. I thought he might be worn out, but they can't wait for me to go away again.'

Ian laughed. 'And school's started again?'

'Oh yes, and there's some interesting school gate gossip,' she said.

He could imagine it. A collection of parents who'd not seen each other for a couple of weeks. There'd be plenty to gossip about. 'Anything in particular?' Juicy bits of scandal perhaps? 'Are you going to tell me about it?' he asked.

She sat down at her desk and grinned at him. 'They're saying Murriemuir House is haunted.'

That was interesting. It had been worth employing Molly for the school gate gossip alone. He hardly needed surveillance. He could probably learn all he wanted to know just by hanging round outside the school. On the other hand, hanging around at school gates wasn't generally a good thing to do. Fine for Molly, who was one of the crowd. For a single middle-aged man, possibly less fine.

'Really?' He wondered if Stewart and Freya knew about that. Like buried corpses, it probably wasn't something that had cropped up in the conveyancing searches. 'Haunted how?' he asked. It was an old, isolated house. There were probably quite a few unexplained events; creaking floorboards, strange shadows, weird sounds from ancient plumbing. He'd had a few of those here. Not so many since the plumber had finished. But anyone of a suggestable disposition could well have suspected visits from the supernatural.

'It's since they dug up the bones,' said Molly.

Coincidence probably. Something like that happens and people start noticing things that they'd never paid any attention to before.

'Apparently really weird things have been happening,' Molly continued.

'What sort of things?' Ghostly figures in white sheets? Clanking chains? Objects flinging themselves around?

'Well, Valerie, one of the mums, goes to a yoga class there and she said there was a lot of noise from the singing bowls.'

That didn't sound very ghostly. 'They teach that, don't they? It was probably someone practising.'

'No, she said the bowls were all set out in the yoga room and started this ringing noise even though there was no one near them. They were doing the end of class relaxation when they started so they were all lying on the floor. There'd been nothing before that.'

'Probably just some strange vibrations. Don't they do some kind of chanting in yoga classes? Perhaps that was enough to set the bowls off. Or perhaps there was a draught. Did they get too hot and open the windows?'

'No idea. I've never done yoga. Aren't the studios usually kept very warm?'

He didn't know either, never having done yoga himself. 'I don't think that's enough to start assuming there are ghosts.'

'But that's not all. Some of the resident guests heard a baby crying in the attic one night.'

'One of the children?' he suggested.

'They said it was definitely a baby.'

'Don't they sound the same?'

'Of course not. They're quite different.' Molly looked at him and sighed. 'Don't you believe in ghosts at all?' she asked.

'Not the sort that make strange noises at night.'

'I didn't think I did really, but it sounded quite scary, and it made me wonder if I was wrong. Valerie said it all started after the bones were dug up. It's a bit of a coincidence, isn't it? Don't you think digging up a body could have disturbed something in the house?'

He was sceptical. 'They didn't hear dogs barking or cats meowing as well, did they?' He tried not to laugh, but it was difficult to take seriously. Weren't they all just a bit sensitive about it? Yes, they'd dug up a skeleton. But it was also coming up to Halloween. They were surrounded by ghosts, witches, pumpkins and all manner of spooky paraphernalia. It was on every child's mind right now, probably most of their parents' as well. They'd been watching too many ghost films or listening to stories of hauntings.

'You're laughing at me,' said Molly. 'I'm only telling you what I heard.'

'No, I wasn't laughing at you. It just seems a bit far-fetched. But you were right to tell me about it. I don't suppose you came across anything in your research about the house that might suggest any kind of haunting?'

'No, I'd have told you if I had.'

She *would* have noticed that. And told him about it. She'd probably have added anecdotal accounts to her report along with any photos she'd managed to find.

'I suppose it might put people off going to the classes there,' she said. 'Although Valerie doesn't seem to have been put off by it.'

'I don't know if it would put people off. It could even attract them.

Your friend Valerie doesn't seem to mind, and she probably isn't the only one.'

'Like ghost watchers?'

'Possibly.' Or sceptics like himself who just wanted to brazen it out and prove there was nothing there. But from what Molly told him it seemed they had opened the centre as planned. There had been some doubt about it, but Stewart claimed he would be able to have a word with *some people* and the crime scene had been cleared up in double quick time. They had spent a couple of days with drones searching for disturbed areas of ground where there could be more bodies buried, but had found nothing. As Duncan had expected, they weren't investigating any further than trying to discover who had missed Clover. That could change if they discovered she'd disappeared in suspicious circumstances, but for now no further action was planned.

Ghosts at Murriemuir? It could, Ian supposed, be someone playing tricks. But he couldn't imagine that Freya had upset anyone. The local wellness community didn't look particularly competitive and the idea of espionage from rivals sat uneasily with mindfulness, meditation and living in the moment. Perhaps Stewart had upset someone. A business colleague possibly, who saw this as a way of getting his own back. Offshore wind farming seemed innocent enough, but Ian knew nothing about the kind of cut-throat circles his brother moved in. Was someone trying to drive them away by targeting his wife's business? A shame for Freya if they were. She'd worked hard to get the centre up and running. It would be just like Stewart to have done something to mess it all up for her. But he was being unfair to his brother. There was nothing to suggest that he'd made enemies. He'd just made a lot of money.

'I'll go and see Freya,' he told Molly. 'Just to check that the rumours are only harmless gossip.' He could drive over there tomorrow afternoon and see how things were going. He might ask Will if he'd help him take Lottie for a walk.

12

'Is it okay if I come in late tomorrow?' asked Molly, looking up from her phone.

'Sure,' said Ian. That would suit him well. The new computer was being delivered first thing in the morning and he'd be able to have it all set up for her when she did come in. It was a surprise for her and one that he'd taken a while to decide on. Should he get another desktop? Or would a laptop be better? Deciding it could be useful to have a computer they could use away from the office, he settled on a large state-of-the-art laptop. He would network it to his own desktop so both of them could use either depending on where they were. He looked up and grinned at her. 'Doing something nice?' Perhaps Jeanie's young constable was making headway after all. Or was it another visit to Alan at the archive? *Mind your own business,* he told himself. He didn't much like other people interfering in his own love life. He should respect Molly's privacy and let her decide for herself when she was ready to try dating again. He was sure she would. She'd had a nasty experience but that shouldn't put her off men for life. She was young and lively, and she deserved some fun. He knew she loved her father but living with Nigel and *fun* didn't really go hand in hand.

'It's work, actually,' she said, putting on her coat. 'I talked to that woman again.'

Ian watched as she wrapped a long scarf around her neck. *One of Lainie's,* he thought. The two of them had become quite chatty recently, sharing biscuit recipes and moaning about the noise the builders made. It was a bright, chilly morning. Breezy but not yet winter. Molly was adding extra layers of clothing every day now. What would she wear in a couple of months when it was really cold? He was distracted by thoughts of long winter walks scrunching through snow with Lottie. 'Which woman is that?' he asked.

'The one who was selling dolls at the autumn sale. You know, the one we had at school before the break. I told you about her.'

'Oh yes, Valerie.'

'No, Valerie does yoga at Murriemuir and told me about the haunting there. This is Viv. She's the one who makes the dolls.'

'Like the one we dug up?'

'Yes. We went for a coffee the other day and I asked her how long she'd been making them. She told me she learnt how to do it from her mother, who used to make them for presents and charities.'

'How long ago was that?'

'She started making them when she was at school in the eighties and stopped when she needed to wear reading glasses and couldn't see so well in dim light. That's when she taught Viv how to do it. She also said her mum used to sell a few in the Murriemuir village shop, which was near where she lived.'

'Interesting,' he said.

'I thought it would be good to go and talk to Mrs Smart who runs the shop now.'

'Excellent idea. Although you might not find out very much. They probably won't keep records of sales from that long ago.'

'But you don't mind me going?'

'Of course not, go for it.' It was good to see her so keen and going out talking to people was doing her good. So far it had been useful as well. Which was more than he could say for his own progress. A few background checks his one contribution, and those hadn't revealed anything out of the ordinary. It was very unlikely that the four prospective employees had any kind of link to the remains found in the garden.

∽

The next day Molly arrived mid-morning looking flushed and excited. 'Good timing,' he said. 'I've just set up the new laptop.'

'Wow,' she said, opening it cautiously and peering at the desktop picture he'd used. A view over the estuary from the office window. 'It's a top-of-the-range one, isn't it?'

'No point in being penny-pinching. We rely on computers for so much of our work. Have a play with it while I go and make the coffee.'

When he returned with a tray of coffee and biscuits, she was busy typing. He poured her a cup of coffee and sat down. 'How was your morning?' he asked, biting into a gingernut.

Molly took a sip of coffee and put the mug down on the desk next to her notebook. 'Really interesting,' she said. 'I'm just typing up my notes.'

'And relevant?'

'I think so. Mrs Smart is very talkative. She had lots to tell me.'

'Mrs Smart?' He really should have made notes of his own. He was losing track of who was who.

'She runs the shop in Murriemuir. It's been there for years, although it was going to close down last year.'

'That would have been a shame.' It was only since he had lived in Greyport that he'd realised how precious village shops were.

'The residents in the village got together and saved it. It's running as a cooperative now. Apparently, your brother was asked for a donation when he moved there, and he paid for new fittings. Mrs Smart is very proud of them. Sustainable timber, she said. For every set of shelves they put up, a tree is planted to replace the timber that was used.'

Good for Stewart. *No doubt he now gets a discount and free advertising,* Ian thought, telling himself not to be so cynical. Considering how little *he* did for the environment, he would do well to follow his brother's example, although right now he couldn't see how.

'They don't sell the dolls any more,' Molly continued, 'but when I showed her the one I'd bought she was able to tell me quite a lot about them. They always had two or three sitting in the window. They didn't sell very many. I suppose all the local kids had one already. But there is one sale she remembered very well.' She grinned at him, keeping him in suspense.

'Why was it so memorable?' he asked.

'Two reasons. The first was that she sold it to an Indian gentleman. He wasn't local. He was on holiday, just spending a couple of days in the area looking up an old friend.'

'And the second reason?'

'He didn't want to take it with him. He asked if it could be delivered to Charles Buckland-Kerr at Murriemuir House.'

Ian was suddenly alert. Why was an Indian gentleman sending dolls to a reclusive Scot? Did they know each other? Was Charles the old friend he was looking up? And why should he want a doll? Unless it was for a little girl.

'Apparently, deliveries to the house weren't that unusual. Mrs Smart said they were phoned through about once a week. Usually by Mr Buckland-Kerr but occasionally by a woman.'

'So there was someone living at the house with Buckland-Kerr?'

'It looks like it. And someone who wasn't on the voter role. Mrs Smart said they hardly ever saw anyone. They left deliveries on the doorstep. Mr Buckland-Kerr had an account at the shop that dated back to his father's time, but it was rarely paid. When he died, they made quite a big claim on the estate. But by then it was more or less bankrupt, and they never got their money.'

'There must have been gossip in the village if there was a possibility of a woman in the house.'

'There was, but they were also scared of Buckland-Kerr. He went a bit mad in his final days – Mrs Smart's words, not mine - and was sometimes seen roaming round the fields with a shotgun.'

'No mention of a child?'

Molly shook her head.

'And the Indian gentleman. Did he say where he was from?'

'He said he was from Glasgow and owned a restaurant.'

'When was this?'

'1996. She remembers because they were celebrating her parents' golden wedding anniversary.'

'No name or address?' Probably too much to hope for, but Molly was looking particularly pleased with herself.

She scrolled through some pictures on her phone and passed it to him. She'd taken a photo of a flyer. 'He gave it to Mrs Smart,' she said. 'She thinks he must have been very proud of his restaurant. Perhaps he hoped she'd recommend it to her friends, although Glasgow would be a long way to go for a meal. She had put the flyer away in a drawer behind the counter and forgotten about it until today. Seems she doesn't tidy up very often. She heaved out a load of stuff and found this right at the bottom.'

Ian took the phone from her and enlarged the picture. The flyer was crumpled and faded but he was able to make out the words *Panchuli Palace, finest Punjabi cuisine.*

Panchuli. A familiar name. It took him a moment or two to remember where he'd seen it. Then he clicked open a file on his computer. The background checks he had done for Freya. He scrolled down until he came to the notes he'd made about Arkash. The young man from a family of Indian cooks. A young man who was interested in special effects for a local drama group and conjuring tricks for children's parties. Arkash Panchuli, son of Hunar Panchuli. Perhaps there were hundreds of Panchulis in Glasgow. Or could this be the same family? And if so, why hadn't he declared a connection to Murriemuir in his job application? 'Very well done, Molly,' he said. 'I think you've found a really useful lead. Finish your report and then we'll decide what to print. I always work better if I can see the evidence spread out in front of me.'

'Photos as well?'

'Any you think might be useful. The flyer definitely, photos of the dolls – both the remains and the new one. And keep a list of names. Anyone connected with Murriemuir. And people you've spoken to with notes about what they told you. I'll do the same.' Although right now he didn't have all that much to add. It was time to go and talk to Freya and hear her opinion on the so-called hauntings. He'd take a look at where it had happened, maybe get some useful photos. That would give him a much better idea of what was going on there. He suspected school gate rumours could get exaggerated. It was probably just a few creaks and groans from the fabric of the building. But if there was more to it, he needed to talk to Arkash, who right now was heading his list of *people playing tricks on Freya* suspects. Why had he not mentioned a family connection to Murriemuir? Why had he applied for the job there?

He called Freya. 'I need to come and see you,' he said. 'And make sure young Arkash is there. I've a few questions for him.'

13

As Ian pulled up on the drive at Murriemuir a group of ponytailed women were coming down the front steps with rolled up mats under their arms. Freya, dressed in leggings and a t-shirt with an elaborately jewelled elephant on the front, stood at the top of the steps and waved them off as they climbed into people carriers and drove away. Ian wondered vaguely if the cars were electric. He clicked his keys to lock his own car. Should he replace it with an electric one? His brother, although probably with more consideration for his income than global warming, had switched his career from oil to wind power and now drove an expensive all-electric Mercedes. And here was Ian still filling up with planet-destroying petrol once a week.

Lottie, released from the car, bounded up the steps and greeted Freya like an old friend. 'Nice to see you, Ian,' she said. 'Have you come with news about our body in the woods?'

'Possibly,' he said. 'But I'm also interested in a rumour I've heard about your house being haunted.'

Freya didn't look worried. 'A few weird things have happened. Mostly in the evenings. We had a residential course last week and a couple of people who had attic bedrooms said they heard a baby crying. Stewart thinks it was more likely to have been the plumbing. We had it checked and the plumber did say that old pipes sometimes make strange and unexpected noises.'

'And something about the yoga room?'

'Yes, that was odd. Sharon had just started her end of class relaxation when they heard the singing bowls. But meditation can cause hallucinations and sometimes people hear singing.'

'Collectively?' That surprised him. Was this an example of mass hysteria?

She shrugged. 'It's not a big deal. We've not had anyone frightened away and we've had one or two enquiries about doing ghost weekends. All good for business, I guess.'

'Can I see the yoga room?' Perhaps seeing it for himself might give him a clue about what had happened there.

'Of course,' she said, leading him into the house and down a flight of wooden steps to the cellar. 'This was horrible when we moved in,' she said. 'It had been a wine cellar at one time, but as the owner's finances declined and he'd drunk all the wine, it was used to store stuff. This was our first project after we moved in. I think it's quite successful.'

More than quite *successful,* Ian thought. This room was stunning. 'How do you keep it so warm?' he asked. Cellars were usually damp and gloomy. It was hard to believe this had ever been like that.

'Under floor heating,' said Freya. 'We dug out the stone floor and laid a new base with pipes set into the concrete. It's all heated by a ground source heat pump, which is buried just the other side of the wall.'

The ceiling was supported by a series of brick arches, which were painted white and lit by uplighters placed at the base of each one. 'All solar powered,' said Freya. She tapped her phone and Ian watched as the lights changed colour. 'Different colours for different moods,' she told him. 'I've done a lot of reading about the effects of colour on mood. Anyone teaching a class can change them to suit what they are doing. For example, at the end of a yoga class I like to use blue or lilac for relaxing. Some people find red is good for concentration and bright white for energy.'

'And those are the singing bowls?' he asked, pointing to six brass bowls of different sizes that were arranged on a table at the far end of the room. 'Tell me how they work.'

'I've not quite got the knack of it,' said Freya. 'I'm sure Sharon could show you if you are interested.'

'Just give me the basics.'

She picked up a wooden beater and chose the biggest bowl. 'You tap the side like this, and then stroke around the rim of the bowl until it starts to hum. A clever practitioner can get them all humming together.'

'So presumably something vibrating on the correct wavelength could set them off on their own?'

'I've never known that to happen, but I suppose it's possible.'

Ian turned each bowl over. He moved the silk cloth they were resting on and studied the table underneath. It was a solid oak coffee table. The kind he'd seen in upmarket coffee shops. He bent down and looked underneath. No sign of wires or switches. He tapped one of the bowls and it pinged in the way any metal object would ping if tapped. He tried whistling at it and then singing. Again, nothing happened. He wondered about all the technology that surrounded him in the room. Was there some way they could have been set off remotely? He couldn't see how, but perhaps there was a phone app that could set things vibrating. It seemed far-fetched and Stewart would probably have already checked it out. And if he had, he would certainly have told everyone about it.

'We've all puzzled over it,' said Freya. 'And no one's come up with a solution.'

'And it only happened once?'

'So far.'

She led him upstairs to a lounge where people were relaxing on couches and sipping fruit juice. 'Grab a juice,' said Freya, 'and we'll go to my office.'

Ian picked up a glass of something thick and green decorated with slices of cucumber and a sprinkling of pomegranate seeds. He followed Freya into a small room with floor-level Japanese-style seating and a computer on a low table. Freya passed him a cushion and he lowered himself to the floor and sat down beside her, trying not to spill his drink. 'You want to talk to Arkash?' she said.

He nodded and Freya turned to a small, white, golf-ball-like object. She tapped the top of it and a light flashed. 'Intercom Arkash. Meeting in my office,' she said to it.

How does that work? Ian wondered as Arkash appeared within seconds.

'Wonders of technology,' said Freya. 'They're all over the house. They can control everything from heating to the music we play, and as you saw, paging people.'

He wondered if it could also arrange ghostly manifestations.

'Arkash,' said Freya. 'Ian would like to talk to you.' She turned to Ian. 'Do you want me to stay or is it private?' she asked.

'No, stay,' said Ian. 'I just have a few questions.'

Arkash chose a lime green cushion with a gold fringe and sat down cross-legged. Ian envied him. Had *he* ever been that supple? 'Arkash,' he said. 'Can you tell me why you applied for the job here?'

He looked surprised to be asked. Presumably it had been one of Freya's first interview questions. 'I wanted some experience away from the family business,' said Arkash.

'That was on his application,' said Freya. 'It's in his notes.'

'No other reason?' Ian asked.

Arkash shook his head. 'It seemed like a nice place,' he said. 'And I'd be in charge of all the menu decisions. I wanted a bit of responsibility.'

That was reasonable. But why here and how had he known about it? 'How did you know about the job?' Ian asked. 'Did you respond to an advert or was it through an agency?'

'It was advertised online,' he said.

Freya nodded in agreement. 'I put it on a site that specialises in catering jobs.'

'Actually,' said Arkash. 'It was my dada, my grandfather, who found it. He spends a lot of time online, silver surfing, innit?'

Ian wondered why Arkash's grandfather had been looking on a site for jobs in catering. Looking for people he could employ himself, he supposed. 'And did your grandfather ever visit Murriemuir?'

'Not that I know of. But he knew quite a lot about it. I assumed he'd found stuff online. He didn't say he'd been here, but he didn't say he hadn't, either. He just likes to interfere.'

'And where is your grandfather now?'

'He's in Glasgow with the rest of the family. He's eighty-five but still does the books.'

'This is at your father's restaurant?'

'My father and grandfather are joint owners.'

'And the family's been there a long time?'

'For as long as I can remember. My grandfather worked there when he was young. He met my grandma there. She was the daughter of the owner at the time. I guess he took over from my great-grandfather. I don't know much more than that.'

Ian was sure Arkash was telling the truth, although it was odd that his grandfather hadn't mentioned visiting Murriemuir. 'Tell me about your special effects with the drama group.'

'Why do you want to know about that?'

'Just interested. What kind of things do you do?'

'We do computer-generated sound effects, dry ice, wire for flying, that kind of thing, and conjuring tricks.'

'No singing bowls or babies crying?'

Arkash looked genuinely horrified. 'I had nothing to do with that, honestly. I'd never play tricks on Freya, or the guests.'

Ian believed him. 'You were very sick in the woods that day – do you remember why?'

'Yeah, we'd just dug up a body. I've not much experience of corpses.'

Ian patted his shoulder. 'Fair enough,' he said. This lad, he was sure, had been genuinely upset. Surprising, really, that none of the rest of them had felt like that. 'Okay, Arkash,' he said. 'Thanks for talking to me.'

'Can I go?' he asked. 'I've got dinner to prepare.'

'Of course,' said Ian. 'Sorry to have taken your time.'

Arkash stood up, added his cushion to a pile by the door and left.

'Is there a problem?' asked Freya, looking worried. 'He's a brilliant chef. I'd hate to lose him.'

'No, I don't think so. There was nothing in his background that you needed to worry about. It's probably just coincidence, but it looks as if his grandfather might have been here at some time in the past.'

'Really? Does he have anything to do with the body?'

'I doubt it. But he might just be able to tell us a bit more about who she is.'

14

Ian checked out the Panchuli Palace website and wondered how much it had changed since the flyer had been left with Mrs Smart. He clicked through the gallery and found pictures of a stylish place with understated décor and plants in brass pots. Tables were laid with silver cutlery, starched white tablecloths and napkins, the floor was polished wood, and picture windows overlooked a garden with fountains. Ian was surprised. He still had an image of flock wallpaper in deep red and velour-covered bench seats. But when had he last visited an Indian restaurant? He and Caroline often ordered takeaway curries, but these were always delivered. As far as he could remember, his last visit to an actual restaurant must have been when he was working in Leith and that was a while back.

The website also offered him the history of Panchuli Palace. It had opened as the Star of India in 1955 and was one of the first Indian restaurants in Glasgow. The name had been changed in 1965 by Jivin Panchuli and had been run by the Panchuli family ever since. It boasted good made-from-scratch authentic Punjabi cuisine. He found a family photograph, Jivin sitting on a throne-like chair, his son Hunar and grandsons standing to attention around him. Ian recognised Arkash as one of the grandsons. He checked the menu and made a mental note of it as somewhere he would definitely have a meal should he ever be in Glasgow and hungry. Today, though, he was going on business. The delights of made-from-scratch Punjabi food would have to wait. He found a number on the website and called it, asking if Jivin Panchuli might be available to speak to him later that day. One of Arkash's brothers answered the phone and Ian noted a hint of excitement in his voice at the prospect of a visit from a private investigator. This was usually a sign of a clear conscience and Ian was assured that Panchuli senior would be happy to meet him later that afternoon. He left Lottie with Lainie and set out for Glasgow.

The area around the Panchuli Palace was in a part of Glasgow that was very much on the up in the recently gentrified area of the city. Ian guessed that the restaurant had evolved as the area around it developed into a street of upmarket shops. From the outside it looked inviting but expensive. He found a menu inside a glass frame at the side of an imposing mahogany door, either side of which were two stone tigers. He opened the door, went inside and found himself in a lobby with low upholstered seats and a glass coffee table. A young woman dressed in a black suit worn with a red and purple silk shirt greeted him. It was the middle of the afternoon and the place was empty, although he detected a bustle of activity in the dining room that was visible beyond the reception desk. Preparing for a busy evening, he supposed.

'Mr Skair?' the woman asked. He nodded and handed her his card. 'Take a seat,' she said. 'I'll see if Mr Panchuli is ready for you.' She turned and left the room, leaving Ian to sit and watch shoppers in the street outside.

After a few moments she returned. 'This way, please,' she said, leading him through the dining room and upstairs to a comfortable sitting room, where an elderly man sat in a chair reading a newspaper through a pair of Gandhi-style spectacles.

He took off his glasses and stood up as Ian came in. 'Welcome,' he said, pointing to a chair. 'Please, sit.' Then he turned to the woman. 'Ameera, my dear, would you bring us some tea and some of your laddu?'

'Yes, Babaji,' she said with a nod, as she turned to leave the room.

'You have come from Fife and wish to speak with me?' the man asked as the door closed.

Ian nodded. 'I'm making some enquiries into events at a house called Murriemuir.'

'Ah, yes. Murriemuir. I lived there for a while.'

He'd lived there! When? And why hadn't Arkash told him that?

'And now my grandson is there,' Jivin continued. 'And what are these events you talk about? Nothing to do with my grandson, I hope?'

Why would they be? Was Arkash considered a troublemaker by his family? 'Arkash hasn't told you?' he asked, noticing Jivin's puzzled expression. Apparently not, but that didn't mean anything. Arkash was busy and probably hadn't had time off to visit his family. In any case, Ian was beginning to think that given time off, spending it with the family probably wasn't high on Arkash's list of leisure activities.

'I haven't seen him since he started work there. And he's not a great communicator when he is here. His head's too full of all that theatre and conjuring nonsense. Thinks he can make a career out of it.'

Ian was beginning to feel sorry for Arkash. He might be a brilliant chef, but it looked as if he'd not had much say in his choice of career.

'No thought for family tradition,' Jivin was saying. 'I didn't build up this business for him to waste his time on a lot of theatrical rubbish.'

It was time to steer the old man away from family rebelliousness and back to Murriemuir. 'Some human bones were found recently in the garden at Murriemuir,' Ian said.

'How very unfortunate,' said Jivin, not seeming at all perturbed. A reaction very different from his grandson's.

They were interrupted by Ameera returning with a brass tray, which she placed on a small table next to Jivin's chair. On the tray were two white china cups, a silver teapot and a plate of small, round cakes. 'Thank you, my dear,' said Jivin. 'Ameera is married to my eldest grandson,' he explained. He patted Ameera's hand. 'Good to know some of the family know where their duty lies. She has a degree in economics and will take over the financial side of the business when I retire.' Ameera didn't look upset at the idea of Jivin retiring. Why would she? She'd be handling the finances of a hugely successful business.

But Ian hadn't come to discuss the restaurant. He wanted to know more about Jivin's connection to Murriemuir. 'You say you lived there? Arkash didn't mention that.'

'He didn't know. Arkash was looking for a job, so I kept an eye on the possibilities. I saw the position at Murriemuir advertised and it seemed like a lucky omen. A sign. Arkash needs to be away from the family for a while. To make his own way. Only then will he be able to come back and take his place with us.'

And to clear his head of any notions of going in a different direction. *Jivin needs to be in control,* Ian thought.

'I insisted on it for all my grandsons,' said Jivin. 'One grandson I sent to London for a year. The other to Birmingham. Now they have returned and settled well into their roles. For my son it was different. We were still a small concern then. We didn't have the luxury of being able to send him away to train.'

Not exactly what Arkash had written on his application. Ian had got the impression that Arkash couldn't wait to get away. 'When did you live at Murriemuir?'

'I went there in 1947 and stayed there for nine years.'

'1947. The year that...'

'The year of partition in India. That's correct. My father worked for a Major Buckland-Kerr in the British army.' Ian looked at him in surprise. He hadn't expected a family connection. 'He was preparing to leave India and arranged for my family to return to Amritsar. But we never arrived there. Our train was attacked, and the rest of my family murdered. I survived by hiding under a blanket. I was uninjured but traumatised and taken back to the army base in Faisalabad by a nurse who had been travelling on the same train. By a miracle the major recognised me. I don't know how he organised it, but he brought me back to Scotland with him and took me to live with his cousin at Murriemuir.'

Ian wished he'd brought Molly's notes with him. 'His cousin owned Murriemuir?'

'That's right. Malcolm Buckland-Kerr, a widower living there with his son, Charles. He took me in, and I worked for them on the farm. Charles was only a few years younger than me and we became friends. Well, I say friends. Charlie was an odd sort. Didn't really make friends, but we rubbed along okay.'

'And when did you leave?'

'In 1962, when Malcolm died. I'd never wanted to be a farmer so there was not a lot to keep me there. I hitched lifts to Glasgow and found work right here. Although it was a run-down area in those days. I started working as a kitchen hand, but I was a quick learner and soon became the best chef in the city. I married the boss's daughter and took over when he died. Been on the up ever since.'

Ian looked around at the expensive furnishings. A combination of hard work and the good fortune of being in an area ripe for gentrification had indeed made him – the whole family – a success. 'And you returned to Murriemuir for a visit in 1996?' he asked.

It was Jivin's turn to look surprised. 'How did you know that?'

'Mrs Smart in the village shop remembered you buying a doll there.'

'Ah, yes, the doll.' He took a bite of laddu. 'That was the least I could do. A small gift. I felt a little guilty, you see.'

'Why should you feel guilty?'

'I'd taken a short holiday. I'd barely left Glasgow in thirty years and thought I'd like to see a bit more of Scotland. Hunar had just married and was doing well growing the business, so I thought it would be good to leave him on his own for a week or two. I began by going to Edinburgh and then thought I'd go and see how Charlie was.'

'And how was he?'

'Dreadful. I'd left a thriving farm and in less than forty years it had gone to ruin. Charlie was struggling to run the place with a couple of good-for-nothing labourers and as far as I could tell he was heavily in debt. The house was falling apart – leaking roof, broken windows. I should have offered to help somehow, but what could I do? Nothing. I turned my back and left. I called in at the shop for some food and saw the dolls. It was the kiddie I felt sorry for. I bought one and asked for it to be delivered to Murriemuir.'

'Kiddie?' said Ian. 'You didn't mention a child.'

'A little girl. They seemed fond of each other. I assumed she was his daughter.'

'How old was she?'

'Maybe two or three. A skinny, timid little thing.'

'And no sign of a mother?'

'Not that I saw. I assumed she was in the kitchen or out buying food.' Mr Panchuli senior, it seemed, had traditional views on the place of women.

'You didn't ask about her?' Two old friends, reunited after many years. Wouldn't they ask each other about family, marriage, children? It seemed not. A pity. It would have made his search a hell of a lot easier.

'No. I suppose I should have taken more of an interest. But Charlie, well, he was barely coherent. I wasn't sure he even remembered me.'

'And the child that you assumed was his daughter, did you ask her name?'

Jivin shook his head. 'I wasn't wanted there. It was a mistake visiting Charlie. I'd left in a hurry after Malcolm died. I should have known better than to return and expect a welcome.'

He could have shown a bit more concern for the child. But what could he have done? Called social services? That wouldn't have been Jivin's way. He expected families to stick together, even if some of its members were unwilling. Jivin would have been out of his depth with a reclusive man and a strange child. A moment of conscience when he spotted the dolls in the shop and then he'd have walked away and not given it another thought until he spotted the advert for a chef at the house he remembered from his distant past.

Ian thanked Jivin for his time and left.

Driving home, he mulled over what he had learnt. He'd discovered that there had been a child at Murriemuir, a girl who could be the right age for the body they'd dug up. Could this be Clover? And was Charles Buckland-Kerr her father? The child must, at some time, have had a mother. Was that the mysterious housekeeper? And if so, how could he find out more?

15

Ian was still trying to puzzle it all out that evening. He went back over Molly's notes about the house, hoping that he might have missed something and that some detail would leap out at him. But there was nothing. All that had happened between Malcolm Buckland-Kerr's death in 1962 and the sale of the house to the university in 2004 was that his son, Charles Buckland-Kerr, had pretty much ruined everything his father and grandfather had built up.

Ian thought about cooking himself a meal to try to stop his imagination creating bleak and sinister narratives. Could Charles Buckland-Kerr have kidnapped a little girl, kept her in the house long enough to meet an old friend and receive the gift of a doll, before murdering her and burying her in the garden? And if so, why mark the grave with an elaborate headstone? Ian made a note to research local stonemasons. He might be able to trace whoever had carved the animal stones. Perhaps they'd remember a commission for a stone for Clover.

But that didn't account for the rumours of a woman living in the house. Mrs Smart had remembered what she assumed was a housekeeper phoning through orders for Murriemuir, so there must have been a woman there. Perhaps there were other people in the village who remembered her.

He cast his mind back to the book Caroline had been reading. The story of a young woman kidnapped and kept prisoner by a man who kept her captive in his cellar. She'd escaped with her child, only to find it difficult living in the outside world, particularly for the child. There had been a few similar reports of real-life incidents like this. Had there been a similar story right here on his doorstep? It made him shudder.

He was still puzzling over this when Freya called him to report two more strange events. The previous evening had been very mild for October, she told him, and they'd decided on an unscheduled forest bathing session at sunset. Sonia led a group of people through a mindfulness exercise in the glade, then left them to relax and lie in silence under the gently falling leaves. Three of the residents had joined the session, taking blankets that they spread out under the trees. The ground had been repaired once it was released by the SOCO team after the removal of the graves. Guy had laid new turf and tidied up the edges of the glade with some ferns and late flowering Japanese anemones. As far as Freya knew, no one had been aware that this was the site of the animal cemetery or that it was also where Clover's bones had been discovered. The three of them had been enjoying a quiet meditation for about ten minutes when they became aware of a strong perfume wafting down from a chestnut tree. All three experienced it, although they disagreed about what kind of perfume it was. One said it reminded her of lilies of the valley, another said it was more of a pine scent and the third said it reminded her of Johnson's baby powder. All three agreed that it had been a soothing experience and assumed it was the result of a heightened sensitivity arising from the depth of their meditation. Freya was inclined to disagree. Raised sensual awareness during meditation was not unusual. Three people experiencing it in the same way was. Stewart and Guy had examined the area the following morning but found nothing unusual.

Freya also told him that they had heard a child singing during their evening meal. It was a silent meal, which Freya explained they held during residential sessions as it allowed the diners to experience mindful eating; a chance to concentrate on the flavours of the spices Arkash had prepared for them. Arkash and Stewart had searched the room once the meal was over but again had found nothing.

'Very strange,' said Ian, wondering what he could do about it. If Stewart, Arkash and Guy had found nothing, it was unlikely that *he* could. He wasn't sure about Arkash, but he was certain that his brother would have no time for the haunting theory that had excited the school pick-up mums. Guy, too, had seemed like a down-to-earth, practical type. 'What do you think?' he asked Freya. 'Do you believe in ghosts?'

'I think the news that we found a body in the garden could play tricks in people's brains. But it would be a personal thing and we all heard the singing. I really don't believe we are part of some kind of group hysteria.'

'I agree. And I know how sceptical Stewart is about anything of that sort.'

'He thinks it's someone playing very clever tricks on us. He sees it as challenge. You know what he's like – no such thing as a problem that can't be solved with the right kind of knowledge.'

For once Ian agreed with his brother. No such thing as the supernatural although Fife, and the rest of Scotland, were littered with places believed to be haunted. But there was always an explanation. They were the product of an overactive imagination, or weird noises and tricks of the light in old buildings. Stewart was right. Someone was playing tricks on them. There would be a perfectly rational explanation. Although on this occasion he couldn't imagine how he was going to find it.

Freya wasn't worried. 'It all seems quite benign,' she said. 'I just hope it stays that way.'

'Or just stops altogether,' he said. 'Let me know if anything else happens, won't you?'

He ended the call and googled *how to fake supernatural events*. He found plenty of stories of people who had been misled into believing they had seen ghosts and most of these were explainable. He couldn't find much about how to deliberately trick people and assumed that was not something that was posted on the internet. Not much point in luring people into believing something if you then told the world how you did it.

He realised it was getting late. He still hadn't eaten, and Lottie hadn't been walked. Well, there was nothing like multitasking. He and Lottie would walk to the pub. The Pigeon had started up their themed supper nights again and this evening it would be pie night. Just what he fancied. To ease his conscience, he'd take the longer route through the park. Lottie could chase squirrels for a bit. They'd still be in time for a pie and mash supper.

The bar was busy. It felt strange after so many months of wearing masks and staying two metres away from people. Ian still found himself keeping his distance, but as evenings became colder, he supposed they would all get used to socialising again.

As he waited for his meal, he noticed some flyers that had been left in a rack by the door. It was time to find out what was going on now the world was moving again, so he picked up a handful of leaflets and started reading them. One in particular drew his attention. It was a picture of man dressed in a Victorian frock coat and top hat and carrying a cane. He was walking through a moonlit garden with the shadowy silhouette of a large house in the distance. Ian read the text:

The Ghosts of Buchan House
Join fellow ghoulish thrillseekers for dinner and a walk to remember.
Enjoy a spine-chilling experience as you meet our resident ghosts.

Two dates were mentioned. The first, with an earlier start, suitable for children. The second was recommended only for over fifteens. Dinner would be Scottish sausages and spicy mash – a vegetarian option was available – followed by a dessert of cobweb brownie served with a blood-red plum coulis.

He'd been to Buchan House to buy plants. It was an eighteenth-century manor house with a walled garden, which had been turned into a plant nursery with a number of spin-off businesses attached – a florist, small bakery and cheese shop, pet food supplier and a horse vet. It was a few miles to the north of Dundee, off the beaten track with a drive through a pine forest – a supplier of Christmas trees. No doubt becoming less remote as staff and customers made sure the track was now being well and truly beaten. But Ian could imagine it as a creepy place at night when the businesses were closed, and everyone had gone home. As far as he knew, the house itself was occupied only by the owner and his family. He'd no idea of the size of the family, but even a large one would make little impact on an estate this size and they probably stayed firmly indoors after dark. The house was old and probably had creaking floorboards and draughty windows. There were bound to have been stories of family black sheep and suspicious deaths over the last couple of hundred years, so he was certain they'd have a collection of ghost legends and other spooky phenomena. Times were hard. He could understand their desire to cash in on family history with scary entertainments. He would, he hoped, be able to work out how they contrived to scare people. Tomorrow, he decided, he'd call and book tickets. He couldn't go on his own without the risk of giving away his identity as a detective and he wondered if Caroline might enjoy it. They would just be another couple out for an evening's fun. And she would be an extra pair of eyes. He picked up his phone and called her.

'An evening of ghost spotting?' she said. 'Doesn't sound like your sort of thing at all.'

Why not? he wondered. Did she think he was scared or that he was a total sceptic where the supernatural was concerned? He supposed the latter would be about right. 'It's research,' he told her, explaining some of the odd events at Murriemuir. 'I want to work out how they do it.'

There could be no doubt that Halloween was on the way. They were shown to a room that during the day was a cafeteria. It would be busy, Ian imagined, during working hours. He didn't know how many people worked at Buchan, but a navy-blue board with gold lettering at the entrance to the car park listed half a dozen company names, all of which would have employees in need of cups of coffee and cooked lunches. And then there would be customers, hungry and thirsty from loading up trolleys with everything from the smallest cactus to full-size fruit trees, terracotta pots and bags of compost, Christmas trees, potted house plants and bouquets of flowers. There would also, Ian supposed, be owners of ailing horses and of course, walkers. There were a number of trails of various lengths shown on a map at the edge of the car park. None of them were less than three miles long. Lottie would enjoy that. And they could sit down to a good meal at the end of it. He made a mental note to bring her one day.

Now the cafeteria had been decked out ready for the evening's events. They had been guided through a walkway festooned with fake cobwebs, complete with dangling spiders, into a room that was lit by tealights inside more pumpkins than Ian had ever seen in one place before. They were on all the tables, windowsills and shelves that usually housed jars of jam and packets of biscuits. They stood next to the cash register and on either side of the doors to the kitchen. Every windowpane had a spider stuck to it and there were more cobwebs dangling from the ceiling. The whole place was an arachnophobe's nightmare.

The meal itself was good. At least it tasted good if he tried to ignore the bright orange food colouring in the mashed potato and the fact that someone had thought it would be fun to make the sausages look like severed fingers. They were local sausages, sourced, he thought, from a farm shop he knew well. But he doubted that they sold sausages decorated with fingernails and suspected these were the work of someone in the kitchen right here at Buchan House. But they tasted good. He had often bought sausages like these for himself and Lottie. He didn't admit that to Caroline, who had strict ideas about dog diets.

After the main course they were served brownies decorated with yet more cobwebs. Ian was intrigued by them. They looked horrible but exploring them further he found they tasted sweet and crunchy. 'How do they do that?' he wondered.

'Spun sugar,' said Caroline.

'Is it difficult to spin sugar?' he asked.

'More messy than difficult, I think.'

Perhaps he wouldn't try it. He was a messy enough cook with basic recipes. He looked around at his fellow diners, wondering if there was a ghost-walking type. Probably not. The group around him consisted mostly of couples, but apart from that they were all ages from late teens to elderly. Like him, they were all wrapped up in coats and scarves. Some with gloves, but not him. He needed to keep his hands free to take photos.

As they finished the meal, the door opened and a man appeared. He was dressed like the character on the flyer in a frock coat and top hat, and carrying a silver-topped walking stick, which he waved menacingly at them. His face was an ashen white and he had black kohl rings around his eyes. 'Ladies and gentlemen,' he said in a deep spectral voice. 'Allow me to introduce myself. I am Jonas Buchan. I lived in Buchan house until my death in 1830. Follow me if you dare. Allow me to introduce you to my family.' He cackled at them and waved his stick in the air as they trooped out into the walled garden. 'No talking, if you please. My family are shy and will only appear to you in silence. And,' he added, suddenly landing back in the twenty-first century, 'please turn off your phones and do not take photographs.'

Ian had planned to take photographs in the hope that they would help him work out the tricks they were about to see, but he didn't want to invoke any spectral bouncers, so he put his phone away in his pocket.

They set off in a crocodile, like schoolchildren on a nature walk. Their first stop was at the side of a huge fig tree growing up against a corner of the wall. They waited for several minutes and then became aware of a humming sound, which gradually became louder and then died away again. Not the scariest of manifestations, Ian thought, and easy to do with some artfully concealed speakers, but perhaps there was better to come. It wouldn't do to get the punters too excited at the start.

They moved on to the middle of the garden and gathered around an old-fashioned streetlamp. Jonas waved his stick at it, and it glowed with an orange light and then a face appeared in the glow and leered at them. No one seemed particularly impressed, so Jonas hurried them on. As they passed some bushes, skeletons jumped out at them. One or two of the walkers jumped in surprise, but on closer inspection these were children dressed in black and painted with luminous white bones. The children disappeared into the undergrowth and were replaced by a shadowy figure dragging a set of chains behind him.

Caroline gripped Ian's arm, and he could feel her shaking with suppressed giggles. This was infectious and the couple immediately behind them also started shaking, the young woman burying her face in her partner's coat sleeve in an effort to keep quiet.

'You've started something,' Ian whispered, as he noticed the effect this was having on the people further behind them in the line.

The walk lasted another fifteen minutes as they were treated to a series of pallid young women in white floaty gowns, demonic-looking children with devil horns and painted faces, an old woman rising from a coffin waving her arms at them and a series of shrieks and groans from the undergrowth.

Finally, they arrived back at the house. Jonas stood between them and the door, still waving his stick. 'Stand still,' he ordered. 'As our final apparition I shall release the hound from hell.' He flung the door open with a flourish and through it trotted a large dog, wagging its tail. *As hellhounds go,* Ian thought, *Lottie would probably do a better job.* At least she growled at people she didn't like, particularly if they were trying to deliver something through his letterbox. But this was an amiable dog, it's only concession to the spookiness of the evening a collar adorned with spikes. It greeted its audience with more tail-wagging as it wandered through the crowd, allowing people to pat it on the head before returning through the door, no doubt seeking the warmth and security of a dog basket by the fire.

They were offered black and white humbugs from a bucket decorated with skulls and returned to the car, where Caroline collapsed with laughter. She wiped tears from her eyes. 'That,' she said, 'is the funniest thing I've seen for a very long time.'

She was right and, as far as he could tell, the comedy was entirely unintentional. He felt sorry for Jonas. Did he seriously expect them to be frightened? Murriemuir and its unexplained scents and sounds was way scarier, and this evening had been no help at all. He was no closer to explaining them. But still, Caroline was right. They'd had a pleasant meal and a good laugh.

He started the car and headed for home. 'I wonder if they actually researched anything to do with the house,' he said. 'There must be some interesting history there, but this was just a load of kids' party clichés with the sort of stuff you can buy in Dundee market all through October.'

'Perhaps you could get Molly to dig into the history of the house. You could offer yourself as a consultant for next year.'

16

The Murriemuir investigation was proceeding far too slowly. Ian glanced through his notes, which, apart from Molly's report on the house and its occupants, were a slim and uninformative collection of documents. Ian now knew about the history of the Buckland-Kerr family in the early days of the house, but as time progressed, the information became more and more hard to find. Jivin visited it in 1996 and had seen a child in the house with Charles. But Ian was no nearer to finding out who she was. He was a looking for a child who was probably born around 1993 and died roughly ten years later. Could this be the same child? And was there any chance that the girl could have been Clover? Her age was about right according to the pathologist's report. But without more evidence he shouldn't assume anything. And if it *was* Clover, did that mean she had lived there until her death a few years after Jivin's visit? Wouldn't someone have noticed her? Charles Buckland-Kerr had by all accounts been an odd, reclusive character, but surely if he had been living with a child someone other than Jivin must have seen her.

Jivin infuriated him. He had cared enough to buy the child a doll but hadn't been interested enough to ask her name or who her parents were. Hadn't he been even a little concerned about a small girl living with what by all accounts was a very strange man? And then there was the mysterious housekeeper no one had seen. The only proof that she existed was a few calls to the village shop to place orders. Was there something sinister about her presence in the house? Could the so-called housekeeper have been Clover's mother? And if she was, what had happened to her? There had been no more bodies found in the grounds. Stewart had virtually rebuilt the cellar, which would have been the obvious place to conceal a body inside the house. So had she escaped? If she had, it should be possible to find her. He should ask Duncan to look for records of missing women older than Clover who might give him a clue as to who her mother might have been.

And he was no nearer to explaining the unexpected events at the house now. Were these connected to the child in some way? He didn't see how they could be. No one had noticed them before the bones were dug up. Had they started then or had there always been strange things happening at Murriemuir? He should have asked Jivin if he remembered anything from his time there as a young boy.

Stewart had bought the house from a bankrupt hotel owner who, as far as Ian knew, he had never met. He'd worked through an agent and presumably unexplained supernatural events weren't something to add to sales brochures.

He wondered if the hotel guests staying at Murriemuir had experienced anything. He checked it on TripAdvisor and found plenty of very bad reviews, but they were about poor food, uncomfortable beds and bad-tempered staff. Not a word about hauntings. Ian wondered if TripAdvisor even accepted comments about resident ghosts or if they were only concerned with prices and facilities. He checked on Google and discovered someone had written a whole book of ghost stories taken from TripAdvisor comments. People didn't hold back. If they stayed in a haunted room, they wasted no time describing it on the site. And there was not so much as an unexplained creaking door reported on the Murriemuir page. That could just mean they had all slept like babies, although the report of uncomfortable beds didn't suggest it. He was quite disappointed. It would have been good to be able to contact someone who had experienced spooky happenings years ago. It wouldn't help explain them, but it would deflect attention away from the current staff and guests.

Before it became a hotel, the house had been home to PhD students. Maybe some of those were still around and might remember things happening there. And Ian knew exactly the right person to help him. Several months before the first lockdown, and while he was hunting for the Drumlychtoun ring, one of his first cases in the area, Ian had met Adrian Walter, a maths lecturer at the university. A down-to-earth, jovial type, they had become friends. Ian called him and found himself invited for lunch, St Andrews lecturers still working mainly from home.

Adrian lived with his wife, son and an enormous dog called Hector, in a village a few miles from the university. Ian was greeted with a slap on the back and was led into the living room he remembered from eighteen months ago. A room full of books and big armchairs, a piano, and some guitars on stands. His last visit had been in the summer and now there was a wood-burning stove with a warm glow and a lightly smoky smell.

'I'd offer you a beer,' said Adrian, 'but I've a Zoom seminar this afternoon and I need to stay awake. Coffee's on the go if you'd like a cup.'

'Coffee would be lovely,' said Ian, remembering the sleep-inducing Zoom sessions run by Nigel.

Adrian poured him a cup. 'So what can I do for you?' he asked.

Ian told him a little about the events at Murriemuir. 'I'd like to know if these are recent or if there's a history of ghost sightings. If you know any of the students who'd lived there, they might be able to tell me if there were any rumours.'

'I remember one or two philosophy and maths graduates who lived there,' he said. 'But I've lost touch with them. Most of them move on once they've qualified. But I tell you what I can do. There's a WhatsApp group for doctorate alumni. I'll post a message on that and ask anyone who remembers the place to get in touch.'

'That would be great, thanks.'

'Okay if I pass on your number?'

Ian was fine with that. He sat back and enjoyed his coffee. Any information about the house would be helpful. He might just start making some progress at last.

He asked after Adrian's son, Robin. A nice boy who had been a student during the Drumlychtoun case.

'He's fine,' said Adrian. 'Thankfully things are getting back to normal again for his final year. And he's got a new girlfriend. Anna's a sweet girl, but they were both far too young to be getting so serious. Robin had a fantastic summer with her family in France though, and I'm sure they will always be friends.'

Inevitable, Ian supposed, thinking of Drumlychtoun and Anna, Robin's girlfriend of two summers ago, who would one day inherit the castle. Anna hadn't returned to St Andrews. She'd gone home as soon as the first lockdown looked likely and spent the rest of the year working online. She'd decided not to return for her final year. Her mother and stepfather persuaded her to complete her degree at the University of Perpignan. She was badly missed by her Scottish family. She was missed by Ian as well. And if she did come back, he was sure she'd get a rapturous welcome from Lottie.

Two days later he had a call from Paul Baker, an environmental studies lecturer at Dundee University who had responded to Adrian's WhatsApp post. 'You wanted to talk to people who'd lived at Murriemuir,' he said. 'I was there for a year until the university sold it. If you'd like to meet up in Dundee sometime, I've got some photos you might find helpful.'

Paul had an office at the university and Ian arranged to call on him the next day.

The department he was looking for was housed in a modern block built in what Ian thought of as brutalist style. And with inadequate parking. He was directed a few hundred yards to a car park that was spacious and not too full, but which was guarded by a barrier that required him to punch a number into a keypad. Paul Baker had failed to mention it and Ian wondered if he should call him and ask for a number. But perhaps on-campus parking was strictly for university staff. They'd want to keep out the unacademic hoi polloi, wouldn't they? He had arrived early and had plenty of time to find somewhere in one of the surrounding streets. After twenty minutes of driving around the edge of the campus, he spotted a van pulling out of a parking space and slid his car into it before anyone else had the same idea. After a few moments of trying to work out some baffling regulations about parking on different sides of the road on alternate days of the week, not staying for more than two hours and not returning within twenty-four hours unless he possessed a resident's permit, he decided to take a chance. He could tell the space was on the correct side of the road because that's where all the other cars were parked. There were no traffic wardens in sight so he could probably stretch the two hours a bit and a glance at his watch told him he'd need to step on it a bit or he'd be late. Luckily, although he felt he'd been searching for a long time, he'd been driving in a circle. Over the roofs of houses, he could see the top of the building just a couple of streets away.

Arriving at the entrance, he was asked to sign in and was given a visitor's pass (not to be used for parking, it said in big black capital letters on the back). He swiped himself through another barrier and studied a map. The office he wanted was on the fourth floor. He could either climb an imposing staircase or take a lift. He decided, purely on the grounds of shortage of time, to take the lift. Emerging on the fourth floor, he found himself in a long corridor of identical grey doors, which luckily had names on them. Paul Baker's was at the far end of the corridor next to a window that looked out over the still half-empty car park. Ian tapped on the door and was invited inside.

Paul Baker was sitting at a desk in front of a computer screen with a coffee machine gurgling next to it. There were a few books on a shelf above the desk, but the room was otherwise surprisingly uncluttered. Ian had expected piles of student essays and huge folders of notes, but he supposed everything was online these days. Paul was pretty much what he'd expected an environmental studies lecturer to look like; tall and skinny with shaggy hair and horn-rimmed spectacles. He was wearing what had become known a few years ago as a Sarah Lund jumper. Ian knew about them because Lainie had offered to knit him one during lockdown. They were made from Icelandic wool and designed to keep out a cold Nordic wind.

Paul jumped up and pulled up a chair. 'Have a seat,' he said. 'But I wouldn't take your coat off. The heating's on the blink.'

Ian sat down and rubbed his hands. It was colder in here than it had been outside. 'Lucky you've got the jumper for it,' he said, laughing.

'You can't beat a bit of Icelandic alpaca for warmth,' Paul said, pouring a mug of coffee and handing it to Ian, who wrapped his hands around it to warm them up.

'Why are you interested in Murriemuir?' Paul asked.

'I'm investigating some recent findings at the house,' said Ian, not sure how much to give away. 'What was it like when you lived there?'

'A mixture of Bohemian freedom and squalor,' said Paul. 'The old fellow who owned it had died there. Up to his ears in debt and the house was sold just as it was, furniture and all. Possibly the most uncomfortable place I've ever lived. Ancient plumbing, dodgy wiring, leaky windows, not seen a coat of paint for God knows how long. But we were young. We made the most of it. We were miles from the nearest neighbours so we could have as many noisy parties as we wanted. No one bothered about cleaning and basically we loafed around and got drunk.'

Ian laughed. 'Did you do any work?'

'We all got our degrees so I suppose work must have come into it at some point.'

'Do you remember anything unusual going on there? Any suggestion it was haunted?'

Paul looked at him in surprise. 'No. It was a creaky old place and sometimes we played tricks on each other, but none of us took it seriously. Is that why you're here? Are you a ghost buster?'

Ian laughed. 'No, nothing like that.' Although after recent events perhaps he should consider becoming one. He took a sip of his very strong, very hot coffee. Adrian made coffee like that. Was this a lecturer thing? Or just one of the necessities of working in old university buildings with unreliable heating? 'Do you remember the pet cemetery?' he asked.

'Yeah, we used to joke about that. Poor old Rex and his friends.'

'Did you know that human remains have been found there?'

Paul looked shocked. 'You're joking. You mean we were sharing the place with a dead body?'

'Been there about fifteen or twenty years when we discovered it a few weeks ago.'

'Do you know who it was?'

'That's what I'm trying to find out. Do you know anything about who lived in the house before the university bought it?'

'Only what I just told you about the old guy dying there, but there were one or two odd things about the place.'

'What sort of things?'

'A few toys in one of the attic rooms, some drawings on the wall.' He found some photos on his phone and passed it to Ian. 'I took those when we left. Don't suppose I'll get to live anywhere that weird again. I thought it would be nice to have a record of it.'

Ian studied the pictures. They looked like a child's drawings in wax crayon. Trees perhaps, and an animal with stick legs. He didn't know enough about children to guess the age of the child who had done the drawing. It was probably a very young child, too young to understand that drawing on walls was not a good idea. He'd been severely punished by his father for doing just that. He must have been about three or four. It was one of his earliest memories and he was sure he'd never done it again. Unlikely, then, that an older child would draw on the wall because they started to understand rules once they'd stopped being toddlers and could understand words like *don't do that*. Paul's photos certainly suggested that there had been a child in the house, possibly just someone visiting with a small child, but one who had drawn pictures on the wall and who had left toys behind? It seemed unlikely. 'Was there anything to suggest anyone else had been living there?' Ian asked.

'Hard to say. We found generations of rubbish there, some old clothes, a few books, and toys.'

'But no children singing, strange perfumes, that kind of thing?'

Paul smiled. 'No, sorry. Apart from being old and dingy the place was quite normal. I do have this, though. We found it screwed up in a drawer and I photographed it.'

Ian looked at the picture of a crumpled sheet of paper with some writing on it. It looked Chinese, he thought, although his knowledge of oriental scripts was limited. 'Could you send me these?' he asked, writing down his email.

'Of course,' said Paul, as Ian got up to leave. 'Has any of what I told you helped?'

Ian nodded. But had it? He wasn't sure. There had been a child in the house but he'd no idea how long she had been there and there wasn't much to connect her with the bones in the garden. Surely if a child had died in the house, there would be a record of it. It also looked as if the odd manifestations, hauntings, whatever one called them, had only started recently. If anyone was susceptible to supernatural events it would be a group of drunk students. Or hotel guests. People who stayed in remote hotels in Scotland would not only be susceptible but would probably consider ghosts a necessity. But there had been no mention of them, sceptical or otherwise. Which suggested that nothing inexplicable had happened. Not until his brother had moved into Murriemuir. And not until they disturbed the occupants of a pet cemetery.

17

'Molly,' said Ian, the morning after his visit to Paul. 'Can you find someone to translate this?' He pointed to the photo he'd taken of the Chinese symbols.

'Sure,' said Molly, opening the file on her computer and enlarging the image. She stared at it and started clicking keys.

It would take her a while, he supposed, and while she was searching, he could tidy up what was on the whiteboard and summarise what they knew. So far, they had a collection of snippets that didn't appear to relate to each other. He needed to find out who Clover was as well as what was going on at Murriemuir. Were they linked? And if so how, and why? Should he concentrate on finding a connection or would his time be better spent on two different lines of enquiry?

He started with a list:

<u>Who was Clover?</u>

Related to Charles? Her name suggests that she might be. Is she the child that Jivin had seen with Charles?

Cause of death – apparently not violent. Natural causes? The pathologist report doesn't suggest what they might be. Difficult to know without a death certificate.

Jivin said she was delicate and timid, but also content and fond of Charles, which suggests she wasn't being held against her will.

Was she the daughter of the mysterious housekeeper no one had met? She must have had a mother and if she lived at Murriemuir the housekeeper was the only possibility. Village gossips would definitely have known about it if there had been regular women visitors to the house. Mrs Smart at the shop would have said something to Molly if there had been.

<u>Haunted?</u>

No record of supernatural events before the body was found.

Who is causing them and what do they hope to gain?

They started after Stewart's family and their staff moved in. Does someone resent them being there and are they using the moving of the pet cemetery as a way of frightening them? If that's the case, are they being unsuccessful? Freya and Stewart are intrigued but not in the least frightened. But maybe this is just the start and things are about to become much more menacing.

<u>Timing of events.</u>

Baby crying – around midnight, only guests with top-floor rooms heard it. Nothing found when the rooms were searched.

Wafting perfume in cemetery grove – three forest bathers all experienced different perfumes, nothing found when the area was searched.

Singing bowls – during yoga class, six people plus Sharon who was teaching the session were present.

Child singing – six guests plus resident staff in dining room, room searched, nothing found.

<u>Paul's evidence</u>

Child's drawings - same child? Or could they be Charles' own drawings from when he was a child? He'd no way of dating them but wax crayons had been around for a while.

Paper with Chinese script.

Ian read through what he had written and tried to puzzle out a connection. He googled wax crayons and discovered they'd been invented by Edwin Binney in 1903. So the drawings could have been there for more than a century. The attic rooms might have been a nursery. Paul told him the house was in a terrible state and hadn't been decorated for many years. And who bothers with an attic anyway? It was probably just used as a place to store stuff.

He put his thoughts about Clover to one side and turned to more recent events. Was the time of day important? Most had happened at night or in the evening when the light would have been poor. Who was in the house at the time? He'd need to check that with Freya. Anyone who had been there for all of them would be a suspect. This probably let the guests off the hook, but he needed to check for any that turned up regularly. He'd checked the residential staff and he couldn't think of any possible motive for them to play tricks. Quite the opposite. They'd want to hold on to their jobs. Playing tricks on their employers should be the last thing on their minds.

He put his pen down and yawned. List-making usually cleared his head and made him feel better but looking at this list he didn't think he'd made much progress and his head was as muddled as ever. 'How are you getting on?' he asked Molly, who had been fiddling with her phone and was now printing something.

'Great,' she said. 'I found this app that translates Chinese symbols. These are Mandarin. I'm just printing it for you.' She gathered up the two sheets of paper and fixed them side by side to the board.

Ian studied them. 'A list of plants?' No help at all. Were they in danger of disappearing up a blind alley of horticulture? It was Chinese gardening, which helped even less. It was probably a scheme of some earlier Buckland-Kerr to introduce an oriental feel to the grounds. Chinese gardens had been fashionable at the beginning of the twentieth century. Or was that Japanese gardens? Either way it didn't help them very much.

'I checked them out on Google,' said Molly. 'They are all used in Chinese remedies.'

That made sense and helped them more than the gardening idea. Was someone in the house in need of a cure for something? He recognised some of the plants; ginseng and magnolia, but there were others he'd not heard of. 'Did you check what they're used for?'

Molly nodded. 'I tried but it's complicated. Chinese practitioners make up their own concoctions after getting to know all about the patient. Weird things like how their tongues look and if they prefer to be hot or cold. But some of these plants are known to help depression and anxiety.'

Murriemuir sounded like a deeply depressing place to be before it was sold. If he'd had to live there, Ian thought, he'd be screaming for any kind of remedy he could lay his hands on. 'That page of script suggests someone in the house was familiar with the language.' Was there any way he could find out if there had been Chinese visitors to the house? Another one that had called in at the village shop was too much to hope for. On the other hand, there probably weren't too many Mandarin speakers in the area. It was something that would be remembered. He looked at the picture again. As far as it was possible to tell from a photograph taken on a phone fifteen years ago, when phone cameras were not what they were today, it looked like a printed page torn out of a book. He'd think about that. It might be worth a visit to the library to see if anyone could identify it or at least give him a clue about where it had come from.

He printed the photo of the child's drawing and passed it to Molly. 'What do you make of this?' he asked. She would know more about children's drawings than he did.

Molly looked at it and laughed. The drawings were on a white-washed wall just below a window. 'Most children draw on a wall at some time,' she told him. 'Ryan did once. He used felt pens and we had a hell of a job cleaning it off before his dad came home.'

'How old was he?'

'About three, I think. He's not done it since. It's probably not encouraged at school and Dad has set him up with rolls of lining paper and washable crayons.'

Ian wondered if Nigel had done the same for Molly when she was small. He was definitely one for heading off problems before they became problems. He felt a moment of affection for Nigel and wished his own father had been as sensible. 'What age do you think the child was when it drew this?'

'Well,' said Molly. 'Ryan's nearly six and he can draw a lot better than that. They start to draw people when they're about four and this looks like a person.' She pointed to one of the stick figures; a woman wearing a triangle-shaped skirt and a green hat on top of a mass of frizzy hair. The woman had a wide grin, which, along with the bright colours, made Ian think this was someone the child had been fond of.

'Let's assume this was done by a four-year-old child. And we know there was a child in the house in 1996 when Jivin visited. This could be her mother.'

'It might be her father wearing a kilt,' Molly suggested.

Good point, Ian thought.

'Do you think they could be Clover's drawings?' she asked.

'That's what I'm wondering.' Were they, he wondered, edging a little closer to discovering who Clover was and how long she'd been there?

Two Clovers. One born in 1938 who died at the age of seven. The other, if it *was* Clover, seen by Jivin in 1996 when she was three or four, and who died about six years later. What was the connection between them? An unusual name like that couldn't be a coincidence. There must be a family association. Charles Buckland-Kerr had never married but that didn't mean he hadn't fathered a daughter. Ian ran a check on Buckland-Kerr births in the 1990s and found nothing. Then he ran another check for deaths but the only name that came up was Charles himself and they already knew he'd died in 2003.

Ian looked at his watch. Molly was taking time off to take Ryan to the dentist. A job she wanted to do herself rather than leave it to Nigel, who was probably perfectly willing to do it, but as Molly explained, dentist visits were a mum's job. It was also time for him to walk Lottie. He watched as Molly tidied her desk and shut down her computer. Then he found Lottie's lead and set off. Winter was on the way, he thought, rubbing his hands. The café in the village served warming home-made soup. Just what he needed after a brisk walk on a cold day. But he couldn't expect Lottie to sit and watch him eat unless she'd had a good walk first, so he decided to take the long route down to the village; through the park and churchyard, then a shortcut through an alley between the houses, which would take them to the back of the café.

The children were all at school now and the park was quiet. He threw Lottie's ball for her a few times then put her back on her lead to walk through the churchyard. There was nothing to say that dogs should be on leads there, but it seemed disrespectful to let her run free among the gravestones. They took their time as Ian paused to read the inscriptions. It was an early Victorian church, the graveyard adhering strictly to the class system of the time. And money, he supposed. The rich landowning types had elaborate memorials with praying angels sitting on marble plinths. The less well-heeled had simpler gravestones, often inscribed with sentimental epitaphs. What was striking was the number of family graves. Not so much recently but a hundred or so years ago. Generations of the same family must have lived their entire lives in the village and then died here. He stood sadly at the grave of one family who had lost three young children all within a few years.

Family graves probably didn't exist now. Except perhaps for royalty. Grandad had been cremated; his ashes scattered somewhere in Morningside cemetery. Ian had no idea where any of the rest of his family were buried, and he didn't imagine that in years to come he and his brother would be found cosying up together for all eternity alongside their parents.

Lottie was getting impatient and started tugging at her lead. She wasn't stupid. She knew lunch was imminent and obviously saw no reason for delaying it. That's how she was, all dogs probably. Walking, eating, sleeping and barking at delivery people was what they did. No patience for contemplation. And on a breezy day like this she was probably right. They carried on down the hill and into the café, which was warm and smelt of fresh bread and bacon. A problem. He'd been set on a healthy bowl of vegetable soup, but the smell of cooking bacon was too much for him and he decided on a bacon buttie instead. He'd heard somewhere that bacon had been described as the gateway drug for vegetarians and he could understand why. Lottie probably agreed with him. And when it arrived, he broke off a piece of bacon and fed it to her. If he'd had soup, she'd only have got a piece of bread. He was doing them both a favour. He silently vowed not to tell Caroline and promised himself a plant-based supper that evening.

They took the short route home. There was now a strong wind blowing in from the estuary and looking across the water he could see dark clouds. The wind was strong enough to ruffle Lottie's fur and he wondered why he hadn't worn a scarf, but a short walk and they would be home and thankful for an efficient heating system. And anyway, walking through the churchyard had made him sad. No one was immortal, but losing three children must have been devastating.

That thought stayed with him as he sat at his desk puzzling over Clover, with the idea of a family connection still niggling at his brain. He opened Molly's file and went once again through the records of the family. He pulled out the copy of the earlier Clover's death certificate. She'd died of an infection when she was seven. Sadly, that probably wasn't unusual at the time. But what caught his attention was that she hadn't died at home. The place of death had been recorded as St Maghread's hospital. He'd heard of St Maghread's recently. It was the name of the school his niece Lyra went to. It was in Glenrothes, not far from Murriemuir. He searched for the school website and found that it was a *sought-after private school for girls, with a reputation for excellence both academic and sporting and with an ethos of hard work, facilitating every girl to reach her full potential*. Of course it was. Stewart would settle for nothing less. He clicked on *History* and read the page with interest. The school had been founded in 1947 by Deoiridh Grimmond and aimed to be, in Deoiridh's own words, *a Scottish Cheltenham Ladies' College*. At the top of the page was a portrait of Ms Grimmond wearing a tweed suit, thick mud-coloured stockings, brogues and the kind of expression likely to engender nightmares in small girls. The school had opened thanks to generous donations from local dignitaries, concerned for the education of their daughters, on the site of St Maghread's hospital, which until the mid

1940s had been a private asylum for simple-minded children. Ian shuddered. He'd known that people with learning difficulties had been locked away by families too ashamed to acknowledge them. Thank goodness that was a thing of the past. Too late for poor Clover though. Then he remembered another name from Molly's report and checked it again. Janet Buckland-Kerr. Daughter of Andrew, who had built Murriemuir, and his wife, Hilda. Janet died in 1903 at the age of thirteen. He checked the copy Molly had made of her death certificate. Janet had also died of infection and, like Clover, she had died in St Maghread's.

A bit of googling led him to admission records for Scottish lunatic asylums between the years of 1856 and 1945. They were both there. Janet admitted in 1903 and Clover in 1942. Both recorded as 'imbecile'. The word jumped off the page at him. How could anyone do that to a small child? No wonder Charles had been, as Jivin had said, difficult to get on with. He must have been haunted by the fate of a sister he had never really known. She would only have been four when she was sent away. Charles himself only a couple of years younger. Was this an inherited condition? Whether it was or wasn't, Charles might well have thought so. Was that why he never married?

18

Ian was going round in circles with the Buckland-Kerrs and it was getting him nowhere. It was, he thought, time to put Clover and her identity aside for a while and concentrate on what was going on at Murriemuir House right now. His idea that what had happened so far was just the start, and that it all might be about to get very much worse, made him think he needed to find out what was going on quickly and put an end to it. After all his questions and searches about Murriemuir he was now convinced that the apparently supernatural events had only started recently. It was nothing caused by the house itself; no rumbling plumbing, strange vibrations caused by an aged heating system or odours brought about by dried vegetation. In the house maybe, where they might use joss sticks for meditation, or place bowls of potpourri on tables. But the perfume event had happened in the garden in the autumn when there were, as far as his limited knowledge of horticulture suggested, no highly scented plants in flower. He firmly ruled out actual haunting. He refused to believe that disturbing a few graves, mostly animal ones, would stir any kind of supernatural events. Scotland was full of ghost sightings, and he believed there was *always* a rational explanation for them. No, whatever was happening at Murriemuir was deliberate and carefully planned by a flesh and blood human. He just needed to find out *which* human and stop them before they did anything serious.

Who were his suspects? Top of his list was still Arkash, who had both the opportunity and the know-how. But he had no motive and Ian had believed him when he denied it.

Could it be the children? Lyra possibly. She was bright enough and could probably persuade Will to do anything she told him to. But why would they? They got on well with their parents and had everything they could possibly want, so why risk it?

Stewart and Freya? A publicity stunt perhaps. But again, why would they? They were doing well and had plenty of bookings. He hadn't sensed any tension between them and there was no reason to think Stewart resented his wife's success. He wasn't that devious, and in any case, Ian suspected he had heavily invested financially in Freya's plans. Ian envied their closeness. If Stewart had married Stephanie things might have turned out very differently. But Stephanie had, for reasons Ian never quite understood, married *him*. She'd quite likely had her sights set on Stewart until he met Freya, and at that point she'd had to make do with his younger brother. Pity it wasn't the other way around. He could easily have fallen for Freya if his brother hadn't got there first.

His mind was drifting in an uncomfortable direction. He should look for suspects outside the family and that left the staff. He knew a little about all their backgrounds but not a lot about them as people. If he was going to accuse any of them, he should find out more and get to know them better. Quite how he was going to do that he didn't know, but he'd start with the obvious and go and talk to Freya. She'd had time to get to know them as individuals rather than names and employment histories.

He looked at his watch. Mid-morning, and it was mid-week. There would be no resident guests and Freya's morning yoga class would have finished. Molly was updating some client records, which would keep her busy for the rest of the day. She would probably be quite glad to have the office to herself for a while and would work faster without him under her feet.

'You okay if I pop over to Murriemuir for a bit?' he asked.

'Of course. There's plenty to do here. Do you want to leave Lottie?'

Lottie pricked up her ears at the sound of her name. 'No,' he said. 'I'll take her with me. Then you can get off home if I'm not back by the time you finish.'

'Okay,' she said, smiling at him and turning back to her computer screen.

It was good to have someone so reliable, he thought as he gathered up his car keys and phone. He still hadn't got around to enrolling her on a course. He'd check that out when he got back.

There were few cars parked in the drive when he arrived at Murriemuir. A quiet time, he supposed. Morning classes had finished, and a few remaining students were relaxing in the lounge, dressed in yoga gear and sipping healthy drinks.

Freya greeted him with a sisterly kiss and led him into her study, which was very warm. He slipped off his jacket and slung it over the back of a chair.

'Sorry,' said Freya, adjusting the thermostat. 'I've been doing accounts in here. That always makes me feel cold.'

Accounts tended to make him feel hot, especially round the collar, but everyone was different.

Freya poured him a cup of coffee and they sat down. 'How are you getting on?' she asked. 'Have you found out who Clover was?'

'I'm going a bit slowly,' he admitted. He opened his folder of notes and showed her what he knew of the Buckland-Kerrs.

She studied the family tree Molly had made and pointed to the entry for Clover (Clover the first, as he thought of her now). 'That's interesting,' she said.

'It's very interesting. It looks like a family name. And a little girl was seen with Charles right here in this house in 1996.'

'Do you think that was our Clover?'

'We think it might have been, but I haven't been able to find any record of her, or a possible mother.'

'Do you think Clover could have been one of the family, Charles' daughter?'

'She'd have been an illegitimate daughter, but it's possible. There's no birth certificate with Charles named as her father.'

'Then we need to find her mother.'

'We do, but right now I'm more concerned with your supernatural manifestations.' He told her about the ghost evening.

Freya laughed. 'Sounds fun. Perhaps we should do that. Although our ghosts aren't so reliable. We've no idea when things are going to happen.'

'Or how,' said Ian. 'I'd hoped to discover some of the tricks of the haunting trade, but everything at Buchan House was glaringly obvious. Your ghosts are much cleverer.'

'They don't seem to work to any schedule though, do they?'

'I'm trying to find something that connects them all. Can you tell me who was here each time? If we find one person who was at all of them, we might be on to something.'

'Well,' said Freya, 'me, obviously, and the children.'

'Stewart?'

'No, he was working the day of the singing bowls.'

Pity, Ian thought. He'd quite fancied uncovering his brother as a trickster. 'You don't think it could have been the children?'

'I'd skin them alive if it was. But no. Will's too much of a goody-goody. Lyra's clever but I think she feels she's a bit above it all. I'm afraid she's inherited her grandmother's snobbishness. In any case I've searched their rooms and checked up on their internet history.'

'And the residents?'

Freya shook her head. 'Different groups each time. We've had one or two returning but no one who's been to all of them.'

'The staff then?'

'We've a couple of part-timers in the kitchen, but they're only here at mealtimes. A cleaner who does mornings only and Guy, but I've never seen him in the house at all. The resident staff were all here except Zhang Ming, who just comes at weekends.'

'I'm not sure we can rule him out. He's here often enough to set something up. Perhaps he's working with one of the others. Remind me who they are.'

'Shining Lotus, also known as Sharon, Sonia Greenlow and Arkash.'

'Arkash interests me,' said Ian. 'You remember he told us it was his grandfather who had found the details of the job here?'

Freya nodded.

'Well, there was more to it. Turns out Arkash's grandad, Jivin, used to live here.'

Freya gazed at him open-mouthed. 'Really? Why didn't Arkash tell us?'

'I don't think he knew. Nothing very secretive, they just don't communicate that much.'

'But you'd think he would have mentioned it when he knew Arkash was coming to work here.'

'Jivin was brought here by a Buckland-Kerr uncle during partition. I don't think it was a very happy time for him.'

'But he encouraged Arkash to come here.'

'He has rather old-fashioned ideas about the young not having a life that's too comfortable. Perhaps he thought being here would be a taste of his own hardship. I don't know. I'm just guessing. Who knows how his mind works? But there's more.'

'About Arkash?'

'About Jivin. He was the one who saw the little girl with Charles. He'd taken a short holiday and dropped in to see how Charles was.'

'You don't think they could be in it together, Jivin and Arkash? Getting back at the house for the miserable time he had here?'

'Jivin may have had mixed feelings about his time here, but I don't think it was that bad. I can't see that he'd want to take revenge on a house. And I've talked to Arkash. He's into special effects and conjuring tricks, but I do believe him when he says he had nothing to do with it.'

'Are you sure he didn't? He seems to have the skill and a connection to the past.'

'He's no motive. Jivin might have, but Arkash was desperate to get away from his family so he's hardly like to risk his job just to play a few tricks. And he comes across as an uncomplicated, honest type.'

'You think it's one of the others?'

'It has to be. Everything started after they began working here.'

'And after we moved the graves. Do you think one of them knew about Clover?'

'Possibly, but apart from Arkash none of them were here when the graves were moved.'

'Apart from Guy,' Freya said.

'What do you know about him?' Ian asked.

'He was already working here when we moved in. He'd looked after the grounds for the hotel owner.'

'And before that?'

She shook her head. 'He was working in the Highlands on an estate somewhere.'

'And you inherited him, so you probably didn't do any reference checks on him?'

'I've got all his details. I can send them to you.'

'I need to find out more about all of them.'

'You've not met Sonia or Sharon, have you? Would you like to? I can call them in.'

'I think I'll lie low for a bit longer. I'm not sure how to approach it yet.' And an idea was taking shape in his head.

'Let's get some lunch first. The dining room isn't open today, but I can make you a sandwich in the kitchen.'

Lottie trotted after them as they made their way to the kitchen. She sat looking hopefully up at Freya while she sliced granary bread and made cold pheasant sandwiches.

'Not gone veggie then?' Ian asked.

'We have a non-meat menu for guests,' she said. 'But when we're on our own we're closet carnivores.'

That figured. He couldn't see Stewart existing on plants in spite of his new-found concern for the environment.

They finished their lunch and returned to Freya's office, which thankfully was now much cooler. Freya flicked through files in a metal filing cabinet and eventually pulled out the one she was looking for. It had given Ian an idea. 'How do you manage all the admin?' he asked. 'Do you have help?'

Freya shrugged. 'Are you suggesting I need it?' she said, handing him the folder. 'Guy's details,' she said. 'I do it all myself. It's probably time I digitised it. But right now, we're too busy. It will have to wait until the Christmas break.'

'I was thinking I might send you my assistant, Molly, for a few days. She could help you out with paperwork and keep an eye on things.'

'Spy on my staff, you mean.'

'Well, yes.' Freya wasn't going to like that, he thought. It was probably a stupid suggestion. 'Your trickster will be careful around you but someone new could look around without arousing any suspicion.'

'Great idea,' said Freya. 'We've a three-day residential coming up. She could help with registration, show people to their rooms, check social distancing plans, stuff like that. It would give her a chance to see what goes on outside classes. And the staff are always popping in and out of the office. Would she be able to stay here for a few days?'

He'd wondered about that. Would Molly be able to stay overnight? If not, he could be there himself in the evenings. He was family, after all, and it wouldn't seem suspicious, although he suspected that Molly would do a far better job at getting people to let slip interesting pieces of information about themselves. 'I'll talk to Molly about it. Even if nothing happens during those three days, she'll get to know the staff and that might give us a better idea of what we're looking for.'

He looked around for his jacket, which he was sure he had left on the chair. It had been moved and hung on a hook on the back of the door. A cleaner tidying the room, he supposed, checking that nothing had fallen out of the pockets. 'I'll be in touch in a day or two,' he told Freya.

'I'll look forward to it,' she said, walking with him to the front door.

. . .

As he walked down the steps, Ian noticed Will and Arkash sitting on the wall at the edge of the lily pond. Will was watching, fascinated, as Arkash played with some two pound coins, making them disappear apparently into thin air, and then finding them behind Will's ear. Ian paused to watch. He'd had an uncle who had done the same trick. In those days it was five pence pieces. Inflation, he supposed, wondering what the going rate for the tooth fairy was these days. It was all sleight of hand and Arkash was very good at it. A two pound coin was a lot bigger and heavier than a five pence piece. Far harder to conceal.

Will noticed Ian watching. He looked up and grinned at him. 'It's magic,' he said. 'Arkash is a really good magician. Show Uncle Ian,' he said, turning back to Arkash.

Arkash held his fist towards Ian and opened it to reveal the coin. Then he closed his fist and opened it again with a flourish to show that it was now empty. Then he reached behind Ian's left ear, opened his palm again and revealed the coin. It was an old trick but very effective.

Will heard Freya calling him. 'Got to go and do homework,' he said. 'Can we do more magic later?'

'Shall I make your rabbits disappear and pull them out of a hat?' Arkash asked.

Will nodded enthusiastically. 'But promise you'll make them reappear and not put them in a curry instead. And can you make Lyra disappear? I don't mind if she doesn't come back. Not for a while, anyway.' He ran towards the house, waving to them as he went.

'That was very clever,' said Ian. 'Where did you learn to do it?'

'I joined a conjuring club years ago. Done a few live gigs. I've got a website,' he said proudly.

Ian already knew that. He'd found it when he was doing his background checks. 'Does it pay well?' he asked.

'Not well enough to give up cooking for a living. It might if I could work up an act and get on something like *Britain's Got Talent*. Trouble is the family don't approve so I'll probably just end up doing kids' parties in my spare time.'

'What other tricks do you do?'

Arkash looked at him and sighed. 'Not stuff with singing and strange perfume. I told you I had nothing to do with that.'

'And I believe you,' said Ian. 'But you must have an idea how it was done.'

'Of course,' said Arkash. 'Magic's all about playing with people's expectations and getting them to focus on what's irrelevant. Young Will was so busy thinking about where the coin was going that he didn't think to watch my hand movements.'

That went for Ian as well. 'So how do you explain what's been going on here?'

'The crying baby and singing child are easy. Just conceal a recording and set it on a timer.'

'But Stewart searched the rooms and found nothing.'

'You think whoever did this didn't know there would be a search? Of course they did, but think of the time involved. There must have been fifteen minutes at least after the singing stopped. Lots of chatter about who it was and where it was coming from and then Stewart deciding to search. Plenty of time to remove the evidence. Even longer with the crying in the attic. No one would have leapt out of bed to search while the crying was happening. They probably didn't say anything until they compared notes at breakfast the next morning.'

This was far more useful than watching the Buchan ghost efforts. Why hadn't he thought of asking Arkash before? 'Okay,' said Ian. 'What about the perfume?'

'That was most likely some kind of balloon and a timer set to puncture it.'

'Wouldn't there have been remains, bits of rubber?'

'They wouldn't have used rubber party balloons. Have you ever seen that stuff that blows bubbles out of a pipe? It's made from a compactable resin. It comes in a tube and with a blob on the end of an air pipe you can blow a bubble. It would be easy to fill with perfumed powder and once it's punctured it shrinks back to almost nothing. Anyone who knew what they were looking for would have found remains in the trees and residue from the powder, but by the time the group had come back inside and started talking about it everything would have blown away.'

'All right,' said Ian, becoming more and more intrigued. 'What about the singing bowls?' There was no way they could have been set off remotely.

'That's a bit more difficult, but my guess is that it relied on perceptions of sound location. Remember they were all lying on the floor, not looking at the bowls.'

'I'm not sure what you mean.'

'Think of surround sound in a cinema. You're watching a film, so it seems like the sound of the actors speaking is coming from their mouths, but really it's coming from the sides and back of the auditorium.'

'So people saw the singing bowls in front of them and when they heard them they assumed that's where the sound was coming from.'

'Exactly. Like I said, it's all about playing tricks on people's perceptions.'

'And you really had nothing to do with it?'

Arkash grinned at him. 'Scout's honour,' he said, jumping up. 'Nice talking but I've got pakoras to cook.' He ran round the side of the house and in through the kitchen door, whistling as he went.

Could he be trusted or was this a double bluff? But he'd hardly be giving away all these trade secrets if he was planning more tricks. Unless he was becoming over-confident. Ian had heard of crimes where the criminals teased the police. Misleading them with bits of information and giving away clues about their identity while continuing to commit their crimes undetected. He'd listened to the gossip among his colleagues when he'd been in the police and had envied them their role in solving crimes while he was out rounding up drunks and school evaders. But perhaps they were just establishing their superior roles by echoing what happened on TV crime dramas where the criminals were a lot cleverer than your average thug on the street. On TV, no matter how clever the criminals were, the police always caught up with them in the end. He wasn't so sure about real-life crime.

He gave Lottie a quick run around the garden, hoping he might meet Guy. But there was no one else there that afternoon and, in any case, he wasn't sure what he would have asked Guy. It would be better to go through his notes first and hope for some glimmer of his past that he could question him about.

He and Lottie drove back to the office, where Molly was tidying up before leaving to collect Ryan. He was glad she hadn't left. He was impatient to ask her about his latest idea. 'Do you fancy working undercover for a bit?' he asked.

Molly stared at him wide-eyed. 'Really?'

'It's perfectly safe,' he assured her. 'I just need you to watch what's going at Murriemuir.'

'What will my cover be?'

'You'll be there to help Freya in the office. She's got a course coming up and it's possible someone's planning some more tricks. But I don't want you to get involved. Just observe.'

'How long will it be for?' she asked.

'Three days while they run one of the residential courses.'

'I'll have to stay overnight?'

'Not if you don't want to. I can be there in the evening but it's more likely that they will set things up during the day.'

'I don't mind staying there for a couple of nights. Dad liked looking after Ryan. He's always saying I should take another break. I think he really likes having Ryan to himself.'

'Won't Ryan mind?'

'I can talk to him on FaceTime. He'll think it's an adventure.'

'Well, if you're sure.'

Molly nodded enthusiastically. 'I can record things that happen, but I won't be able to work out how it's all set up.'

'You don't need to. Just keep an eye on the staff members. Report on anything that seems odd about them. What do you think? Up for it?'

'Definitely.'

'Great. And if you enjoy it, we'll start looking for a course you can do after Christmas. Work towards your PI licence.'

She looked thrilled as she put her coat on and bounded down the garden path, keen to give Ryan and Nigel the news that they were going to spend three days together. Three days when they could do exactly as they liked without her insisting on boring things like bedtimes and eating carrots.

Ian wasn't surprised to get a call from Nigel later that day. They arranged to meet in the pub that evening and there was nothing unusual about that. It was something they did every couple of weeks or so. But Ian guessed that choosing the very day he'd asked Molly to go undercover wasn't a coincidence. He'd want to know why Ian was sending Molly to Murriemuir and was showing a fatherly concern for her. She'd probably told him she was going for a weekend of pampering. And in a way she was, but Nigel was a lot more perceptive than everyone gave him credit for. At least he was where Molly was concerned; Ian was unsure about other areas of his life. He was known to be thick-skinned and not altogether tactful when he wanted things done in the village. But with Molly and Ryan he was a caring and admirable father and grandfather. In this case Ian sympathised. He assumed Molly hadn't given him any details and he thought Nigel should know that she wasn't skiving off for a girly weekend. She was taking the job seriously; even planning to make a career of it. And Nigel should be aware of that. He was, Ian thought, just a wee bit patronising; patting her on the head and telling her to run off and have fun. Very nice of him and no doubt Molly appreciated it up to a point. But she was developing a career for herself, and she deserved respect for doing it under trying circumstances.

. . .

He bought a couple of pints and carried them to where Nigel was sitting.

Nigel took a gulp of beer. 'How's my Molly getting on?' he asked. 'She's enjoying the work. Tells me she's going to be a proper detective and do some undercover work.'

Had Ian underestimated Nigel after all? It was hard to stop thinking of him as an irritating busybody who got under everyone's skin. He'd not asked Molly to keep her assignment a secret from her father. There were going to be times when she'd need to do that, but this wasn't one of them. They'd deal with that when it happened. They would have to be tactful; he couldn't have Nigel digging into every case Molly was involved in. But for now, it was fine. It was unlikely that Nigel knew anyone in the wellness world. It didn't sound like him at all. He was far more into getting on with things with *none of this airy-fairy touchy-feely nonsense*. The idea of Nigel standing on his head or even in downward dog wasn't something easily visualised. Ian couldn't even imagine him lying under trees meditating. It was more likely that he'd be thinking about the best way to prune them and whether the ground he was lying on was damp.

'She'll be staying with my brother and his wife for three days,' he said. 'She's going to be in the background observing some of the staff and making notes.'

'Nothing risky, I hope?'

So he had been worried. Everyone had this idea that private investigation involved rushing into dangerous situations and fighting off baddies that were too much for the police. In fact, although he had been in a couple of dangerous situations himself, it was rare and usually because he hadn't planned properly. The reality was that they spent most of their time sitting in front of computer screens, making case notes, and drinking a lot of coffee.

'I rarely get involved with anything dangerous,' he said. 'And I'd never send Molly to do something I thought was risky. She'll be well looked after by my brother and his wife. It's a calm, gentle place. We just need to know a little more about the people who work there.'

'Not like on *Line of Duty* then?'

That was a surprise. He'd always thought of Nigel as more of a *Midsomer Murders* type. Characters who went undercover in *Line of Duty* rarely came out of it well, or even alive. If that was what Nigel was expecting, Ian couldn't blame him for being worried. 'Absolutely not,' he said. 'You can call her any time while she's there. She's already said she'll FaceTime Ryan. You can even drop in on her if you like. I'm sure Freya and Stewart would be happy to treat you to a meal. They have an excellent Indian chef.' That should reassure him.

'Nah, can't have her old dad popping in on her at work.'

'I'm sure she wouldn't mind.' Although Nigel was probably right. Molly wouldn't want her dad checking up on her. But she wouldn't want him worrying about her either.

'Anyway,' said Nigel, 'I can't be doing with all that spicy cooking. Gives me indigestion. And Molly's a grown woman. She's had a tough time, but she needs to know I think she's doing a great job at getting back to her old self. Can't treat her like a kiddie, can I?'

He was right and once again Ian marvelled at his ability to talk perfect sense and be thoroughly irritating at the same time.

'We've been talking about her going on a PI course. She would learn a lot and get herself licensed. She enjoys the work and is very good at it.'

'Set up on her own, you mean?'

'Well, that would be an option, but she'd probably want to get a lot more experience working with me first.'

'You could go into partnership,' he said. Ian had had the same idea, but he hoped Nigel wasn't going to suggest putting money into it. He'd have to be careful. Much as he liked working with Molly, he had no intention of becoming financially indebted to her father. But it was way too soon to be thinking like that.

'She did well joining that support group,' said Nigel. 'It's really drawn her out. I thought it was going to be all crying on each other's shoulders, hating all men, that kind of thing. But they seem to have a lot of fun. She's made some good friends there.'

Ian took a gulp of beer. 'I think women are better at that kind of thing than men,' he said, wishing he'd had a support group after he'd been shot, and Stephanie had left him. Nigel was right about the friendships. Molly, he thought, had adopted Caroline as a role model and in Ian's opinion she couldn't have chosen anyone better for independence and toughness. Both Molly and Caroline had made a far better job of pulling their lives back together again than he had. *Stop that*, he thought. Must be the beer making him feel sorry for himself. Lottie hopped up onto his lap and looked longingly at his packet of crisps. He patted her thoughtfully on the head. Two years ago, Stephanie had thrust Lottie into his unwilling arms. It was quite possibly the best thing she had ever done for him. Hell, it was the only good thing she had ever done for him.

He glanced across at Nigel, who was gazing at his empty glass. 'Whatever Molly decides to do with her life,' he said, misty-eyed, 'it's given me time with Ryan, and I can't imagine anything I value more than that.'

19

Ian had plenty to do during the three days Molly was away at Murriemuir. The months since the end of lockdown, with people working in offices again, children all back at school and the freedom to stay in hotels once more gave plenty of excuses for wandering spouses to catch up with activities they had been forced to curtail. It was also a time of extreme suspicion. Couples who had been shut up at home together for long periods and knew each other's whereabouts twenty-four hours a day now became suspicious about partners who went off on their own for even the shortest amount of time. Ian had been deluged with enquiries about spying on husbands or wives and while most of these suspicions were unfounded, he still had to write up reports, explain the lack of photographic evidence and generally calm down those who had lost trust in their nearest and dearest.

The three days that Molly wasn't in the office went slowly. Ian found himself tempted to check up on her every half hour or so. But he knew that was the best way to lose her. She knew what she was doing, and he must learn to let her get on with it. He did allow himself evening phone calls to Freya, who assured him Molly was fine. She had quickly become part of the resident staff group, sharing a table for meals, walking to the pub in the village after evening classes and gossiping round the kitchen table before bed.

'If anyone can get to know their secrets, Molly can,' said Freya. 'She's great at the admin as well. I might even poach her from you permanently. The clients love her, and the office has never looked so tidy.'

'Don't you dare,' he said, laughing. 'My office could definitely not manage without her.'

All he could do while she was away was tidy up his own cases and wait for her report. It was a long three days, during which Lottie found herself being walked more than usual. And although Lottie was never going to complain about extra walks, he suspected she too would be glad to see Molly back in the office.

The day she was due to return, he and Lottie walked to the shop, bought a bag of pastries, and met her as she parked her car. He held up the bag. 'Debriefing over coffee and buns?' he suggested.

They walked up the path together, Lottie not straying far from the bag of buns. Not, thought Ian, that she was likely to get any. He'd have to find her a dog chew instead. He couldn't have her feeling left out, but he couldn't risk her putting on weight either. She'd not hold back if offered a bun and her waistline would expand alarmingly even with all the extra walking she'd had recently.

Molly unpacked her bag; a notebook and several sheets of paper, which she organised into four piles. One for each person she had been watching, he guessed.

'How did it go?' he asked, turning the coffee machine on, waiting impatiently for it to bubble and puff out coffee-scented steam. She was keeping him in suspense. No coffee, no report. Fair enough. He'd be the same if he had interesting information to share. He cleared a space on his desk and poured two cups of coffee.

'It was good,' said Molly at last, sitting down and opening her notebook.

'Any supernatural events?' he asked. Would he be pleased if Molly had witnessed one of them or disappointed that he had missed it himself?

'No, nothing like that unfortunately.'

'So was it a waste of time?'

'Not at all. I discovered some interesting things about several of the staff.'

'Right,' he said, sitting down at his own desk. 'Who's first?'

He expected her to talk about Arkash and his magic tricks. He still couldn't quite let go of the idea that the Panchulis were behind it all. But she surprised him.

'Stewart,' she said, looking at him for a reaction. She wasn't disappointed.

'What? You can't be serious. You're accusing my brother of trying to ruin his own business?'

'Freya's business,' she corrected him. 'And no. I'm not accusing him. Not at all. But I think he could be the target.'

'Whatever makes you think that? I know there may be people who don't like him, but they'd be work colleagues or rivals in the offshore wind industry. Why would they target him at home?'

'You know he's running a seminar at the COP conference in a couple of weeks?'

'Yes, Freya did mention that. A symposium on offshore wind. Are you saying you think someone is trying to disrupt it? But that doesn't make sense. Why would they target him at home?'

'His COP pass was stolen. He'd just been sent it by recorded delivery. It was a lanyard with a card clipped to it. It's like a credit card with a magnetic strip that was programmed to let him into various conference rooms. He left it on a table in the lounge while he went to check out a problem one of the guests had with their bathroom. He was only out of the room for a few minutes, but when he came back it had gone.'

'Did he call the police?'

'He called the COP office and they told him it wasn't necessary. They'd cancel it and send him another one. They gave him a bit of an earful about being more careful. He was quite annoyed about that.'

Yes, Ian could imagine that. His brother had never responded well to a ticking off. 'So where was everyone when this happened?'

'All over the place. It was before the first session on Saturday morning. A few guests were still in the dining room having breakfast, some had gone back to their rooms, and a few had gone for a walk.'

'What about the staff?'

'I know where they should have been but the only one I can be sure about was Arkash because I was with him in the kitchen. Ming left breakfast early, saying he had to prepare for his first consultation. He was using one of the small rooms on the ground floor. Sonia was probably printing out notes for her meditation session. I didn't see her, but I could hear the printer.'

'That was in the office?'

'Yes. It's quite close to the lounge so she could have popped out for a moment while she was waiting for the printing to finish. That goes for Ming as well. His room is right next to the lounge.'

'And Sharon?'

'Down in the yoga studio getting ready for her first class.'

'Are you sure that's where she was?'

'I saw her going downstairs but she might not have stayed there. Like I said, I was in the kitchen with Arkash.'

'How long were you there?'

'About ten minutes.' She blushed. 'I came up when I heard Stewart shouting about his pass.'

'What were you doing in the kitchen?' he asked with a smile, noticing her blushes.

'Just chatting.'

'What about the children?'

'Lyra had just left to catch the bus to school. She had a hockey match. And Will was playing with his kite in the garden.'

This was all rather baffling. Who would steal a pass that could easily be cancelled and replaced? Presumably someone who didn't know that. Was there a black market for COP passes? 'Who do *you* think might have taken it?' he asked.

'Shining Lotus,' she said, tapping a name in her notebook and reaching for a page of notes.

'Sharon, the yoga teacher?' He thought she was the least suspicious of their suspects. Her background was straightforward. He'd traced her way back to when she had left school. And if she was down in the cellar, she'd have been the furthest away. 'Why do you think that?'

'She's asked for time off. First two weeks in November.'

A little surprising, he thought. She'd only been working there for six weeks. But was that really grounds for suspicion? 'Do you know why?' he asked.

Molly shook her head. 'There's no reason why she should tell us if she doesn't want to. She's taking it unpaid, and Freya wasn't too bothered. There are no residentials then and Freya herself can cover her classes.'

There must be more. Something to draw Molly's attention to her.

'It's during the conference in Glasgow,' she said.

And she'd pinched Stewart's pass so she could attend a meeting about wind power? It seemed unlikely and he didn't see any reason to worry about it. Glasgow was going to be full of world leaders and they expected crowds of climate demonstrators. But security would be tight. They were very unlikely to cause much trouble. It would be all dressing up as trees and dancing in the street. They'd be kept well away from anyone important. Sharon was known as an eco-protester. She'd never tried to hide it. There was no reason why she shouldn't go dancing in the streets for something she felt strongly about. He didn't know why she'd kept quiet about it. Stewart and Freya might even approve. Stewart's move from oil to wind power might have been an astute career move in terms of income but no one could argue about its green credentials.

'I don't really see how that could have anything to do with what's going on at Murriemuir,' he said.

'I'm not sure it does,' said Molly. 'But I don't think Sharon is who she says she is. I found this.' She turned to a page she had printed from Facebook. He recognised the photo of Sharon and thought he recognised the man standing next to her but couldn't remember why. 'I was checking her Facebook activity, and this was tagged. The man calls himself John Bull. It's not his real name.'

John Bull. He recognised *that* name. A cartoon character, personification of Englishness, usually depicted with a fat stomach and wearing a Union Jack waistcoat. But more alarmingly, it was the alias used by the leader of a nasty bunch of white supremacists who had turned up at Black Lives Matter meetings with cudgels and painted Union Jack faces. They'd also tweeted in support of the January 6th riots in Washington. An unlikely friend for someone who actively protested on environmental issues. He tried to remember what he knew about far-right groups and didn't think they were notable objectors to new airport runways and rail links. In other words, the last person he expected to be close to someone who called herself Shining Lotus and who sat down in front of bulldozers. And in this photograph, they did look close. Shaven-headed John Bull had his arm around Sharon's shoulders, and she was leaning against him in a way that didn't suggest an abhorrence of those holding right-wing opinions.

Infiltration was the word that came into his head. But who was infiltrating who?

'Do you know where this was taken?' he asked.

'In London about three months ago. It was at a party but there's not much detail about that.'

It was worrying. Either Sharon was not who she said she was, or she was playing a very dangerous game. Could there be plans to disrupt COP? Perhaps Sharon was planning to smuggle John Bull supporters into the previously harmless demonstration. Then he wondered about Stewart's company. Could there be a plan to attack an offshore windfarm? It seemed unlikely but he knew nothing about it. This was too much for him and Molly. He needed to talk to Duncan, and it was their pub evening. But he didn't want to alarm Molly. 'We'll put Sharon to one side for the moment,' he said. 'Are any of the others a cause for concern?'

'There are a couple of things. I don't know if they are important.'

'Tell me. We should consider everything.'

'Well, Sonia seems to know the house better than someone who's only been there a short time.'

'In what way?'

'There are some hidden passageways and a concealed staircase. Freya told me about them. It was from when the house had loads of servants, a way for them to get around without disturbing the toffs. Sonia was using them to take shortcuts. I watched her coming out of a hidden door into the dining room. It was a cut through from the kitchen.'

'I suppose Freya could have told her about it.'

'She could, but she told me she didn't want them used and was thinking of locking them.'

He'd warn Freya but couldn't see that it was anything to worry about. You found a shortcut? You'd use it to make life easier.

'And,' Molly continued, 'I think she and Ming knew each other before.'

'What makes you think that?'

'They don't seem to like each other. I overheard Ming telling Sonia she shouldn't be there, and I thought she sounded quite threatening. I don't know. I could be wrong.'

Ian couldn't really see that it would matter if they had or hadn't met before. They moved in alternative medicine circles so it would surprise him if they hadn't met. And if they didn't like each other? Unfortunate if they were working together but hardly grounds for playing tricks on the clients. But again, it was something to keep an eye on.

'You did really well,' he told Molly. 'I'm amazed how much you found out in just three days.' He flicked through the pages of her report. 'All beautifully presented as well.'

'I enjoyed doing it,' she said, yawning.

She did look tired, and he wasn't surprised. 'That's great. I've found some training courses for you to look at but first, you worked all weekend so you must take a couple of days off.'

'I wouldn't mind,' she said. 'Ryan and Dad had a great time together, and the house looks like it's been hit by a tornado. But I'll work tomorrow. I've to finish one or two reports on the knock-off handbag case.'

'Okay,' he agreed. That had been a tedious case that involved trailing around markets tracking the source of fake designer handbags. It had been a good case for Molly though. Her knowledge of handbags was far greater than his and she was good at chatting up stallholders and getting them to reveal the names of their suppliers. If he had still been working on his own, he wouldn't have accepted the case, but the amount it had brought in fees for that case alone had already made it worth employing Molly. He could see them widening their caseload in the future, using their different interests and areas of expertise. 'Make sure you take a couple of days off at the end of the week. And don't spend them on housework.'

She laughed. 'I won't. I'll get Ryan and Dad to do it. I'm planning on going Christmas shopping.'

'Really?' he said, looking at her in surprise. 'In October?'

'Best time. The shops won't be too crowded. And who knows? We might be in lockdown again by December.'

He really hoped not. Surely with vaccination they'd got it all under control. Molly was being alarmist, wasn't she?

Later that day he closed the office and strolled with Lottie to the Pigeon, where they had lit the first fire of the year and Duncan was waiting for him with a pint and a packet of bacon flavoured crisps. *Well done, Duncan*, Ian thought. He'd remembered they were Lottie's favourite and he'd managed to grab a table close to the log fire, which was glowing in a pleasant evening with friends, snooze-inducing kind of way. Ian took his coat off and settled into a comfortable armchair with Lottie curled up at his side. He couldn't imagine anything better right now. Good company, good beer, and a hint of wood smoke. He thought back to the last time he'd sat by a fire in a pub. That would have been during his first winter here, nearly two years ago, and something he'd missed during lockdown.

'How's your case going?' Duncan asked. 'Sorted the Murriemuir poltergeist yet?'

'Just someone playing tricks. It'll probably all settle down once

Halloween is over. But more importantly, I haven't made very much progress on the identity of the skeleton.'

'No one has come forward, although we've posted on all the missing person websites and sent posters round to hospitals and refuges. Thanks for the report, by the way. A very thorough job.'

'Not very helpful though,' Ian said, reaching down to give Lottie a crisp. 'Although we've learnt a bit more since I sent it.'

'Anything that helps us identify the remains?'

'Possibly. Did you notice the name Clover in our report? She was Charles Buckland-Kerr's sister who died very young.'

'Quite a coincidence.'

'And I talked to a man who saw a child at the house back in 1996. He gave her a doll like the one we found with the skeleton, so it looks like she could have been the Clover we dug up. I'm wondering if our Clover might have been Charles' daughter.'

'So there was a little girl at the house?' Duncan asked.

Ian nodded. 'And possibly the right age to be our victim. But I've no idea how we could prove she was his daughter. There's nothing left of him in the house so no chance of a DNA test. I can't find any other Buckland-Kerrs still alive, which means we can't even look for a family match. I don't imagine there'd be a case for exhumation.' He looked at Duncan hopefully.

'Very unlikely,' said Duncan. 'Any idea who the mother could have been?'

'Only that a Mrs Smart who works in the village shop remembers taking telephone orders from a woman at the house. That would have been a few years before Charlie died.'

'Hmm,' said Duncan. 'It's sad, but we might have to accept that we'll never know who she was. At least the pathologist said there was nothing to suggest a violent death. We don't have grounds for a murder hunt.'

Ian drained his glass and went to the bar for a refill. 'There's something else I wanted to talk to you about,' he said as he sat down.

'Connected to Murriemuir?'

'Not exactly, although it is about one of their employees.'

'A criminal connection?'

'No. I did a background search, and she was clean, but my assistant came across something that worried us. It may be nothing.'

'I can't advise you unless you tell me about it.'

'I don't want to arouse unnecessary suspicion, so I'll not tell you her name right now. As I say, I ran a background check and discovered that this woman belonged to an environmental action group. She's been at demonstrations against HS2 and a new Heathrow runway.'

'Nothing wrong with that,' said Duncan. 'Bit of a policing nuisance sometimes but most of the time they are law-abiding, peaceful people.'

'She's asked for time off at the beginning of November.'

'I don't really see—'

'It's during the COP conference.'

Duncan shrugged. 'So she's going to join a demo. There are going to be a lot of those. Again, nothing much to worry about.'

'I thought so as well, until we found a photo of her on Facebook with her arms around the leader of a far-right action group.'

'Odd, but we can't lay down the law about who people choose as their friends.'

'And Stewart's COP pass was stolen.'

'Did he report it?'

'Not to you. The COP people told him it wasn't necessary.'

Duncan's expression told him he thought otherwise. 'He should have told us,' he said.

'It's no big deal apparently. They just cancel it and give him another. But it's worrying that there might be a thief in the house.'

'Do you think this eco woman stole it?'

'I've no reason to suspect her apart from the fact that she's asked for leave during COP.'

Duncan gazed thoughtfully into his beer. 'Not enough to accuse her, certainly. And we wouldn't get a search warrant with so little evidence. Och, it was probably just the kids being nosy or one of the cleaners binning it by mistake. And it's no good to anyone now it's been cancelled. I'd say there was nothing to worry about.'

Ian supposed not, but at least he'd raised it. If Duncan wasn't worried, then he probably shouldn't be either. He was hungry and went to the bar to order pie and chips for both of them. When he returned to his seat, Duncan was scrolling through notes on his phone, looking thoughtful. 'These two protesters of yours,' he said. 'You might want to talk to Kezia about them.'

Kezia Wallace, the detective inspector with all the charm of an angry crocodile and a degree of contempt for Ian, was the last person he wanted to talk to.

'Come on,' said Duncan. 'Don't scowl at me like that. Didn't you work together a while back?'

'For three days and she had me doing paperwork for the last of those.' And then he'd had to spend an evening in the pub with her. An experience he hoped he'd never have to repeat, although he'd been impressed with her ability to sink countless pints with whisky chasers and remain upright. 'Why would I talk to her?'

'She's been seconded to the counter terrorist squad for the duration of the conference.'

She might well be interested in an unlikely pairing of an environment campaigner and a white supremacist, Ian supposed. 'I could email her,' he said, unwilling to have more to do with her than was absolutely necessary.

'Come on, laddie. She's not that scary. Get a grip and go and see her.'

'Glasgow's a long way.' He wouldn't walk down the road to see Kezia, never mind a fifty-mile drive to Glasgow with all the hassle of extra traffic and draconian parking restrictions.

'She's not there. The city's a nightmare right now so she's coordinating from her office in Montrose.'

'And the last time I went to her with information she told me I was wasting police time. You were there, remember?'

'*I* thought you were wasting our time as well. But it turns out you weren't and didn't Kezia admit that?'

'Only when facing a cliff-edge arrest.'

'Look,' said Duncan. 'I'll come with you. I've to be in Montrose tomorrow. We'll go and see her together and you can tell her it was my idea to pass on the information. I'll pick you up nine sharp tomorrow morning.'

'I suppose I don't have a choice,' he said, draining his beer and giving his last chip to Lottie.

He and Lottie walked home together. Once home, Lottie curled up and went to sleep on the sofa. Ian sat at his desk and put together a file with everything he had on Sharon/Shining Lotus and John Bull – aka, he had discovered, Sean Trotter, age forty-two and with a record of fines for minor violence.

20

'Morning, young Molly.' Duncan bustled into the office rubbing his hands and reaching down to stroke Lottie. 'It's very quiet,' he said. 'Have your builders finished?'

'The plastering is done,' said Ian. 'We have to wait for it to dry before the decorators can start. I thought it might be a few days, but it seems like it's going to be a few weeks.'

'Frustrating,' said Duncan. 'But that's builders for you. They've been busy since everyone started working from home.'

'Can't be helped,' said Ian. 'At least the noise has stopped.'

'Would you like some coffee?' Molly asked. 'I've just got the machine going.'

'Not this time,' said Duncan. 'I'm here to take your boss away for a wee while.'

'You okay with that?' Ian asked, rather hoping she would say she wasn't.

'Sure,' said Molly. 'I've plenty to get on with. I've got all the fake handbag photos to download and the reports to send out. Then I thought I'd have a good tidy up while the office is empty.'

'You don't mind looking after Lottie?' Ian asked. 'Lainie's off to her knit and natter group this morning.'

'Of course not. We'll have fun, won't we, Lottie?' Lottie wagged her tail and glanced hopefully towards the biscuit tin.

'That's the spirit,' said Duncan. 'Jeanie's cooking lunch for us so I'll drop him back early this afternoon.'

'Are you sure you don't mind?' Ian asked in one final effort to put off the day's visit.

'Och, away with you both now. I'll be fine.'

Duncan slapped Ian on the back. 'I don't really think it's you he's worrying about. He's just scared.'

Molly laughed. 'She can't be that bad.'

'She is that bad,' said Ian. 'She'd like to see me locked up.'

'Rubbish,' said Duncan. 'Now into that car with you. It'll all be over before you know it.'

They walked down the garden to Duncan's car and strapped themselves in, Ian clutching the folder of notes he had made.

'That's a good wee lass you've got there,' said Duncan as he drove out of the village towards the bridge.

'She is. Very efficient and works like a trooper. Easy to get along with as well.'

'Not too much like her dad?'

'Nigel's okay once you get to know him. And not nearly so bothered about speed bumps since he's had Molly and Ryan living with him.'

They drove over the bridge and out of the city towards Montrose. It was a drive Ian always enjoyed, even when he knew he'd be facing Kezia Wallace at the end of it. Nothing could spoil the enjoyment of this lovely stretch of coastline.

'Ryan sounds like a lively wee chap,' said Duncan. 'He's been helping Jeanie with her safety posters.'

'Molly tells me he loves school,' said Ian, thinking school was very different from when he'd been Ryan's age. Children actually enjoyed being there. 'He seems quite unscarred by all that went on a few months back. Nigel's a new man, too. Out playing football, volunteering with the Cubs – last week he did a sponsored walk over the bridge with the school kids to raise money for a beaver sanctuary. Probably never been so fit before.'

'Sounds like you've got to like him.'

He had. Ian was sure Nigel's tendency to irritate was still there somewhere, but he'd seen a lot less of it since he'd been a major player in Ryan's life.

Kezia appeared to be in a friendly mood when she greeted the two of them. 'Coffee?' she asked as they sat down. 'I'll send someone out. What would you like? Cappuccino okay?'

They both nodded.

'Right,' said Kezia, sitting down behind her desk. 'You've something to show me?'

'We're not sure if it's important or not,' said Duncan.

'It could be nothing,' Ian added.

'We didn't want to waste your time,' said Duncan. 'But we thought you should know about it.'

'And since you are going to be working in Glasgow…'

'For God's sake, just spit it out,' said Kezia. 'What's got into the pair of you?'

Being shouted at, or worse, for wasting police time, Ian thought. Or being threatened with arrest. Thank God Duncan was with him. He opened his folder and talked Kezia through Molly's research as well as the notes he'd made following his own research on Sean Trotter, alias John Bull.

Their coffee arrived and they sipped it in silence, watching as Kezia nibbled a biscuit, scanned through the notes and then returned to the first page to make some notes of her own in the margin. 'Hmm,' she said.

'Helpful?' Duncan asked cautiously.

She tapped her pencil on the desk in a way that suggested she didn't know how to answer. 'Of course,' she said at last, 'there's no reason why a climate activist shouldn't hold strong right-wing views, or why a hard-line white supremacist shouldn't want to save the planet. But I'll pass it on.' She closed the folder and put it on the side of the desk, still tapping her pencil, which Ian found irritating.

'We've not wasted your time, then?' asked Duncan. 'We did think of emailing it to you.'

'Not at all. You were right to drop in. Things can get lost in the flood of emails we get.' She turned to Ian. 'How did you become involved with this Sharon?'

'I've been doing background checks on her for my sister-in-law. She's employing Sharon as a yoga teacher at her wellness centre at Murriemuir. It was actually my assistant who discovered the photo.'

'You're working at Murriemuir?' She looked at him in what he thought was alarm.

'You know it?' Ian asked.

'I've heard of it, yes.'

'It's where we found the skeleton,' said Duncan.

'Ah yes, the skeleton,' said Kezia, looking relieved. 'But surely you're not investigating Sharon Lofts about that?'

'No,' said Ian. 'There are some odd things going on there.'

'Someone's trying to make out the house is haunted,' Duncan added.

'Just Halloween tricks, surely? I'd concentrate on finding out who the skeleton belonged to. A child, wasn't it? Any idea who it might have been?'

'We think there could be a connection to someone who was living in the house. A family member who died in 2003.'

'The investigation is going rather slowly,' said Duncan.

'Hmm,' said Kezia again. It seemed to be her word of the day. 'There was an incident, wasn't there, Duncan? Some time back, maybe mid-nineties. Before my time here but I remember reading the case notes when I first arrived. I was trying to familiarise myself with the area and what goes on here.'

'Way before my time too. I was still in Edinburgh then,' said Duncan.

Kezia tapped some keys on her computer. It was several minutes before she looked up. 'Archive files,' she said. 'Takes a while to find what you want. Ah, here we go.' She turned the screen to face them. 'A very sad case. A baby died in the village and a woman was arrested for acting as an unregistered midwife. She was suspected of delivering quite a few babies in the village. Luckily there were no other deaths.'

'Why would they use an unregistered midwife when there are perfectly good official maternity services?' Duncan asked.

'According to witness statements, she was a kind, motherly type. And close to home. Getting to the maternity hospital meant a long bus ride and women complained that they were never seen by the same midwife twice.'

'What happened to her?' Ian asked.

'Convicted of manslaughter and given a suspended sentence. It says here she moved to Edinburgh after that. That could be a useful line of enquiry for you. More productive than looking for ghosts.'

She was right. That could be very useful information. But why was she so keen for him to stop his hunt to discover the cause of the strange happenings at the house? Too fanciful for her, Ian supposed. He would certainly follow up the case of the fake midwife, but he'd carry on trying to find out what was going on in the house now. And Sharon Lofts was as likely a suspect as any of them.

'What was her name?' asked Duncan. 'The woman posing as a midwife?'

'It says here she was Elizabeth Jones.'

Ian scribbled the name in his notebook. There'd be newspaper and court reports he could look at.

'Right,' said Kezia, standing up and walking towards the door. 'I'll pass on what you've told me and be in touch.'

A clear dismissal. At least she hadn't accused him of wasting police time and threatened to charge him. He was relieved to be leaving relatively unscathed.

'You're quiet,' said Duncan, as they drove towards his house in St Andrews.

'Yeah, Kezia has given me something to think about.'

'That must be a first,' said Duncan, grinning.

'I'm wondering if this fake midwife knows anything about Clover's birth.'

'Hard to track down, I should think.'

'I told you we'd been thinking Clover could have been Buckland-Kerr's daughter. But we've not been able to find any birth with his name on it. And nothing for anyone in Murriemuir.'

'Most births are registered through hospitals and maternity homes. And it could've been registered by the mother, who didn't name the father. If you don't know *her* name it's going to be impossible.'

'But we know Clover, or at least a child of the right age, was at Murriemuir with Charles in 1996, so why would there be any reason to leave his name off the birth certificate?'

'Could be a lot of reasons. You can't be sure that the child your Indian bloke saw *was* Clover. You don't know that she lived there. She could have just been visiting.'

'Or she could have been delivered by an unregistered midwife and the birth never recorded.'

Duncan scratched his head. 'It's illegal not to register a birth.'

'But it couldn't be registered without paperwork and an unregistered midwife wouldn't be able to do that,' said Ian.

'And the child would have no birth certificate. They wouldn't be able to take her to a doctor or even send her to school.'

She'd be a non-person, Ian thought. No proof that she'd ever existed. Was that why she was buried in the garden? Had she become ill and died because they had no access to medical treatment? Or could it be something even worse? It was a chilling thought.

'From what I remember of the law,' Duncan was saying, 'an unassisted birth is not illegal, although it may be questioned by social services. But acting as a midwife when not registered is a crime that carries a fine. Don't take my word for it, though. I've never had to deal with anything like that.'

While Duncan was driving Ian reached into his bag for a notebook and made a list. What chance was there of finding Elizabeth Jones in Edinburgh? There must be quite a few women called Elizabeth Jones. What kind of job might she have now? Pretty menial, he assumed. She'd not be allowed anywhere near any kind of nursing or carer role. Her name would come up like a red flag the moment anyone checked her background. He'd spend tomorrow searching for newspaper reports and find out what he could about the case. There might be a photo of Elizabeth. She'd have changed, of course. This was more than twenty years ago. But it might give him an idea of the woman he was looking for. Of course, if she had been an elderly woman at the time, she might not even be alive.

There might be people in the village who remembered her. Perhaps even children she'd delivered. Not that they would remember, but their parents might. He and Molly could start searching tomorrow. He was convinced there was a connection to Clover.

By now Duncan had turned into his drive and the idea of a home-cooked lunch drove thoughts of midwives, registered or not, from their minds. They entered the house and were greeted with the mouth-watering smell of Irish stew. Jeanie sat them down and dished out generous plates of it with mashed potato and carrots.

'I can see that a morning with DI Wallace has given you an both an appetite,' she said.

'Relief,' said Duncan. 'Relief that it's over and we don't need to see her again until at least the end of the COP conference.'

'She's not that bad,' said Jeanie.

'She is,' said Ian. 'She's terrifying.'

'What a pair of wusses you are,' said Jeanie. 'Two grown men scared of a wee girl.'

A wee girl? Had Jeanie ever met her?

'And you in particular, Duncan Clyde. What on earth have you got to be scared of? You're the same rank.'

'Not for much longer,' said Duncan, mopping up the last of his gravy and looking longingly at an apple pie and a jug of custard sitting on the sideboard. 'She's up for Deputy Chief Inspector after she's finished at COP. If she gets it, she'll be my boss.'

Ian didn't envy him. As a DI, Duncan would have Kezia breathing down his neck at every opportunity. Some DCIs sat back and let their teams get on with it. He doubted that Kezia Wallace was one of them.

'What's she in Glasgow for?' asked Jeanie.

'She's not in Glasgow. She's coordinating terrorist watch at COP from her office in Montrose,' said Duncan. 'That's going to keep her busy but only for a couple of weeks.'

'How many people will be at COP?' Jeanie asked.

'About 25,000. Quite a lot of them are heads of state. You can see why they're all on terrorist alert. Ian's brother's going. How long will he be there?' he asked Ian.

'Just a couple of days during the second week for a workshop on offshore wind.'

'And this woman, the yoga teacher that's been working for his wife? She's going as well?'

'We don't know that she is. She's asked for leave for the first two weeks in November, but she might just be taking a couple of weeks by the sea somewhere.'

'Right,' said Duncan, scraping the last traces of custard from his plate. 'We'd better make a move. I'll run you home, then I've got criminals to check up on.'

'I could get the bus,' Ian offered, glancing out of the window at the pelting rain and wondering if Jeanie would lend him an umbrella.

'You'll do no such thing,' said Duncan. 'I'm off to Dundee. You're on my way. And you'll want to be getting back to Lottie and young Molly.'

'How's Molly getting on?' Jeanie asked.

'She's great,' said Ian. 'Quite a find. The office runs like clockwork, and she keeps me on my toes.'

'And she's been out in the field, I hear,' said Duncan.

'Just a short stay at Murriemuir. Nothing too difficult and my sister-in-law was glad of her help.'

'And Duncan has a new young constable on his team,' said Jeanie. 'Nice lad – unattached, good looking.'

'There's no stopping her, is there?' said Duncan as he and Ian turned up their coat collars and made a dash for the car.

'At least it takes her mind off me for a bit,' said Ian.

'Don't count on it, laddie. Jeanie's a dab hand at multitasking. Seen Caroline recently?' he asked.

'None of your business,' said Ian, laughing.

The rain was still torrential when they arrived in Greyport. By the time Ian reached his front door he was soaked. Lottie greeted him as usual, as if he'd been away for a week. He took off his coat just as Molly emerged from the office.

'Will I hang that on the radiator for you?' she asked.

He handed it to her. 'I'll just grab some dry clothes,' he said. 'Then we'll catch up on your day.'

By the time he'd changed, Molly had made a pot of tea. 'So,' he said, wrapping his hands round the mug. 'How's your day been?'

'I sent out the last lot of invoices, finished the report on the handbags and a woman called about COP. Her number's on your notepad.'

'Probably for my brother,' he said. But glancing at the name on the pad he knew it wasn't. It was from Elsa Curran. Ian had spent a couple of very pleasant evenings with Elsa before lockdown. She ran a B&B near Glasgow, and as far as he knew she had nothing to do with COP, although he supposed she would be accommodating some of the delegates.

'I'd better be on my way,' said Molly. 'The rain's eased off a bit and I'm picking Ryan up today.'

'Your dad busy?' he asked.

'You know Dad. Got some bee in his bonnet about a plan to paint yellow lines on the road outside the post office.'

'A petition on the way, then?'

'Probably.'

Ian took the tea things into the kitchen and then sat down to call Elsa.

'Ian,' she said. 'Lovely to hear your voice. How are you?'

'Fine,' he told her. 'Busy, and you?'

'Very busy. Bookings picked up in the summer. Loads of people not risking holidays abroad. And now I'm booked up for the first two weeks in November.'

'With COP people?'

'Yes, I've got a delegation from the Galeda Islands booked in for the whole two weeks.'

Ian had never heard of the Galeda Islands. 'Where?' he asked.

'It's a tiny island state in the South Pacific. They're sinking into the sea. I've got their senior government ministers staying here.'

'And they'll be driving into Glasgow every day?'

'I've arranged a minibus for them. But I wanted to talk to you about that. One of them couldn't afford the air fare and cancelled his room. And almost the moment he cancelled I had a request from a woman who wants to stay here with her boyfriend. To be honest I was quite glad to have the cancellation. It's been tremendously hard work. So I told them I couldn't fit them in. The next thing I knew, I had this guy in a suit offering me a load of cash and telling me I would be doing the country a service if I took them.'

'And did you?'

'I didn't feel I had any choice. He told me they had their own car and would be no trouble. But he also told me the woman had got my address from you, so I wondered if you knew who they were.'

'I've no idea,' said Ian. 'Did he tell you his name?'

'No, but the woman called herself Ms Lofts. Does that mean anything to you?'

'I know who she is, but I've never spoken to her.' He had a sudden idea and reached for his wallet. He'd kept Elsa's business card since his last enquiry. He'd needed to call her urgently a while back and the card had stayed in his wallet. But it wasn't there now. He rummaged through one of his desk drawers but couldn't find it. He had Elsa's details on his computer so perhaps Molly had thrown it out when she'd been tidying up. Unlikely. She wouldn't do that without asking him first. And in any case, he was sure he had seen it in his wallet quite recently. Then he remembered the day at

Murriemuir when he had taken his jacket off in Freya's office, and found that it had been moved to a hook on the door when he returned to fetch it. Had Sharon been through the contents of his wallet? And if so, why? And why take a business card and leave plenty of other valuable stuff like credit cards behind?

'I'll look into it for you,' he told Elsa. 'But don't worry. I'm sure there's a perfectly simple explanation.'

He hoped he was right, but he felt uneasy about it. He didn't like the idea of Elsa being forced to take in people she didn't want, and he was alarmed at the idea of her housing a right-wing extremist, although he had no proof that Sharon was planning to stay there with Mr Trotter. And who was the suited gentleman who was prepared to bribe her to let them stay there? There was only one person who could help him. He took a deep breath, told himself not to be a coward and called Kezia. He thought he heard some unrepeatable muttered curses when he mentioned Sharon's name and waited several moments for her to respond.

'You have to let it drop,' she said.

'What do you mean?' he asked. 'I'm just worried about Elsa's safety with strange men in suits offering her money to house right-wing extremists.'

'Your friend is not in any danger,' she said.

'How do you know?'

'Look,' said Kezia. 'I'm going to lay down a few ground rules.'

'Okay,' he said, feeling like a naughty child.

'First, you leave Sharon Lofts alone. I can assure you she's got nothing to do with your supposed hauntings at Murriemuir or the skeleton.'

Who the hell did she think she was? 'Are you telling me I have to drop my case?'

'No, I'm not. You'll be doing everyone a favour if you can find out who this wretched skeleton belonged to. I've even given you a bit of help with it.'

He grudgingly had to admit that her knowledge of the fake

midwife had been helpful. 'But you're asking me to limit my enquiries about Murriemuir?'

'I'm not asking you. I'm ordering you. Search for as many ghosts as you want but leave Sharon alone. She's nothing to do with it.'

'But...'

'Look. I don't want to take out a court order to stop you, but I will if I have to.'

'But why?'

'I can't tell you that.'

'So you're saying I can't carry on my investigation in the way I feel I need to?'

'You can do what the hell you like as long as you leave Sharon out of it. She'll be leaving Murriemuir in a day or two and I absolutely forbid you to follow her or make any further enquiries about her.'

'And what about Elsa? Can I visit her?'

'Call her if you must, but don't go anywhere near the B&B or arrange to meet her.'

He sighed loudly into the phone.

'I'm sorry,' she said, not unkindly. 'I know you're worried about your friend, but believe me when I tell you she's safe. Or she will be if you don't go steaming in stirring things up among her guests.'

She thought he'd find that reassuring? 'For how long?' he asked. 'She's a good friend. You're saying I can't see her any more?'

'Like I said, you can call her in a few days, and she will tell you she's fine. That's a promise. I'll let you know when things are back to normal.'

'I suppose I can talk to Duncan.'

'Of course, but I'll be telling him the same as I've told you. Leave Sharon Lofts alone. Now if you'll excuse me, I have work to do.'

He ended the call. What the hell was going on? Sharon had been his prime suspect and he could do nothing about it. But there was no way he'd risk following up that lead with Kezia breathing down his neck. He'd just have to concentrate on finding out who Clover was and hope that whoever was trying to spook the residents of Murriemuir would get bored and stop doing it.

21

Molly had made brownies. 'Ryan's favourites,' she said. 'Dad's too. But if I let them, they'd finish off the lot before breakfast, so I thought I'd bring some here. We can have them with our coffee.'

'Good idea,' said Ian, with only a slight glance down at his waistline. 'We've a busy day ahead of us. We'll need extra energy by coffee time.'

'What are we doing today?'

'We have to hold back on any more enquiries about Sharon. I've been warned off by the police.'

'Even though she might have stolen Stewart's COP pass?'

'Apparently. It looks as if she might be a suspect in some ongoing police investigation.'

'I thought there was something not quite right about her,' said Molly. 'She wasn't my idea of a typical yoga teacher. Arkash thought the same.'

What was a typical yoga teacher? Ian wondered. When he thought about yoga, he always had an image of Freya in his mind, but that was because she was the only yoga teacher he had come across. Sharon wasn't at all like Freya, but that didn't mean she couldn't be one. There must be all kinds. Just as there were all kinds of private investigator. His own fictional role models stretched from Sherlock Holmes to Miss Marple, taking in Jonathan Creek and Madame Ramotswe on the way. He wasn't like any of those and none of his clients had ever expressed any disappointment that he wasn't. No doubt yoga teachers came in all shapes and sizes. Although he couldn't think of any fictional ones. Perhaps he was just reading the wrong books. Possibly the only thing they had in common was an ability to bend in unusual ways and didn't make for interesting fictional characters.

'Where does that leave our enquiry?' Molly asked.

'We hold back on the supernatural stuff. Nothing's happened recently anyway. We can pick it up again if it does, but for now we concentrate on finding out more about Clover. I've got some interesting info from police records.' He told her about the unregistered midwife in Murriemuir and his theory that she had possibly delivered Buckland-Kerr's baby. 'Her name was Elizabeth Jones,' he said. 'We need to find her.'

Molly gaped at him. 'From thirty years ago? How are we going to do that? It's not like it's an uncommon name.'

'Just as well we have the new laptop. We can both search at the same time.'

A crash from upstairs made Molly jump. 'Are the builders back?' she asked. 'I thought painting and decorating would be quiet.'

'Snagging,' said Ian.

'What's snagging?'

'No idea. It's what Dennis said they'd be doing this morning. Has to be done before the painting can start, apparently.'

'I hope they don't cut off the electricity again,' said Molly. 'We're really going to need it for all this internet searching.'

'If that happens, we'll to move to plan B.'

'Plan B?'

Ian picked up a marker pen and wrote a list on the whiteboard:

. . .

Plan A

Search for newspaper articles – date of trial, make notes of witnesses etc., name for parents of dead baby.

Voter rolls for Murriemuir area pre-trial date.

Voter rolls for Edinburgh post-trial date – list likely names and addresses.

Plan B

Visit Murriemuir village shop – chat to owner and visit any residents she thinks have been there for more than thirty years.

He looked out of the window and hoped they wouldn't need plan B. It was a wet and windy day. Not much fun traipsing round the village knocking on doors in the hope of finding someone who had lived there thirty years ago. Perhaps Molly could bribe the builders with her brownies and persuade them to be extra careful. 'You take the newspapers,' he said, passing her his login details for the archive. 'You'll be able to print off anything that might be useful. I'll check the voter rolls.'

One of the builders appeared at the office door. 'Sorry about the noise,' he said. 'But that's it for now. We're off to buy paint so we'll be out of the way for an hour or so. Can you just confirm the colour you want?'

Ian had chosen a soft dove grey. *Was that too dull?* he wondered, with his usual feeling of insecurity about matters of décor. He passed the colour card over to Molly. 'What do you think?' he asked. 'Too boring?'

'Not at all,' said Molly. 'It'll look great with white woodwork.'

He nodded at the builder. 'Nearly finished then?' he asked. It felt like a lifetime since they had started the work.

'Give us a couple of days and it's all yours.'

Realistically? That probably meant some time towards the end of the week after next. Ian was getting used to the vagaries of building schedules. And then he'd have to sort out all the stuff currently stacked up in his bedroom. The one he was about to vacate. *Don't waste time worrying about that now,* he told himself. *We need to find Elizabeth.* He turned with some relief to his search of voter rolls. He started in 1980 and worked forwards. Why hadn't he asked Kezia if she knew the date of the woman's arrest? That would have made his search a lot easier. But there was no way he was going to call and ask her now. He'd worked his way through more than ten years without finding anyone by the name of Jones in Murriemuir. He'd need to extend the area of his search. She obviously hadn't lived in the village.

He was just thinking it must be coffee time when Molly looked up from her screen. 'I've found something,' she said. 'Report of trial and sentencing in the High Court of Judiciary in Edinburgh of Elizabeth Jones for culpable homicide of baby Edward McGregor in June 1995.'

'Great,' said Ian. 'Print it out.'

Molly printed a copy and Ian read it while she made the coffee.

'Ms Jones, 31, resident of Leven in Fife, was well known among local mothers-to-be as a supporter of natural childbirth. Her normal practice was to befriend expectant mothers and support them up to the time of their delivery, at which point she handed them over to the local domiciliary midwife team. Prosecuting counsel suggested she may have carried out actual deliveries, which would have been against the law, but police had been unable to find any supporting witnesses. On the night of baby Edward's death an ambulance was called but the baby was declared dead on arrival at the Leven maternity unit. Mr McGregor, Edward's father, made a statement to the effect that Ms Jones had refused to call in medical assistance and had delivered the baby herself. A post-mortem suggested that the baby's life might have been saved had the mother been in hospital during labour.

When sentencing, the judge, Hon. Lord Reginald, took into account Jones' guilty plea and her obvious display of remorse. She was given a sentence of three years, non-custodial on condition of her not re-offending.

. . .

turned to another, shorter article.

On the night of June 22nd police were called to an address in Leven, where two men were seen posting a piece of burning cloth through the letterbox. Prompt action on the part of a neighbour, who forced the door open and extinguished the blaze, prevented extensive damage. Two men were later detained, having been identified by other residents in the street. The house is the former residence of Ms Elizabeth Jones, who was recently sentenced for the unlawful killing of a baby. Ms Jones is believed to have moved away immediately after the sentencing and is now staying with friends in Edinburgh.

A cup of coffee and two slices of brownie later and Ian had found a now sixty-three-year-old Elizabeth Jones at an address in Edinburgh. What was even more interesting was the people who lived at the same address, a couple with Chinese names. Could there be a connection to the list of Chinese plants found in the house? *Time,* he thought, *for a visit to Edinburgh.*

'Shall I come with you?' Molly asked.

Ian looked out of the window. The rain had stopped, and he could see a patch of blue sky and the sun glinting on the estuary. 'I think it would be more useful if you could visit your friend Mrs Smart in the Murriemuir shop and see if she remembers any gossip in the village. We don't know for sure that Elizabeth delivered any other babies but there might have been rumours about it. It would also be useful to know how people got in touch with her. Did she do regular house calls? Did she look after mums and babies after the birth?'

'Okay,' said Molly, scribbling down his questions in a notebook. 'I'll pop into Murriemuir House as well and see if there've been any more odd events.'

And no doubt chat to Arkash while she was there. Was this friendship with Arkash ethical? he wondered. But he couldn't see any harm in it. They'd cleared Arkash from the list of suspects and he'd given them some useful information. And they were suspending enquiries into this case for a while anyway. No, it was good for Molly to be making friends and, from what he had seen of Arkash, he thought Molly could do a lot worse. *My God,* he thought, *I'm getting as bad as Jeanie.*

∼

It wasn't one of the nicer parts of Edinburgh. A row of run-down shops with flats on the first and second floors. Ian drove to the back of the shops and found a parking space. He steered himself round a line of dustbins and chained-up bikes to a stone stairway, which led to a balcony that ran along the back of the building. He found the number of the flat he wanted and rang the doorbell. The door, which was on a chain, opened just enough for him to see a wrinkled face peering out at him. He held up his ID badge and the door was shut in his face, to be opened, properly this time, a few moments later by a different person. An elderly woman. If this was Elizabeth Jones, the years hadn't treated her well. She didn't look a day under seventy-five.

'Elizabeth Jones?' he asked.

The woman stared at him. 'Who are you?'

He held up his ID again.

'Nothing to say,' she said, trying to shut the door and finding his foot in the way.

'Please,' said Ian. 'I just want a quick chat.'

'What about?'

'Someone you may have met at a place called Murriemuir.'

She was shaking her head and trying again to shut the door when a very small, very old man appeared next to her. He too scrutinised Ian's ID. 'Let him in, Elizabeth,' he said. 'You've nothing to fear now.'

Elizabeth didn't look convinced but opened the door a little wider and led Ian into an overheated living room full of china ornaments and caged birds. Another woman, also very small and old, sat in a chair next to a table with a mound of dried plants that she was trimming and tying into bundles. Ian thought, but wasn't sure, that it was the woman who had first opened the door.

The old man put his hands together as if praying, bowed to Ian, indicated a chair and said, 'Please sit.' Ian did as he was told, and the old man disappeared.

'He'll be making tea,' said the old woman. 'You'd like a cup?'

'Thank you. That would be very nice.' He turned to the other woman. 'Elizabeth,' he said kindly. 'I've not come here to upset you. Please hear what I have to say and if you feel you have any comment to make, I assure you it will be in confidence.'

The old man returned with a tray and handed round tiny china cups of pale tea. *Jasmine,* Ian thought, taking a sip and deciding he liked it.

'Please,' said the old man. 'Tell us your story. We will listen. And then you may ask your questions.'

Ian told them about finding the body. He stressed as strongly as he could that he wanted to find out the child's identity in order to set minds at rest. Not with any intention of blaming anyone. 'Are you able to help at all?' he asked Elizabeth. 'We only want to give her what she is due, a name and a proper burial.'

Elizabeth bowed her head. 'I didn't deliver the child,' she muttered.

'But you know who she was?'

'Not exactly. I was called to the house late one evening. Someone from the village came to fetch me from my home in Leven. He said my help was needed.'

'Do you remember the date?'

'It was in June in the early 1990s. I don't remember the date. It was a Sunday, I think. I'd been watching *The House of Elliot* on TV. When I arrived at Murriemuir the baby was in a room with her mother and father. She was a few hours old, a poorly, weak little thing. I did what I could for her and then told them she needed to go to hospital.'

'You called for an ambulance?'

She shook her head. 'They told me their phone had been disconnected and they would manage alone. Then they called for the man to drive me home again.'

'Do you know who this man was?'

She shook her head. 'On the way back, he told me he lived near the village and did some gardening at the house. He told me the baby's father was Charles Buckland-Kerr. He didn't know the mother's name. She'd told me to call her Sarah, but I don't think that was her real name.'

'Why did you think that?'

'It was as if she needed to think about it. Most people just say what they are called. They don't have to make decisions about it.'

'And what was she like?'

'It was a long time ago. I'm not sure I remember very much.'

'Her age?'

'Late twenties or early thirties, I think. She told me the birth had been quick and easy, so she was probably quite fit. I remember she was muscular, like she worked out a lot.'

'Did you hear from them again?'

'Yes, I was worried about them, so I drove back and called in a few days later. They hadn't been to hospital, but the baby seemed better. She was feeding and was a little livelier but, I don't know, I've seen a lot of newborns and there was something not quite right about this one.'

'Not right, how?'

'She was full term but very small. She was quite floppy and didn't grip my finger or react when I tickled her feet. And there was no startle response. All things a midwife checks. That's why I told them to take her to hospital. Although, as I said, she was a little better after a few days.'

'Tell me more about the parents. Do you know why they wouldn't call a doctor?'

'I don't know. They seemed very gentle and loving. The baby was being well cared for, which is why I didn't contact anyone. What good would it have done if she had been taken into care?'

'No hint of neglect?'

'No, none at all. They were living very frugally but the room was warm, and they had a few baby clothes and blankets. The baby was sleeping in a cardboard box, but someone had painted birds and flowers on it. They told me they were clover flowers because they had called the baby Clover after her father's sister. She was tucked up safe and warm. They may not have had much, but there was a lot of love for that child.'

'Do you know anything about this?' Ian asked, showing her the picture of the Chinese symbols.

'Yes. I tore it out of my book and gave it to them. Because they were unwilling to go to a regular doctor, I told them to take this to the Chinese practitioner in Dundee who would make it up for them. It was a remedy I had used before for postnatal fatigue. It raises the spirits and helps the flow of milk.'

'You know a lot about Chinese medicine?'

She smiled at him. 'I have studied it and as you can see, I have Chinese friends. Mr and Mrs Lei took me in when I needed a home many years ago and I will stay and care for them now they are old.'

The old man patted her hand. 'Elizabeth is very good to us,' he said.

Ian believed him. This was a woman who cared and whose life had been blighted by one very stupid mistake. 'Do you know a man called Zhang Ming?'

'No,' said Elizabeth abruptly. Ian thought she was lying.

'He has a Chinese medicine practice in Dundee.'

'Many people are called Zhang Ming,' said the old man.

That hadn't answered his question, but they were not going to tell him any more. Ian finished his tea and thanked them. He handed them each one of his cards. The old woman took hers and tucked it into her blouse. 'If you think of anything else you can call me,' he said.

Mr Lei showed him to the door and slipped a piece of paper into his hand. 'My phone number,' he said. 'Call me if you have any news.' Then he watched as Ian limped down the stairs and back to his car.

The visit had given him a lot to think about. He had found Clover and felt a huge sense of relief that she had been loved and wanted. Had Sarah registered the birth or had she been too afraid of admitting that she'd not had any medical help? Was he about to trawl through every birth for that date registered by mothers named Sarah? And he didn't even know that her name *was* Sarah. Elizabeth thought she was lying, and Ian had no reason not to believe her. But why hadn't they registered her birth? Why had they been so frightened of doctors? Charles and Clover were both now dead. But where was Sarah and how on earth was he going to set about finding her?

22

There was an air of gloom in the office. Molly handed Ian a cup of coffee and pushed a tin of shortbread over to his side of the desk. They sat sipping their drinks and looking glumly at each other. At least it was quiet; just the occasional muttering from upstairs and the swish of paint brushes. Ian would soon be able to move into his new quarters, but right now he had little enthusiasm for it.

'We're up against a brick wall,' he said, helping himself to a piece of shortbread.

'Not completely,' said Molly. 'We know who Clover was. Do you think the police will take it any further now?'

'I don't see how they can unless they find Sarah. There's no evidence that any crime was committed.'

'Failure to register a birth and a death?'

'I can't see them using up police funds to pursue that with so little evidence.'

'So we just let it go there?'

'I'll send Duncan our report and we can invoice them for the hours we've spent. We won't be out of pocket.'

'But it's not about the money, is it? I can see you're upset,' Molly said.

'I'm upset about Sarah. This poor woman has lost her child and the man she was living with. And she's just wandered off into thin air. Anything could have happened to her. She could be in prison, in long-term care, in an abusive relationship, out of her head on drugs...'

'Or she could be happily married with a good job and three more children. People do recover, you know.'

'I just wish we knew,' he said sadly.

'Then we have to find her,' said Molly with a tone of determination that surprised him.

'How?' he asked. 'We don't know her name, what she looks like or where she went when she left Murriemuir. We don't even know how long she was there.'

'Come on,' she said. 'This isn't like you.' She jumped up, grabbed a pen and cleared a space on the whiteboard. 'We'll start with a list. That's what *you* always do.'

'Okay,' he sighed, deciding to humour her.

'We'll start with Elizabeth. What did she tell you about Sarah?'

'She was in her late twenties or early thirties. She'd had an easy birth, which probably meant she was quite fit. And she looked as if she worked out.'

Molly wrote it down.

'We don't know how long she'd been at Murriemuir, or why she was there. She probably didn't have a car, or it would have been noticed in the village.' She tapped her pen on the board thoughtfully for a moment. 'Could she have been a runaway? That would explain why she didn't want anyone to know she was there.'

'A bit old for a runaway,' he said, and regretted it immediately.

Molly frowned at him. 'It's not only teenagers who run away,' she said. 'She could have been in a miserable situation. It would have been brave to escape.'

'Yes. I'm sorry. Of course, you're right. But it's not an obvious place to run to. Murriemuir is quite remote. How would she have got there?'

'By bus? Or perhaps someone gave her a lift.'

'She might have known someone there.'

'You think she already knew Charles? He was the only person living there.'

'She might have done,' said Ian. 'But I don't think he got out and about a lot. I'm not sure how he would have met someone looking for shelter. No, I'm wondering about this bloke who went to fetch Elizabeth in his car. Did you pick up anything useful from Mrs Smart?'

'I was there to ask about Elizabeth, not blokes in cars. Mrs Smart remembered her. She said they used to have coffee mornings in people's houses for pregnant women and mums with their babies, but of course that all stopped after Elizabeth was arrested.'

'The first time you spoke to her, didn't she say that there had been telephone orders made by a woman?'

'Yes, that's right. She did. I'd forgotten.'

'Then we'll go back and talk to her again. Write that on the list.'

Molly did as she was told. 'And we can ask about the man with the car at the same time. She might remember him.' She wrote *man with car* and then remembered *did some gardening*.

'We'll drop in at Murriemuir and ask Guy if he knows anything about who worked in the garden before he went there.'

'See,' said Molly, 'we've already got some leads.'

'We'll go out there tomorrow and talk to people in the village.' He was becoming quite hopeful again, catching Molly's optimism. 'Oh, and there's this Chinese medicine connection. We should talk to Ming. Do you know if he'll be there tomorrow?'

'I'll call Freya and ask.'

'We should invite ourselves for lunch,' he said. 'We might be there for a while.'

'What about asking Duncan to run a check on missing women in around 1993?' said Molly. 'We're assuming Charles was Clover's father, but perhaps she ran away because she was pregnant, and Charles took her in.'

'Add that to the list. Although from what I've heard about Charles, he doesn't sound like the type to take in pregnant women and shelter them. They were there for seven years, remember? My money's still on Charles being the father. Elizabeth said Clover was named after her father's sister.'

'You're right. I'd forgotten that.'

'Checking on missing women is an excellent idea. You call Freya and I'll talk to Duncan.'

Their plans were coming together at last. Molly talked to Freya while Ian texted Duncan. Ming would be running a surgery the next morning and Freya had invited them for lunch. 'We'll start in the village,' said Ian. 'Then have a quick word with Ming before he leaves.'

'What are you going to ask him?'

'I was sure Elizabeth was lying when she said she didn't know him. I'd like to get to the bottom of that. There's also a chance that he was the one who made up the remedy and that he actually met Sarah.'

An email pinged in from Duncan. *That was quick*, Ian thought. There probably weren't any missing women of the right age. But reading Duncan's message he could see he'd been wrong. He had found someone who might just be the person they were searching for.

Could this be the woman you are looking for? Sarah Jane Grant left her home in Dundee in July 1990 after a row with her boss. She told her family she was going away to look for work. Her father reported her missing a week later when she'd failed to contact them. The local police didn't consider there were suspicious circumstances or that she was vulnerable. She had told friends and family she was leaving and at twenty-nine she could live wherever she wanted to. The Dundee force only knew about it because of a letter her father wrote to the local paper saying how useless the police had been. He was threatening to go to his MP, so the Dundee squad began a rather half-hearted search. From what I can make out it only involved calls to hospitals and placing an advert in the Dundee paper. Sarah Jane worked for an undertaker in Dundee. It is believed she fell out with her employer after a series of disagreements about a commission for a headstone that she disapproved of. She was a little over five-foot-four and of medium build. She was described as fit and healthy and was a member of a local sports club. She had blue eyes and her natural hair colour was light brown. At the time of her departure, it was dyed black. I have attached a photo. It's not known whether she ever made contact with her family, but she is not currently resident in Dundee.

Ian clicked on the photo and Molly leaned over his shoulder to look at it. 'I can't imagine what she looks like now,' said Molly.

Ian agreed. It was a blurred photo of a woman who might be any age from sixteen to sixty. Sarah Jane was wearing thick black eye makeup and lipstick; her hair in braids, which largely obscured what looked like a deathly white complexion. She was dressed from head to toe in black with a series of skulls and crosses hanging from piercings in her ears. The only item they could see clearly was a chunky necklace. It was gold with a fearsome-looking lion's head dangling from it.

'She probably wasn't a frontline member of the undertaking team,' said Ian, unable to visualise her in a sombre grey suit and black tie.

'Unless they specialised in goth funerals,' said Molly, suppressing a giggle.

'I can't really see her in sports gear either,' said Ian. 'She'd need to unload a hell of a lot of jewellery.' She'd probably go down a treat at one of Buchan House's ghost evenings though.

Ian replied to Duncan's email and thanked him for the information. Then he scanned the picture and sent it to Mr Lei, hoping he had a smartphone and would be able to share it with Elizabeth. He tapped in a message: *Can you ask Elizabeth if she recognises this woman?*

The reply came quickly. *Elizabeth is not sure. The woman she saw had short hair and no make-up. But she does recognise the necklace.*

Ian tapped in a quick reply to thank him. Then he turned back to his computer screen. 'What chance do you suppose there is of a birth registered by Sarah Jane Grant?' he said, logging in to the archive.

'Very little, I should think,' said Molly. She was right. There was nothing. But on the plus side, no one of that name and age had died, nor did she appear to have married.

Between them they trawled the internet for Sarah Jane Grants. They found hundreds scattered around the world but none that they were convinced was the one they were looking for. Molly scanned the picture of the necklace and posted it on her Facebook page asking if anyone had seen a similar one. Ian found one on eBay. It wasn't quite the same but close enough for comparison. It was not particularly valuable, so with luck she wouldn't have had to sell it to keep herself going after leaving Murriemuir, and that meant she might still have it.

They left it there for the day, feeling they had made progress.

23

Mrs Smart was delighted to see Molly again. 'Come in, come in,' she said, pulling up a couple of chairs for them. *A quiet day in the shop,* Ian thought.

'We wouldn't want to stop you working,' he said, encouraging Lottie to sit at his feet.

'Not at all. There's always a lull once the school kiddies have been in for their sweeties. Will I make us a nice cup of tea? And a biscuit for the wee dog?'

'We're not stopping,' said Molly. 'We've just got one or two more questions for you. This is my boss,' she said, pointing at Ian.

'Pleased to meet you,' said Mrs Smart, shaking his hand. 'That's a braw wee lassie you've got working for you.' Ian nodded in agreement.

'He's Stewart Skair's brother,' said Molly.

'Then you're all the more welcome,' she said. 'Mr Skair made such a beautiful job of the shop. Well, you can see for yourself.'

Ian glanced around. It was a lovely bit of work; varnished beech shelves, Swedish oak floor, glass-fronted display cabinets. Unlikely that Stewart had been down here in person with a plane and screwdriver. All the same, this was top quality stuff. He'd not have stinted over the expense. 'Very nice, Mrs Smart,' he said. 'And all the better for the lovely produce you're selling.'

'Aye,' she said. 'Mostly made locally. The whole village worked so hard to keep it all going. A village isn't the same without its shop, is it?'

Being a regular customer at the shop in Greyport, he heartily agreed with her.

'So what can I do for you?' she asked.

'You've already been a great help with your Indian visitor.'

'Such a lovely polite gentleman,' she said.

'Yes,' Ian agreed. 'With the information you gave Molly I was able to go and meet him. And now we're wondering if you can help us with any other people you met from Murriemuir House. A few years before that, perhaps?'

'Well, there were never very many. Just Mr Buckland-Kerr.'

'Did you know him well?'

She shook her head. 'He didn't come in much. Mind you, he was that good looking. Some of the village lassies tried to set their caps at him. Get their feet under his table, if you get my meaning. But for all his good looks he was a dour, brooding type.'

That was interesting. Ian hadn't imagined a Mr Rochester or Heathcliff type. 'Did any of them of them, er... get their feet under his table?'

'Not even through the door,' she said. 'And in his last few years he really went downhill. Started prowling the grounds with his shotgun. Let himself go, too. Grew his hair long, never looked very clean. Everyone gave him a wide berth.'

'Mrs Smart,' said Molly. 'You told me orders were sometimes phoned through by a woman.'

'Yes, that's right, I did. Looks like there was at least one lassie to get herself inside the house.'

'Do you remember anything about her?' Ian asked.

'I only spoke to her on the phone. Very polite though, and well spoken.'

'Well spoken?'

'Edinburgh rather than Dundee, if you get my meaning.'

'She didn't tell you her name?'

'No, just said the order was for Murriemuir House and to put it on the account.'

'And did anyone ever speak of a child in the house?'

'No, I don't think so. Oh, wait a moment, some said they'd seen the wee ghost.'

'Ghost?' said Ian, catching Molly's eye.

'Lot of nonsense, of course. But there was a rumour that Mr Charles had a sister who died when she was a wee girl. People said they saw a little girl playing with a dog in the garden.'

'What made them think it was a ghost?'

'She was a little pale thing, by all accounts. Wearing a white dress and looking as if a puff of wind would blow her away. Never believed them myself. Trick of the light, most likely. But it was only a couple of times. There's never been any talk of ghosts at Murriemuir.'

Interesting how many times he'd been told that recently. 'And do you know the man who helped in the garden?'

'Oh, aye, that would be Rod McCulloch.'

'Does he live in the village?'

'No. He popped in now and then for cigarettes but didn't say much. I think he drove here two or three times a week to do the gardening. I doubt there was much for him to do. By the time I met him the farmland was being sold field by field. Sad, really. It was part of the village in Mr Malcolm's day when my mum and dad kept the shop. Plenty of work for the villagers. But once the farm started to fail, they moved away and the commuters moved in and started doing up the houses. Good for trade, of course.'

A very different trade, Ian thought. Cigarette sales would have dropped to be replaced with artisan bread and jars of upmarket chutney. 'Thank you very much, Mrs Smart,' Ian said. 'You've been very helpful.'

'Any time,' she said. 'I'm always pleased to see Molly. Are you away up to the house now?'

'We are,' said Molly. 'We're going for lunch there.'

Mrs Smart reached up for a jar on a shelf behind the counter. 'Can you give this to Mrs Skair for me? It's my home-made raspberry jam. Tell her how much we appreciate the way she and her husband are bringing the village back to life again. And take these for the kiddies.' She reached into a box and handed Ian two bars of chocolate. Then as they were leaving, she pulled another box from under the counter and handed him a bar of something that promised to keep Lottie's teeth strong and her breath sweet.

Turning into the drive to Murriemuir House, he puzzled over the name, McCulloch. He'd heard it before and not all that long ago. He just couldn't remember when or where.

'Interesting that people thought they'd seen a ghost,' said Molly.

It was interesting, but it had probably stopped them from wondering why there was a child in the house. If people had been more curious about that, maybe Clover would still be alive. But at least it was a sign that she had not been kept a prisoner in there. He hoped it meant her mother wasn't either.

As he pulled up by the lily pond, he caught sight of Guy raking up leaves and remembered where he'd heard that name before. Guy McCulloch. He didn't look old enough to have been working here for thirty years. He could well be related to Rod McCulloch though. 'Here', he said, thrusting two bars of chocolate, a dog chew and a jar of raspberry jam at Molly. 'Go on inside. I just want a word with Guy.'

He climbed out of the car and let Lottie run across the grass. Molly made her way into the house, and he strolled over to where Guy was working. 'Morning,' he said. 'Do you remember me?'

Guy stopped raking and stared at him for a moment, looking puzzled. Then he smiled in recognition. 'Aye, you're Stewart's brother. You were here to help with the digging. Stupid business. They should have left well alone.'

'Why do you say that?'

Guy prodded a pile of leaves, pushing them to the edge of the path. 'Stirred up a load of stories, didn't it? Silly stuff about ghosts. Murriemuir's never been haunted.'

No one wanted the place to be haunted. Unlike just about every other old building in Scotland. Were they worried that he'd dig too deep and find out things they'd rather not reveal? 'How long have you worked here?' Ian asked.

'Started when the hotel people were here, about six years ago.'

'And did you take over the job from your father?'

'What? No, my dad's a keeper up near Inverness.'

'But your predecessor was called McCulloch.'

'Oh, aye, that was my uncle. But he wasn't my predecessor. There were a couple of other blokes before I took over.'

'Would it be possible for me to talk to your uncle?'

'You'd have a job. He's been dead for fifteen years.'

A pity. Rod McCulloch sounded like the one person who knew what had gone on there. 'Did he ever talk to you about when he worked here?'

'Not much. He used to say he was the only person who really cared what happened in the house. He was here when old Buckland-Kerr went barmy and shot himself. He left then because there was no money to pay him.'

'Buckland-Kerr killed himself?' That wasn't what was on the death certificate. He couldn't remember the registered cause of death – a heart attack, he thought. It definitely wasn't suicide.

'All hushed up. The doc said he'd had a heart attack while he was out shooting squirrels and the gun had gone off accidentally. But my uncle said he was up to his eyes in debt. Stands to reason he'd top himself,' he said. 'And he knew guns. There's no way a man with his experience would have shot himself by accident.'

'Did your uncle mention anyone else living in the house?'

'Like I said, he didn't talk about it much. I was just a bairn at the time.'

'How did *you* end up working here? Was it because of your uncle?'

'Nah, just coincidence. I'd been doing a bit of landscaping for a hotel group in the Highlands and saw it advertised in the company magazine. It was a head groundsman job. Better pay, you see, more responsibility. Although to be honest I didn't realise the responsibility would be me working on my own. Mind you, things have looked up since Stewart moved in. He's promised to find a lad to help me. An apprentice, he said.'

Good old Stewart, Ian thought. *He's stepping into country squire mode once again.* Probably wouldn't be long before he shelled out and registered himself as the Laird of Murriemuir. Ian had seen it advertised on the internet. It was a way of raising money for conservation. *Buy yourself a chunk of Scottish soil and become a Laird.* And Stewart already owned the requisite chunk of Scotland. He could imagine the pleasure that would give their mother. *Better,* Ian thought, *not to put the idea into his head.*

He whistled to Lottie, and she scampered after him to the house while Guy returned to his raking.

Ian stood in the doorway and looked around. The small consulting room was bright and warm. Simply furnished with a leather-topped desk, two chairs with padded, buttoned seats and a couch covered in deep purple leather. Zhang Ming had finished his consultations and was tidying away his equipment ready to leave. He opened a wooden box with brass hinges that was divided into compartments, into which he placed glass cups, a set of silver needles, some jars of herbs and a small set of scales. 'I'm sorry,' he said, closing the lid and fastening the catches with a click. 'Surgery is finished.'

'We wanted to catch you before you left,' said Molly. 'This is Mr Skair.'

'No,' said Ming, frowning at Ian. 'It isn't.'

'Sorry,' said Molly. 'This is Mr *Ian* Skair. He's Stewart's brother. He would like to ask you some questions.'

'Ah,' he said. 'I didn't know Stewart had a brother. You'd better have a seat.' He indicated one of the chairs. Molly left, closing the door gently behind her. 'I must warn you that a consultation takes much time. I need to know many things before I can treat you.'

'I'm not looking for treatment,' said Ian, while at the same time wondering if Chinese herbs could do anything for his aching leg. 'At least not right now. I wanted to ask if you remembered a lady called Elizabeth Jones.'

'No,' said Ming abruptly. 'Why do you ask?'

'She mentioned that she had worked with a Chinese practitioner in Dundee a while back. I wondered if it was you. She spoke very highly of the man she had worked with,' he added, hoping it might encourage him to open up a bit.

'Could have been my practice,' Ming conceded. 'We see many people, my son and I. Some come to us for treatment. Some are medical professionals looking for alternative remedies.'

'She was a midwife,' said Ian, thinking he had spotted the merest hint of alarm in Ming's eyes.

'I don't think I remember her,' Ming said, lifting his case from the desk and putting it down on the floor. 'But as I said, I have to leave. I've other patients to see.'

'I won't keep you,' said Ian, standing up and rubbing his leg theatrically.

'When I am here again, perhaps we could talk about that,' said Ming, pointing to where Ian was rubbing his shin. 'I have remedies for old injuries.'

How did he know it was an old injury? Ian wondered. 'It seems like a friendly team here,' he said.

'It is,' said Ming, looking a bit more relaxed now they had got to small talk.

'Did you know any of the team before you came here?'

'Not really. I had a brief meeting with Ms, er... Greenlow a few years ago.'

So Molly had been right. Not that it was relevant. They must move in similar circles.

'I'll let you get on,' said Ian. 'Just one more question. Does the name Sarah Jane Grant mean anything to you?'

Ming looked down at his shoes, then pulled back his shoulders and looked Ian in the eye. 'No,' he said.

He was lying. Ian was sure of it.

He had discovered a lot this morning and it was all buzzing around in his head as he tried to make sense of it. He crossed the hall to the dining room. He'd enjoy a good lunch in good company. Then he'd go home and try to work out how it all fitted together.

24

It was a small gathering for lunch. Ming had muttered some excuses and left as soon as he'd finished talking to Ian.

'That's not like Ming,' said Freya as she cleared his place from the table. 'He usually enjoys his lunch. It'll just be the five of us now. But that will be quite nice. We can catch up on your Clover investigation.'

'Is Stewart in Glasgow?' Ian asked.

'Not yet. His seminar is next week, but he's working long hours getting it all prepared.'

'Has Sharon left already?' Molly asked.

'Yes,' said Freya. 'Her leave started yesterday. Her boyfriend came to pick her up.'

Ian was about to ask about the boyfriend but remembered that Kezia had banned him from showing any interest in Sharon and that no doubt included her friends and acquaintances. Probably just as well she wasn't there, he thought. He'd have been tempted to ask her a lot of questions.

The five, he supposed, would be Molly and Arkash, himself and Freya, and Sonia. He hadn't met Sonia yet and Molly's notes had said little about her. Of the four staff members he had checked, Sonia was the least interesting. A solid background in reiki and meditation going back more than fifteen years. And before that domestic work. He did wonder why Ming had been reluctant to say they knew each other. He could think of no reason why they'd want to hide it. Unless, of course, Sonia had consulted him about some highly embarrassing condition. He speculated on some obscure and unmentionable 'women's trouble' that had baffled conventional medicine. Best not to go there, he told himself.

He was surprised when Will wandered in, still clutching his boat and greeting Lottie like an old friend. 'No school?' Ian asked.

'Staff development day,' said Will.

'Flaming nuisance,' said Freya. 'But Will's very good at amusing himself. I'm lucky really. It's tough for mothers who don't work at home.'

'I was going to have a friend round for the day,' said Will. 'But his dad's got to self-isolate so he couldn't come.'

'It makes me wonder if we'll ever be shot of this wretched disease,' said Freya. 'You and Molly did test yourselves this morning, didn't you? I forgot to remind you. Sorry, I know it's a nuisance but if I'm to keep going, the place has got to be covid-free.'

Ian thought of the blue boxes that popped through his letterbox every week. The morning test was part of his routine now. Like cleaning his teeth and walking Lottie.

'Yes, we're both in the clear.' He could vouch for Molly as well. Nigel insisted on testing all three of them every morning before breakfast. He probably recorded the results on a spreadsheet. At the very least he'd be meticulous about uploading them to the test site. 'Sonia not joining us?'

'She's fasting today. She'll be in her room meditating.'

'Is that a religious thing?' he asked.

'No, she fasts one day a week. She says it clears her of toxins, or something.'

Arkash arrived with a tray of Punjabi delicacies; pakoras and bhajis Ian recognised, with several others that he couldn't put names to but couldn't wait to sample. No doubt it would do no favours to his toxin count, but he didn't care. *Sonia probably doesn't realise what she's missing,* he thought as he helped himself enthusiastically, dipping each mouthful into one of the chutneys Arkash had served on a silver tray, while enjoying the scent of garlic and spices. Ian wondered how anyone managed to fast with the wonderful aroma of exotic food wafting through the house.

'You were going to tell us what you've found out about Clover,' said Freya.

Ian spooned mango chutney onto his plate and dipped in a particularly delicious onion bhaji. 'We're fairly sure that she was Charles Buckland-Kerr's daughter,' he said. 'And we think it's likely that her mother was a woman called Sarah Jane Grant.' Put like that it seemed very little. 'There's not a scrap of paperwork,' he added, 'so it's all speculation.'

'And you've still no idea how she died?'

'That's not really up to us. It's a decision the Crown Office will make but I don't think we have enough information yet for them to hold an enquiry.'

'Does that mean nothing can happen to the remains? The poor little thing doesn't get a proper burial?'

'I'm afraid it does,' he said sadly.

'Unless we can find her mother,' said Molly. 'We're still searching for her.'

'We don't have much to go on yet,' said Ian. 'Apart from Mrs Smart in the shop telling us she was well spoken and polite.'

'Someone must have seen her while she was here,' said Freya. 'I only have to pop into the shop for people to start quizzing me on my life history.'

'Charles was very reclusive,' said Ian. 'I think people in the village were scared of him.'

'I've heard people saying he was a bit unbalanced for the few years before he died,' said Freya. 'Not that there are many people who remember him.'

'I've spoken to a woman who came to treat the baby just after she was born,' said Ian. 'She thinks she recognises Sarah Jane from a rather blurred photo we have of her.'

'Some people saw a child in the garden,' said Molly. 'They thought it was the ghost of Charles' sister.'

'Why would it be a ghost?' asked Freya.

'She was very pale and wearing a white dress,' Molly explained. 'And we don't think Charles had been in the pub wetting the baby's head so not many people knew about her. Just the gardener who used to run errands. Oh, and Arkash's grandfather.'

Arkash looked up from his plate of food. 'Really?' he said. 'He didn't tell me.'

'Did he tell you he lived here for a while?'

'Not a word,' said Arkash. 'He's a secretive old codger. When did he live here and why?'

'It was a long time ago, when he first left India after partition.'

'Partition was complete hell,' said Arkash. 'None of the olds want to talk about it.'

Ian wasn't surprised. It had been traumatic for so many. For a while everyone ate in silence as they contemplated this, accompanied only by the clatter of forks on plates.

'We should have a vigil for the animals,' Will piped up suddenly. 'We can't do anything for Clover until we know who her mother is, but we can for them. They've been disturbed. That's why all these strange things are going on.'

'They've been dead a long time,' his mother argued. 'And it's not like they were people who need to be remembered for things they did.'

'They were someone's pets,' said Will. 'People loved them, and they need to be remembered.'

'In some religions,' said Arkash, as he started to clear away the plates, 'animals have souls just like people. And many people believe that they were reincarnated, so they'd believe the animals in the garden might once have been people.'

'Is that true?' asked Will. 'Was I an animal once?'

'It's just what some people believe,' said Freya. 'It doesn't mean it's true.'

'I had an uncle who was told he had been an elephant in a former life,' said Arkash. 'He was sure he was going to be a snake in the next one.'

'How did he know?' Will asked.

'A wise man in India told him.'

'How did the wise man know?'

'He worked out my uncle's horoscope,' said Arkash. 'It's very complicated and cost him a lot of money.' Arkash disappeared into the kitchen, no doubt hoping to head off requests from Will to work out a horoscope for him.

'Can we do the animals' horoscopes and find out if they were people once?'

He was a persistent little chap, Ian thought. 'I don't think the residents of Fife really go in for horoscopes,' he said.

'Are wise men only in India?' Will asked as Arkash returned with glass bowls of kulfi.

'Um...' said Arkash.

'Yes,' said Freya firmly. 'I don't think there's a single one in Scotland. Rather the opposite, if the men around here are anything to go by.'

'But we should still do something to celebrate them, or they might come back as people and be very angry with us.'

Ian was not sure that this was helping. Did they really want some kind of ceremony in the garden? Wouldn't it just remind them of the day they'd discovered the bones?

'We were going to have a party the day we moved them but then we had to stop because of finding Clover. And Daddy promised we could have one for bonfire night.'

'He did,' Freya agreed. 'And I'm sorry you had to miss the party. You're quite right, Will. A party would help to cheer us all up. We'll ask Daddy when he gets home.'

. . .

Ian and Molly spent a discouraging afternoon knocking on doors in the village but not finding a single person who had seen either Sarah Jane or her child. They returned to the house in the early evening when it was getting dark and found that Stewart and Lyra had arrived home.

Stewart was keen on the idea of a celebration. 'Who knows if we'll get to have Christmas this year, with all the infection that's going to spread during COP. We could all be in lockdown again by December, so let's have a party now.'

'We can find some poems about dogs and cats and make posies of flowers,' said Freya.

'I can bring my guitar,' said Lyra, who up until that moment had been looking scornful about the whole idea. 'I'll sing some sad songs.'

'We'll do it on Sunday, before Stewart goes to Glasgow,' said Freya. 'We've no residential this weekend so it'll only be a few of us. And it's close enough to Guy Fawkes Night for few fireworks and a bonfire. You'll come, won't you, Ian? Caroline as well if you like. And you, Molly, and your little boy.'

'I could do a lightshow,' Arkash offered. 'It can be a Diwali celebration as well. I'll make some traditional sweets,' he added.

A bit of a mash-up of cultures, Ian thought. Did Stewart really think they'd be back in lockdown again? Would he spend another Christmas sharing his dinner over the fence with Lainie? That wouldn't be so bad. Lottie wouldn't object and he'd enjoyed it last year. He glanced at Molly, who looked excited by the idea and was offering to help Arkash with the catering. Well, it could be fun. As long as they didn't discover any more bodies.

He arrived home with something nagging at his brain. Something about his chat to Ming that left him feeling uneasy. First that Ming had stumbled over Sonia's name and then the denial that he'd ever heard of Sarah Jane Grant.

25

Sunday started as a day of squalls with rain lashing against the windows, the estuary barely visible through the clouds. Ian wondered if they'd cancel what everyone was now calling the *light for the animals* evening. He and Caroline had spent Saturday together sorting out his new upstairs quarters, the builders having moved out on Friday. They had been out for a meal in the evening and Caroline stayed over with the intention of helping him to tidy the garden before winter set in.

A pity, he thought, as he climbed out of bed and looked through the window, *that on my first morning in my new room I don't get to see the Tay in its full glory*.

It was still early, and Lottie was curled up asleep with Caroline's dog at the foot of the bed. None of them was keen on a walk in the rain. A quick dash to the village for the papers and then a day spent slouching on the sofa reading. He looked forward to it. The garden could wait. He expected a call from Freya to say the party was off but by three o'clock the rain had stopped, the wind dropped, and the sun made a weak appearance. The image of a quiet afternoon on the sofa in a nice warm house receded. Oh well, there'd be plenty of other wet Sundays over the coming winter.

. . .

They arrived at Murriemuir at the same time as Molly, Nigel and an overexcited Ryan, who was wrapped up in a fur hooded parka, a bobble hat and wellies that looked like frogs. Nigel was wearing a similar outfit but without the frog wellies.

'This looks a lot better than the last time I was here,' said Caroline.

It did look pretty. Arkash had lit small oil lamps on each grave and Lyra was mustering a group of children, handing out posies of flowers, each one labelled with the name of one of the animals. *Bossy like her grandmother*, Ian thought uncharitably, but then she surprised him by taking Ryan by the hand and leading him to where a line of children waited, each one holding a bunch of flowers and a drawing of an animal. Lyra had organised this and had sent Molly a message asking if Ryan could draw a cat. Perhaps Ian had misjudged his niece.

Ryan proudly held up his picture for her to see. 'That's really good, Ryan,' she said, passing him a small bunch of dahlias and pointing to one of the stones, which was inscribed with the outline of a cat and the name *Archie*. 'Arkash will read out the names of all the animals and wish them well in their new lives. When he reads out Archie's name you put your flowers and your drawing down next to the stone and read out your poem. Do you understand?' Ryan nodded and smiled at her.

Stewart arrived with a tray of drinks. 'The children are having a fruit Halloween drink that Freya's mum used to make. I thought the adults could do with something a bit more warming.' He held out the tray and Ian and Caroline took a glass each.

Caroline took a cautious sip. 'It's delicious,' she said. 'But I'd better not have too much. I'm driving.'

She was right, Ian thought, taking a swig from his own glass. This had quite a kick. He was lucky to have Caroline to drive him home. He noticed she had slipped her drink back onto the tray and had helped herself to a glass of the children's drink.

Ian had never imagined his brother as a mixer of cocktails. He'd assumed he was more of a whisky man. 'It is good,' he said as he took another sip. 'Your own recipe?'

'Something I used to knock up for the lads at the end of a stint on the rigs. There's a lot of rum in it,' he added, taking a hearty gulp and looking at the group of children. 'You both ready for the celebration?' he asked. 'Arkash has put himself in charge, thank God. I don't think I'd be able to take it seriously.'

'The lights are lovely,' said Caroline.

'Diwali lamps. Borrowed from his family, who don't use them in the restaurant any more because of health and safety. They have a battery-powered version now. He's also planned a surprise finale.'

Ian looked around at the adults in the gathering. There were not very many. As Freya had said, there were no residential guests this weekend. There were a few regulars from classes; women with ponytails, bright coloured puffa jackets and children with names like Fergus and Anoushka. Guy was standing by the bonfire with his wife and son, Alistair. A boy of about thirteen who needed the services of a good orthodontist and who trotted after an oblivious Lyra like a cringing puppy dog waiting to be kicked out of the way. Guy had built the bonfire and had been put in charge of the fireworks, which were housed in what looked like milk crates in a double-fenced pen that he'd built. 'Exactly fifteen metres square,' he told Ian. 'As specified in the local bye-laws.'

There were bye-laws about letting off fireworks? Ian hadn't known that. But then it was something he had never done, and it was reassuring to know that Guy had the children's safety in mind. He just hoped none of them were the adventurous type. Guy's fence wasn't strong enough to withstand a determined child. Even an undetermined one would be able to shuffle its way in with very little effort.

Ian shone his torch at the fireworks that had names – *pyro-spectacular*, one was called, and *rainbow of thrills* was another. 'So you light one crate at a time?' Ian asked Guy.

'They're called cakes,' said Guy. 'They are programmed to go off in sequence. There's just one fuse, which starts a four-and-a-half-minute display. 'Stewart and I bought them on the internet. They were couriered up from Queensferry yesterday.'

Ian wondered if they'd been sitting out here in the rain since they'd arrived. If so, the display could become something of... well, a damp squib.

'We covered them with a tarpaulin,' said Guy, who must have been reading his thoughts.

Caroline was helping Freya hand out sausage rolls. Ian took one and wandered over to where Sonia was standing on her own, looking, Ian thought, bad-tempered.

Is she who she says she is? he suddenly wondered. Sonia was quiet and serious, intense, Ian thought. Not someone it was easy to strike up a casual conversation with and certainly not someone you could suddenly accuse of being a different person altogether. He found it hard to imagine reiki sessions. Did they involve chatting to clients the way hairdressers did? Or was it carried out in contemplative silence? She also ran mindfulness and meditation sessions, which he assumed involved a deal of silence, so perhaps reiki was the same.

'I'm Ian,' he said, holding out his hand, but then, remembering that no one shook hands any more, pushing it into his pocket. 'Stewart's brother.'

She nodded at him, keeping her gloved hands clenched.

She was well wrapped up in a dark coat, scarf, black wellington boots and an incongruous knitted hat with a cat's ears, nose and whiskers.

'You're not drinking,' said Ian. 'Would you like me to get you one?'

She shook her head.

'Something to eat? The sausage rolls are delicious.'

She didn't answer. She removed one of her gloves, pulled her phone out of her pocket and stared at it like someone trying to decide whether or not to make a difficult call.

He was relieved when Caroline ran up to him and grabbed his hand. 'Come and watch the children,' she said. 'They're so sweet.'

'Are you coming?' he asked Sonia in a last desperate attempt to draw her into the festivities. She shook her head and went on staring at her phone.

Arkash clapped his hands to get their attention. This was his moment to take centre stage. He was wearing the jewelled turban that Ian recognised from his website, but rather than the magician's cloak he'd gone for a thick black jumper and jeans. He had mustered the children into a group, and they trailed along behind him as he approached the graves. At each grave he said a few words about the animal that was buried there. He couldn't possibly know anything about them, but he had made up a little story for each one, which he read out and then stood back as the chosen child read a short poem and laid their flowers and pictures by each stone. Last in the line was Ryan. Arkash stood next to him and put a hand on his shoulder. 'Finally,' he said. 'We come to Archie. We can imagine him as an expert mouser. Perhaps in the kitchen where he kept them away from all the bags of rice and flour. And when his day's work was done, he liked nothing better than to curl up in front of a fire with a saucer of cream.'

Ryan stepped forward with his offering and lisped his way through a poem he'd written himself with help, Ian suspected, from Nigel. It was called *Good Cat Archie*. It rhymed badly and didn't scan. But it was mercifully short. Nigel looked on proudly and Molly took a photo of him on her phone. This was the cue for Lyra to reach for her guitar and sing. She started with *Old Dog Tray* and moved on to *Memory*. When she'd finished, she put her guitar down to a round of polite applause and stood to take a bow. Arkash took out his phone and pressed a button and at that moment they heard a cry from the trees. 'Mama.' Arkash looked startled and pressed some more buttons on his phone. Then they heard it again, louder this time. 'Mama, Mama.' It was a ghostly, unsettling voice.

'No,' said Arkash, staring in disbelief at his phone. 'That's not right.' He stared up at the trees as the voice continued.

'What's he playing at?' Stewart hissed. 'He told us it would be a light show.'

At that moment Arkash must have pressed the correct button and looked with relief at the fence behind the animal graves as it lit up and revealed a line of cats and dogs in pastel colours prancing around like circus animals.

But the voice continued its cry. 'Mama, Mama.'

Suddenly there was a scream. Sonia flung her phone into the bushes, screamed again and ran towards the house with her hands over her ears as the cries of 'Mama, Mama,' continued.

Arkash, to everyone's surprise, leapt towards one of the trees and started climbing into its branches. He reappeared a moment later and jumped down to the ground with a flurry of leaves and twigs and clutching an iPod and a small speaker, which he laid on the grass in front of them. He clicked a button and the cries stopped. 'Must have been a crossed channel,' he said. 'Somehow it connected to my phone and turned the sound on.' He looked at the surprised faces. 'This was nothing to do with me,' he said. 'The light show was mine, not the voice.'

'So,' said Stewart, stepping forward. 'You're saying this was a trick someone planned?'

'Must be,' said Arkash. 'I promise I had nothing to do with it. Why would I want to scare the children?'

The children, Ian noticed, looked anything but scared. Ryan in particular was running round in circles in excitement. Suddenly he stopped running, stared across the garden towards the house and grabbed Molly's sleeve. 'Look, Mummy,' he said. 'There's someone on the roof.'

They all turned to look. Freya was the first to act. She grabbed Guy's arm. 'Get the fireworks started,' she said. 'Stewart, Ian, do something, call the police, whatever...'

Caroline rounded up the children, bribed them with Arkash's plate of sweets and herded them towards the far end of the garden where they could watch the fireworks safely. Guy was having trouble lighting the fuse. 'Won't be a minute,' he muttered, manically striking matches and muttering under his breath.

'Bring your guitar,' Caroline said to Lyra. 'Let's have some loud singing.'

Thank God for trained teachers, Ian thought as she and Lyra launched into *Ten Green Bottles*. The loudest voice, Ian noted, was Nigel's robust baritone.

Ian called for police and an ambulance. 'We can't wait,' he said to Stewart. 'Can you see who it is up there?'

'It's too dark to see,' said Stewart, glancing around at the remaining adults to check who was missing. 'I think it's Sonia.'

'How do I get up there?' Ian asked.

'Up to the attic. There's a staircase at the end of the corridor that leads to a door onto the roof. You can lose your sense of direction a bit but if you turn left out of the door and work your way around the chimney stack, you'll be on a flat roof that leads to a parapet overlooking the garden. I should go myself,' he said, 'or at least come with you.'

'You're better off staying down here,' said Ian. 'Two of us might alarm her.'

'So let me go on my own.'

'I did some training for situations like this,' said Ian, hoping he'd remember the details of the week-long course he'd been to twenty years ago on getting people out of difficult situations. 'The police and ambulance are on the way. I warned them about what had happened, but you need to explain the layout. They'll know to keep evidence of their presence down to the minimum, but they'll be concerned about the children in the garden. You can explain what happened and where everyone is now. They'll be calling round for psychiatric advice and my guess is that they'll keep a low profile until they've found someone to deal with it.'

Stewart nodded. 'Ian,' he said. 'Be careful.'

'I'll just keep her talking,' he promised. 'I'm not planning any heroics.'

He turned towards the empty house, climbed the stairs and made his way towards the roof. The door was open, and he turned on the flashlight on his phone to help him get his bearings. Stewart had been right. He had lost his sense of direction. He turned off the light and put his phone into his pocket, leaving both hands free to feel his way around. He groped his way to the chimney stack and ventured out onto the flat part of the roof. It wasn't quite dark yet and lights from the ground floor windows gave enough of a glow for him to see where he was going. As his eyes adjusted to the gloom, he could see that the walkway he was standing on led straight ahead to where Sonia was sitting on a low parapet. She was facing towards the garden with her legs hanging over the edge.

'Sonia,' he said softly.

She turned to face him. 'Go away,' she said.

He ignored her and perched on the parapet next to her. 'Just tell me why you are here?'

'I wanted to be near my daughter, but she's gone. They took her away and now I don't know where she is.' She took her hat off and threw it over the edge of the roof. They both watched as it fluttered down to the ground. They gazed at the pink shape lying on the stone path below them. 'Stupid hat,' she said. 'I never liked it. One of my patients gave it to me.'

'Your patients must really appreciate what you do for them.'

'Well, I'm not doing it any more.' She shuffled forward and Ian was afraid she was going to push herself over the edge. But she wasn't. She had been sitting on the edge of her scarf. She pulled it free and tossed it down to join the hat. 'Too hot,' she said, turning to face him again.

Below them in the garden the fireworks started, shooting bursts of colour into the sky, exploding as stars fizzed upwards.

'She wouldn't have liked that,' said Sonia. 'She was frightened of loud noises.'

For a second, he caught the glint of light at her neck reflected in the colours from the fireworks. The heavy necklace with the lion's head. He'd been right. Sonia and Sarah Jane were the same person. It was all falling into place, hiding first from her employer and her family, building a new life as someone else. 'Tell me about your daughter,' he said. 'You're Clover's mother, aren't you, Sonia? Or should I call you Sarah Jane?'

'I left Sarah Jane behind years ago. She was a stupid woman.'

'Tell me why you left home.'

'I made a mistake at work and my boss wanted... well, he said he'd go to the police and say I'd stolen some money if I didn't... do what he wanted.'

'That's when you came here?'

'I was going to Leven. A friend told me there was work there.'

'As an undertaker?'

She shook her head. 'As a stone carver. That's what I was doing in Dundee, but the place in Leven was making house signs and garden sculptures.'

Of course, she was a stone carver. She had made the gravestones in the garden.

'But I didn't get as far as Leven. I got off at Murriemuir. I'd eaten a pasty at the bus station in Dundee and it was making me feel sick. I thought I would walk for a bit, get some fresh air and pick up a later bus.'

'You carved the stones for the animals? The ones we moved?'

'Clover loved the animals. We always had dogs and cats when she was small.'

'She chose the pictures for the stones?'

Sonia nodded. 'She had a favourite story book. Charlie read it to her every night. Every night for years. There was a story about a poodle and some kittens. She... she never grew out of those stories. She wasn't like other children.'

She was getting ahead of herself. In a couple of sentences, she had gone from walking through the village feeling sick to living at Murriemuir, the mother of a little girl called Clover. Had she called at the house? he wondered. Attracted Charlie in a way none of the other girls had? Or had he realised she was not local and lured her in with an offer of a drink or somewhere to sit and wait for the next bus?

'He was standing at the end of the drive looking sad. He was the most handsome man I'd ever seen, but sort of... unreal, like he'd stepped out of a movie. And he looked untidy, his clothes were filthy, and his hair was too long. I asked if he wanted help. He told me he couldn't stand the house any longer and he was leaving. But he had nothing with him. He was confused and I don't think he even knew what day it was. I walked him back up the drive, thinking there would be someone in the house to help him. I thought he wasn't right in the head and there'd be a carer or someone. But there was only the gardener, Rod. Well, between us we got him into the house. Rod helped him clean up and I cooked him a meal. There wasn't much, but I found eggs and some potatoes and after he'd eaten, he didn't seem so bad. He was just lonely and worried about the state of things. Rod told me he'd sold off most of his land and was starting on the house – selling paintings and bits of furniture.'

'So you stayed to look after him?'

'I'd nowhere else to go. Even with a job in Leven I'd have had nowhere to live and there was still the worry of my ex-boss, that he might send the police after me. There was less chance of being found here than in Leven. Charlie said he'd no money to pay me, but I told him having a roof over my head was enough. I could move on when things had quietened down a bit and no one was looking for me. That was in October. Clover was born nine months later.'

'Did he force you to have sex with him?'

She looked horrified. 'No, not at all. I wanted it as much as he did.'

'You were never seen in the village. Did he keep you here against your will?'

She considered that for a moment. 'Not really. I was fond of him, maybe in love with him. I could have left at any time but where would I have gone? I had no money and nowhere else to go. And I had to think of Clover. She wasn't... normal. She was better off here with her animals and the garden. Charlie loved her. I think she was the only thing he really cared about.'

'Wouldn't it have been better for Clover if you'd left? The two of you would have been looked after. You could have got treatment for her.'

'Charlie said they would take her away if anyone knew about her.'

'Why would they do that?'

'Because she wasn't right in the head. He said it was something in the family. His sister had been taken away when she was little. He went to visit her once a year at Christmas and she didn't even know who he was. A horrible, gloomy, cold place, he said. He didn't want that to happen to Clover so he said no one must ever know about her.'

'But Rod knew.'

'Charlie said we could trust him. He'd known Rod since he was a child. He came over a couple of times a week. He brought us food sometimes and medicine for Clover.'

'Chinese medicine?' Ian recalled Elizabeth and her list of remedies.

'Sometimes, but mostly things for her cough and something to help her sleep.'

Was that how she'd died? he wondered. An overdose of sleeping pills. 'Sonia,' he asked gently. 'Did Charlie kill Clover?'

'Of course not.' She was almost shouting at him. 'Charlie loved Clover. He would never have hurt her.' She gazed down at the garden below and Ian was convinced for a moment that she was about to jump. 'No,' she said, the tears pouring down her face. 'I killed Clover.'

Ian let her sob for several minutes. 'Tell me what happened.'

He reached for her hand and Sonia clutched it. He eased himself off the wall and squatted uncomfortably on the ground. He was still able to keep hold of her hand, but there was less danger of her taking him with her if she decided to jump.

'She was always getting chest infections, but this was worse than she'd had before. She couldn't sleep. None of us had slept for days with her coughing and crying. That night I took her into bed with me. She was more comfortable if I held her against me and it stopped her crying. Charlie fell asleep and after a while so did I. When I woke up Clover was dead in my arms. I must have fallen against her and suffocated her. We buried her in the garden where the animals were. Next to the dogs and cats she loved to play with. I thought she would be happy there with them.'

'And you told nobody?'

'Rod knew. He helped me dig the grave and watched while I

carved her stone. Then Charlie threw me out. He was so angry. He blamed me for Clover dying. And he was right.'

Ian tightened his grip on her hand. 'It was an accident,' he said. 'You can't blame yourself.'

'I'd broken his heart. I knew I had to leave.'

'You were frightened of Charlie?'

'I don't think he wanted to hurt me, not really, but he was so unpredictable. Even before Clover died. Rod said he'd look after him and that he'd be calmer if I left.'

'But you had nowhere to go.'

'Rod drove me to Dundee.'

'That's when you became Sonia Greenlow?'

She nodded. 'I promised I'd never tell anyone who I really was.'

Ian wasn't going to press her, but he suspected that was why she and Ming pretended not to know each other. During his PI training Ian had learnt a lot about identity theft. Stealing the details of dead children was not uncommon and Ming might well have known how to set her up with a new identity. He'd have learnt about Sonia and Clover from Elizabeth. Presumably it was his remedies that Rod had been sent to collect. Was that also what brought Ming to Murriemuir? To keep a protective eye on Sonia, or to make sure no one knew about her fake identity?

Ian's phone rang, the ringtone jarring noisily against the quiet of the night. It startled both of them and Sonia clung tightly to the edge of the parapet with Ian still holding her hand. He pulled the phone out of his pocket with his free hand and answered it.

'Ian.' It was a voice he didn't recognise. 'My name is Brendon. I'm a negotiator with Police Scotland. Are you able to tell me how things are up there? Are you both okay?'

'Put it on speaker,' Sonia hissed at him.

'We're both fine,' he said, tapping the speaker icon. 'Sonia has asked me to put you on speaker.' Brendon needed to know that she was able to overhear what they were saying.

'That's fine,' said Brendon. 'Sonia, I'd like us to talk, but first, do you need anything? Blankets, a hot drink?'

'No,' said Sonia. 'I'm tired. I've had enough. I just want it all to end.'

'Ian,' he said. 'How much battery do you have?'

Ian looked at his phone. 'It's about seventy percent.'

'That's good,' said Brendon. 'It gives us time to talk.'

'I don't want to talk.'

'What do you want, Sonia?' Brendon asked.

'I want my baby girl back. I want her to have a proper funeral.'

'If you come down, we can talk about that.'

Ian could hear whispered voices.

'Sonia,' said Brendon after a pause. 'Inspector Clyde is here with me. He's explained what happened. How they found your daughter's body.'

'Her name's Clover.'

'Yes, of course, I'm sorry.'

'They moved the animals, and Clover was taken away. She needs to be here. This is the only home she ever knew.'

'Sonia,' said Ian gently. 'Is that why you did what you did? The singing, the perfume, the baby crying?'

'I thought if they knew Clover's spirit was here, they'd bring her back. But this evening she called to me herself. She was crying for me.'

'You're saying that this evening's voice wasn't something you set up?' Was it someone playing a cruel trick on her? He couldn't believe anyone would be that heartless.

'I didn't want to frighten the children,' she said. 'I made the recording, and it was ready in the tree, but I saw all their little faces and I couldn't do it. Then I heard Clover really calling me and now I must join her.'

This probably wasn't the best time to tell her that it wasn't Clover calling her but some crossed channel technology on Arkash's phone.

'Sonia,' said Brendon. 'Don't do it like this. Come down and talk to us. Clover is safe in the mortuary. She's tucked up with her doll. If you come down, we can talk about where she can be buried.'

She let go of Ian's hand and climbed up onto the wall. 'Sonia,' said

Ian. 'You said you didn't want to upset the children. Look down there. Can you see them? They're having a great time.'

'Ian...' Brendon interrupted him, a warning note in his voice.

Ian ignored it. 'What do you think it will do to them if the one thing they remember about tonight is your crushed body lying on the stones down there?'

Had he gone too far? Sonia was teetering dangerously close to the edge. He climbed up onto the wall next to her and put an arm around her shoulder. 'It's time to go,' he said, climbing off the wall and leading her gently down with him just as four policemen charged through the door and pulled them apart, pushing both of them to the ground. Sonia was restrained and carried down to a waiting ambulance. Stewart ran to him and wrapped a blanket around his shoulders. He supported Ian as, his legs shaking, they made their way down the three flights of stairs to the kitchen.

'Where will they take her?' Ian asked as he sat in the kitchen, still wrapped in the blanket, his hands around a mug of hot chocolate. He was shivering. He didn't know why. It wasn't cold in there.

'It's the shock,' said Caroline, who sat next to him. She prised his hands from the mug and put it on the table in front of him. Then she rubbed his hands vigorously until the shivering stopped.

'I thought she was going to jump,' he said.

'We all did,' said Duncan.

'For a moment I thought I'd made it all worse and if she killed herself, it would be my fault.'

'Not quite straight out of the negotiator's manual,' said Brendon. 'But it was the right decision. I couldn't have done it any better. She's safe now.'

'What will happen to her?'

'She'll be detained under the Mental Health Act for assessment,' said Duncan. 'It's going to be a long process. We've no real idea what happened. Now we know who the child was, there can be an enquiry about her death. Any further action will depend on the result of that.'

Ian finished his hot chocolate and wandered out into the garden feeling very, very tired. It looked much the same as it had when they first saw Sonia on the roof. The children were running around laughing and shouting. He could see Molly and Arkash standing next to the bonfire warming their hands in the glow. Nigel had taken charge of the baked potatoes, wrapping them in foil, poking them into the fire to heat and after a few minutes dragging them out again. He cut each one open, added a knob of butter and left them to cool, calling the children over when they were ready to eat. He beckoned to Ian but he'd lost his appetite.

Ian looked around. 'Where's Lottie?' he asked suddenly.

'We left the dogs at home, remember?' said Caroline. 'We thought they'd be worried by the fireworks.'

'Oh yeah,' he said with a yawn. 'I'd forgotten.'

'I think it's time I got you home,' she said, taking his hand. 'It's been quite an evening.'

She wasn't wrong, he thought, wondering if Stewart might one day have a party that didn't end in drama.

26

It was a quiet day in the office. Molly was tidying up the case board. She'd taken down all the Murriemuir photos and spread them out in front of her before arranging them by date and folding them carefully into a cardboard box. 'What shall I do with these?' she asked, looking through the folders of notes Ian had made for Freya.

'We shouldn't keep those,' he said. 'It's confidential information about Freya's staff. We'd better keep Sonia's in case the police need it. Put the rest in a pile for the shredder.'

Molly stacked up three of the folders next to the shredder and opened Sonia's notes. 'I don't understand this,' she said, holding up the copy of Sonia's birth certificate. 'I can understand why she'd want to change her name, but how did she get a different birth certificate?'

Ian looked at it. He'd not seen the original, but Freya's photocopy looked genuine. He ran a quick check online. He was surprised how easy it was to get forged documents, from birth certificates to degrees. Surely that couldn't be legal? All one had to do was send them the relevant details and they would knock up a 'replacement' document rapidly from a vast selection of templates guaranteed to be indistinguishable from the original, and at a price. Did they check the details they were given? They must or the country would be overrun with entirely fictitious people. Which meant only one thing. Somewhere out there would be another Sonia Greenlow, who just happened to have the same birthday and parents. Identity theft. Happened all the time but that was more about fraud. Not just needing to be a different person. It would be a temporary theft, not something that lasted half a lifetime. He couldn't work out how Sarah Jane had done it, but he put the folder aside ready to pass on to Duncan. It was an official police enquiry now.

Molly put everything from the board into in a cardboard box and carried it through to what had been Ian's bedroom.

They had thrown around ideas about the best way to use this room now he had moved upstairs. Ian repeated his offer of a separate office for Molly, but she still didn't like the idea of working on her own and neither, when he thought about it, did Ian. He had offered it to her because he felt it was the right thing to do. She was such an asset that she deserved the status it would give her. But he wasn't sorry when she told him she'd rather they continued to work together in the same room.

'I don't want to be moved into a back office like a Dickensian clerk,' she told him.

She was right, of course. Although he was disappointed that his gesture had been misunderstood. He tried to apologise but she brushed it aside. 'I know you didn't mean it like that,' she said. 'But I like the view from my desk where it is now and it's much easier to mull over ideas if we're together.'

'What do you suggest we do with all the extra space?'

'We could move that lot in there,' she said, pointing to the untidy heap of cardboard boxes that lurked behind his desk in a dark corner of the room where they were easy to ignore.

'We don't really need to keep all that,' he said. 'It's stuff about old cases. Anything important is stored electronically. I might as well shred it all.'

'We should keep it,' she said. 'It's a mess but I can sort it. There'll be a record of everything you've done since you started. It'll be backup in case of computer failure, and we can make a book of interesting cases that prospective clients can browse through. And I can use some of it for case studies when I start my course.'

Ian had enrolled her on a course starting in Edinburgh in January and Molly was as excited as a student about to head off to university. 'We'd need some new boxes,' he said, eyeing the battered cardboard heaps on the floor.

'We can do better than that.' She clicked open a web page and turned the laptop round so that he could look at it.

IKEA Edinburgh.

He groaned. He'd heard of it. A nightmare of a place where you were herded round a series of tasteful rooms selling, he read, *a wide range of simple, well-designed and affordable home furnishings because enjoying a* Wonderful Everyday *starts with a better life at home.* His eyes landed on the phrase, *easy to assemble flat pack furniture with simple instructions.* 'I'm no good at assembling things,' he said.

She showed him a picture of some shelves – square cube shapes with coloured storage boxes. He had to admit they were an improvement on *his* boxes.

'They're really easy to put together,' said Molly. 'And if we get stuck we could get Dad to come and help.'

Yes, Nigel would be a dab hand with an Allen key. 'Well...'

'Come on,' said Molly. 'We can get it all in the back of your car. And we can get lunch there. We could go tomorrow. Leave after I've dropped Ryan at school and be back by early afternoon.'

'And you'll sort all the boxes?' The idea was beginning to appeal to him. Not the IKEA bit, but the thought of a well-ordered archive was an attractive one and keeping a book of cases was a good idea.

'I'll start now,' she said, picking up one of the boxes and carrying it through to the empty room.

She'd persuaded him. It was a good time for a sort out in the lull between cases. Next week they had a couple of surveillances, and some workplace checks to do. But right now, there was not a lot going on. He could also do with kitting out his new laundry room, which currently had only a washing machine and a hook for Lottie's muddy towels. He'd kill two birds with one stone and check out some Swedish laundry accessories. But before he started planning any more major expenditure, he thought he should check his bank balance. He signed in to his account. The payment to the builder had cleared but it left him with rather more money than he expected. Checking further down the statement he found a payment from the police for his Murriemuir research and when he clicked open the payslip they had emailed him, he discovered an extra 10% bonus had been added for 'taxable sundries'. He wasn't sure what the sundries were, but who was he to argue with the police finance department? There was also a payment from *Skair Wellness Centre*. He'd sent Freya an invoice for the background checks he had done but this was for rather more than that. They hadn't discussed a fee for investigating spooky manifestations, but they'd obviously checked out his hourly rate and made a generous assumption about the number of hours he and Molly had spent on it. An unexpected windfall was always welcome. He clicked open his payroll account and added a bonus to Molly's next pay cheque.

He was about to call out and ask her how she was getting on when his phone rang. Duncan's name flashed up on the screen and Ian clicked to take the call.

'Fully recovered from the party?' Duncan asked.

It had shaken Ian up more than he cared to admit. He hoped that his next case would, should anyone need rescuing, involve something at ground level. He'd been concerned about his fear of heights when he first joined the police, but it had never been a problem. He'd never had to deal with anything worse than a flight of stairs. There had been training sessions that involved dangling on ropes, but never any that were more than first floor window height. And yet two recent cases had involved the edge of a forty-foot cliff and the roof of a three-storey building. 'It shook me up a bit, but I'm fine now,' he told Duncan.

'That's good,' he said. 'You looked very pale when you came down from the roof. But I haven't called just to ask after your health. Are you busy this afternoon?'

'Not particularly. Molly and I are having a sort out.' Well, Molly was sorting out. He was sitting at his desk watching her. 'Why?'

'We've been summoned by Kezia,' he said. 'Meeting in her office in an hour.'

That was not good news. 'Oh, hell,' he said. 'What have we done now?'

'I don't think it's anything bad. She sounded quite friendly, just asked if we could drop in. She's got her promotion, by the way. I expect she wants to impress us with her new badges. I can pick you up in about fifteen minutes.'

'Okay, see you soon.'

He ended the call and went to see how Molly was getting on. She was sitting on the floor surrounded by photographs and pieces of paper with notes scribbled on them. Lottie was perched on a windowsill watching her. 'I've got to go and see Inspector Wallace,' he said. 'You okay doing this on your own this afternoon?'

'I've been doing it on my own all morning, so probably, yes.'

'Sorry,' he said. 'I've been checking the accounts. We can afford a slap-up lunch tomorrow.'

She laughed. 'I wasn't getting at you. I'm fine doing it on my own. Although I don't think IKEA goes in for slap-up food.'

'Is it okay if I leave Lottie with you? Kezia doesn't like her very much.'

'How can anyone not like Lottie?' she said, patting her on the head. 'We'll be fine, won't we, Lottie?'

~

'Not brought your dog today?' Kezia asked as she ushered them into her office. Her new office, Ian noticed. It had a bigger desk and a view of the river instead of the car park.

'I left her with my assistant,' he said.

'I hear congratulations are in order,' said Duncan.

'Thank you,' she said, pulling her shoulders back so that the light caught the new silver diamond on her shoulder badge. She now had three diamonds on each shoulder as opposed to Duncan's two. And she wasn't likely to let him forget it.

She's not taken long to settle into her new role, Ian thought. Although to be fair she was smiling at him. Perhaps promotion had softened her.

'I won't keep you long,' she said. 'I thought you were due an explanation. You brought me some useful information.'

'Glad to have helped,' said Ian.

'We knew most of it already,' she said, 'but it was helpful to have it confirmed by someone at ground level.'

Okay, Ian already knew that where Kezia was concerned, he was the lowest of the low.

'If only,' she continued, 'because it gave me the opportunity to ask you not to continue that particular area of enquiry.'

Ordered rather than asked, Ian thought. Under threats of dire consequences, he remembered. Probably best not to mention that, though. 'Is this about Sharon Lofts?'

'I'll explain it all in a minute, but first, Duncan, I must remind you that as a public official you are bound by the Official Secrets Act.'

Duncan nodded.

'And Ian, you will need to sign it.'

Yes, rub in the fact that I'm no longer a public official.

'I'm sure you understand,' she said, in a way he thought patronising. She slid a piece of paper across the desk to him. He signed it and passed it back to her. She glanced at it and sat it under a paperweight that looked as if it could cause severe injury to the majority of those taking part in a medium-sized riot. 'First you should know that we recently averted a serious terrorist attack at the COP conference.'

Well, that's good, Ian thought, but it was what she was there for, wasn't it?

'Yes, we have closed down a terrorist cell and made a number of arrests. One of our agents is someone you know, Ian.'

'Sharon Lofts?'

'Yes, she was trained by MI5 a number of years ago. She has been what I think the best spy novels call a sleeper. Her job at Murriemuir was carefully engineered by ourselves. It was a stroke of luck for us that the job came up there exactly when we needed to place her somewhere local.'

'Local?' Duncan asked, looking up at her in surprise. 'We have terrorist cells in Fife? Why was I not told?'

'As far as I know, you don't. When I said local, I meant Scotland. This group was targeting the COP conference.'

'Was my brother in danger?' Ian asked.

'No, not at all. The planned attack was during the first week, which was when most of the world leaders were there. However, your brother did have an unwitting part to play.'

'His stolen COP pass,' said Ian. He should have realised it was more than just someone wanting to gatecrash Stewart's symposium.

'That's correct. You need to have a word with your brother about his level of security. We assumed he'd make it much harder for us.'

'That's why he was told not to report it to the local police,' said Ian. 'So that DCI Wallace's buddies didn't get hassled by them.'

She smiled at him. 'You're catching on fast. As I said, Sharon was working for us under cover. She was infiltrating a group of far-right activists and with the particular brief to become friendly with one Sean Trotter.'

'Catfishing,' said Ian.

Wallace looked shocked. 'Not at all. A legitimate undercover operation.'

If you say so, he thought. 'But that Facebook photo I showed you was taken months ago.'

She gave him a withering glance. 'We like to plan ahead.'

'Okay, so Sharon chums up with this bloke, steals Stewart's pass and gives it to him. But it had been deactivated. He couldn't use it.'

'She didn't give it to Trotter right away. She handed it over to the COP team who were instructed to program it with an alarm. It would let him through the barrier but unknown to him he would be picked up by our people once he was inside.'

Wasn't that entrapment? Ian decided to keep quiet this time.

'Clever,' said Duncan. 'And because it was a genuine pass

belonging to someone he could check up on, he'd never suspect he was being monitored.'

'What was Trotter going to do once he was in?' asked Ian.

'It was his job to set off the explosives.'

'You mean there were explosives *inside* the conference centre?'

'There were, but they'd all been disabled. Trotter wasn't the only one using a stolen security pass. We'd set up a number of others in the same way.'

'But why didn't you just arrest them on their way in?'

'We needed to catch the ringleader. The kingpin, not just the pawns.'

'Wasn't that very dangerous?'

'It could have been a disaster and gone catastrophically wrong. But our security services are highly trained. I can't take any of the credit for it,' she said with what Ian thought was uncharacteristic modesty. 'MI5 work continuously on world conference security. They do know what they are doing.'

'They managed to divert an attack and disable all these explosives, and no one knew anything about it?'

'Absolutely. I told you they are highly trained experts.'

'And where is Sharon now?'

'I'd imagine she's in a safe house somewhere. She'll be debriefed and then prepared for her next mission, which is likely to be a few years down the line. I'm afraid your sister-in-law will shortly receive a very polite and apologetic email from Sharon with a number of plausible excuses about why Shining Lotus is no longer able to work for her.' She tapped the sheet of paper under the paperweight.

Ian understood the gesture and mimed zipping his mouth. 'You can trust me,' he said.

'I'm sure I can, since disclosing anything I've said today can result in a prison sentence.'

Yeah, right. She'd like nothing better than to see him banged up.

'Wasn't it an odd choice?' Duncan asked. 'Using someone who was better known as a supporter of environmental issues. Wouldn't a far-right group be suspicious?'

'You'd think so, wouldn't you?' said Kezia. 'But it does make sense. There's nothing that makes people with strong ideas happier than the thought that they've made a convert. And Sharon puts on a very good act as a ditsy one-time hairdresser and woolly liberal yoga teacher. You can imagine the self-congratulation going on in camp Trotter.'

'I don't understand why Elsa Curran and the B&B were used,' said Ian.

'That wasn't part of the original plan. We were set up to monitor the hotel Sharon and Trotter had booked into, but unfortunately it had to close because of a high number of covid cases among their staff. As you can imagine, finding another room in Glasgow at short notice was a nightmare. Luckily for us you had left a card in your wallet. A place run by a woman who might do you a favour and squeeze in a couple of extra guests.'

'So Sharon went trawling through my wallet on the off-chance she would find details of a nice little B&B that might just have a room free?' Ian didn't know a lot about spying but this seemed implausible.

'You underestimate Sharon. She knew you weren't just Stewart's brother and she also guessed that Molly had been sent into Murriemuir as a spy. She was afraid her cover might have been blown. She was going through your pockets looking for more information about you. She probably thought you were more of a threat to the operation than you really were.'

Was that reassuring? He didn't want to be threatening but this made him sound like a complete wimp. And surely a halfway decent spy would have the sense to put his jacket back where she'd found it. Did she assume he wouldn't have noticed?

'She found Elsa Curran's card,' Kezia continued, 'and called her to book a room.'

'But Elsa told her she didn't have one, so how did Sharon know about the cancellation?'

'Our operatives knew the delegation from the Galeda Islands was smaller than expected so an agent was sent in to put a little pressure on her.'

'The man in the suit.'

'That's right. Not the best move. If you and Elsa hadn't been so trusting it could have ruined the whole operation.'

Elsa, he agreed, was a trusting type who thought the best of everyone. Ian didn't think he was so easily taken in. He'd reported it to Kezia, hadn't he? And at that point he'd been told in no uncertain terms to keep out of it. And where did that leave him now? Elsa had unwittingly housed a dangerous terrorist. She could have been in a lot of danger herself and because of the piece of paper he'd just signed, he'd never be able to tell her the lucky escape she'd had. But perhaps that was for the best. He wouldn't want to frighten her to the extent that she might never take any more bookings. The last eighteen months had been difficult enough for anyone in the hospitality industry without adding to their problems by worrying them about dodgy clients.

Kezia stood up, which suggested they had taken too much of her time. 'It's all turned out very satisfactorily,' she said, ushering them to the door. Not a word about how they'd discovered the identity of the body in the garden or how they'd solved the puzzle of the supposed hauntings. But that was just humdrum local stuff. Kezia had moved on to greater things. Working with MI5, no less. And she already thought she was God's gift to policing. The only consolation was that in her new and exalted role she might now have less time to harass him and Duncan.

~

They climbed into Duncan's car and Ian handed him Sonia's folder. 'It might help you tie up some loose ends,' he said. 'Molly and I were puzzled by the birth certificate and how Sarah Jane was able to use Sonia Greenlow's.'

'It's something we're looking into. Sonia Greenlow died when she was eight months old. There are people on the dark web who sell details of long-dead children to fraudsters and illegal immigrants.'

'You think Sonia did that?'

'More likely someone did it for her, but she's playing up the mental confusion bit when we try to ask her about it.'

'You think she's acting?'

'I think she's being economical with the truth, but there's nothing we can do about it. Anyway,' he said, as they reached the outskirts of Dundee, 'who is Elsa?'

'A friend,' Ian said.

'Oh, yeah? You've kept very quiet about her. Is she a sweet old lady with grey hair who runs a nice little B&B in Glasgow?'

'Not exactly,' said Ian. 'It's in Bearsden.' And she was about thirty-five with spectacular red hair and a wicked sense of humour, but there was no way he was going to tell Duncan that. He'd pass it on to Jeanie and Ian would be quizzed about her for ever more.

'Does Caroline know her?' Duncan asked, obviously not ready to let it go.

'Quite possibly,' he said, knowing perfectly well that she didn't and guiltily wondering if perhaps she should. But what would he tell her? He had a friend called Elsa. Nothing more than that. Even if he did plan to take her out for a slap-up dinner some time soon. He knew a quirky little place up in the Trossacks run by a friend of Elsa's. A man who had helped him with a recent case. It would be perfect. And it would assuage his guilt at having placed her in a possibly dangerous situation. It was no more than that. Definitely.

27

It was a small gathering. Six of them standing around the freshly dug grave on a bright spring morning – just a hint of warmth in the air, a few daffodils coming into flower. Three weeks since the verdict that Clover's death had been accidental, and her body released for cremation.

Sonia was recovering well. After three months in hospital, she had been released on a community treatment order, a room found for her in a sheltered hostel. She had received a police caution for failure to register a birth and a death. The matter of the birth certificate was still part of an open enquiry. Sonia had co-operated with the police at every stage but had claimed loss of memory over the details of her new identity. She gave the name of the website she'd used to buy a new certificate and claimed she'd used the first name that came into her head, suggesting that she might have subconsciously remembered the details from funeral records at work. The police felt there was little to be gained by pursuing it with her. She'd not changed her name for any financial gain, only to prove she had a right to work. A right she had in any case, whatever she chose to call herself. Someone was running an identity theft racket, but it was unlikely that the perpetrator would be found by harassing an already mentally frail woman. Now Sonia was free to continue her life once more.

She stood at the graveside holding a posy of spring flowers, her care worker, Joanne, standing at her side. *A sensible-looking woman,* Ian thought. He and Freya had first met her when they visited Sonia, first in hospital and later in her bedsit in Dunfermline. Joanne and Sonia had driven there together for Clover's funeral in Murriemuir churchyard. Sonia had decided she wanted her daughter's ashes to be scattered over her father's grave. A request eventually granted after Stewart had taken the minister aside and persuaded him that it was his Christian duty to allow it regardless of the child's illegitimacy. Ian suspected this had also involved a significant contribution towards the church roof fund, and a stipulation, one that Sonia had been happy to agree to, that the name *Clover Buckland-Kerr* should be added to the gravestone.

Molly had taken the remains of Clover's doll to her friend Viv, who had replaced its body and hair and reclothed it in a white dress that Sonia had sketched for her, and which she said was similar to one Clover had worn.

The minister said a few words and Sonia tipped out the contents of the urn. Molly handed the doll to Sonia, who placed it along with her posy of flowers on Charles' grave.

As they left the churchyard Freya took Sonia's hand. 'You'll come back to the house for something to eat?' she asked.

Sonia shook her head. 'I'd rather not. I'd just like to remember Clover here, next to her father.'

'Of course,' said Freya.

They watched as Sonia climbed into Joanne's car and they drove away. Then they walked back to the house.

Arkash was waiting for them with bowls of soup. Well-planned comfort food, Ian thought and watched as Arkash put his arms round Molly and gently kissed her cheek. 'You're a bit short-staffed,' he said to Freya.

'We are,' Freya agreed. 'Losing both Sonia and Sharon at the same time was a blow. Sharon had to leave to care for a sick relative somewhere down south. It was all rather sudden.'

'We'd take Sonia back,' said Stewart. 'Once she's fully recovered. But I can understand why she doesn't want to be here.'

'Ming's going to carry on with his clinics here,' said Freya, 'but just once a month. And Arkash is staying.'

'Will you be looking for new staff?' Ian asked.

'In time,' said Stewart. 'We're going to cut down a bit until later in the summer. 'Freya's going to carry on with her yoga classes and we're starting some one-day events. A morning of yoga followed by a Punjabi cookery class.'

28

Ian eased himself into a chair and looked out of his bedroom window at a view he would never tire of. The same view that he had from the office downstairs but more so. Here he could see over the roofs of houses and down to the estuary. It was as if he had been tipped at an angle that had changed his perspective and flattened out the view in front of him.

It was a time of year he always liked. The clocks had just gone forward, and the extra hour of evening daylight was striking. Not so good in the morning, of course, but he was never much good at mornings anyway. From now until the autumn he would watch the sunset, the time varying by a few minutes every day until the clocks went back again and his working day would extend into a dark late afternoon. This was normally a time when he could relax and think calm, optimistic thoughts. Plan the next day perhaps, the next week or even the rest of his life. But this evening he felt uneasy. He'd been in Dundee all afternoon, returned home to cook a meal, walk Lottie and finally have a shower. All of which should have calmed the thoughts churning round in his brain. But it hadn't worked. The reason it hadn't worked was sitting on the windowsill in front of him. A small ceramic jar with a picture of a tiger and some Chinese script.

Zhang Ming had called him the day after Clover's funeral. 'Mr Skair,' he said. 'I thought we might arrange a time for your free consultation.'

'Sorry?'

'The offer I made you some weeks ago. To see perhaps if I might be able to ease the pain in your leg.'

Yes, of course. He remembered now. It was a kind offer but after all this time he doubted that there was much that could be done. 'It's really not so bad,' said Ian. 'It took a long time to heal but I'm not in much pain from it now. Most of the time it's fine.'

'But,' said Ming, clearly not willing to give up. 'My experience of injury tells me that it will still trouble you from time to time. When you are tired perhaps, or cold or when the weather is wet.'

'Well, yes...'

'Then why not take up my offer? I may have ways to help. And if I don't, it will be a free session. You have nothing to lose. Would tomorrow afternoon suit you? At around four o'clock?'

Why not? He had nothing much to do tomorrow and Ming was right. His leg did still trouble him occasionally.

He parked in the Overgate car park and strolled past the shops, paused to buy a cappuccino at Costa, which he carried outside and listened to a man with a straggly beard playing *Stranger on the Shore* on a dented saxophone. He searched through his pockets unsuccessfully for some small change. Who used cash these days? He hadn't been near a cash machine for two years. Not since it was suspected that covid could be carried on coins and bank notes. It didn't matter anyway, since the busker had nothing to collect money in. All he had was a scruffy card with a QR code. Ian scanned it with his phone and the man nodded at him without losing a beat of the song he was playing.

Ian crossed the road away from the glossy Overgate shops and down a narrow side street to Ming's consulting room. The window was covered with lists of the conditions Ming dealt with; depression, arthritis, high blood pressure, obesity, infertility... and peering through the window Ian could see shelves with jars of herbs and ointments. Could anyone treat so many different complaints? He looked again at the list on the window. There was no mention of painful legs. But he was here now. And as Ming had said, what harm could it do? He opened the door and went inside.

He was shown into a small room at the back of the shop, where Ming sat behind a mahogany desk, and Ian was offered a leather armchair.

'I'm pleased that you are here,' said Ming. 'There are things we need to discuss.'

The thought flashed into Ian's mind that Ming was about to offer him a new case. 'I thought you were going to help with my leg.'

'That too,' he said. 'In fact, I will begin with that. I shall ask you some questions that will help me decide on suitable treatment.'

Ian patiently answered questions about his diet, how often he was thirsty, whether he preferred to be hot or cold, how well he slept and the general state of his digestion. Nothing at all related to his injury, although he was occasionally kept awake by the throbbing in his leg and still, even after all these years, had nightmares.

Ming's next question had even less to do with the state of his health.

'The case of Clover's death. That is all finished?'

'Yes, the body was released after the inquest. We scattered Clover's ashes yesterday.'

'She was cremated?'

'It was what Sonia wanted.'

'Of course, it would have been what she wanted.'

Ian stared at him. What was he saying? 'I'm not sure what you are getting at.'

'You are forgetting that I knew Sonia when she was Sarah Jane Grant. I met her only twice, but she wrote to me often to ask for medication for the child. Medication that was collected from here by Mr McCulloch.'

What the hell was he trying to say? 'Yes. That all came out in the police enquiry. Sarah Jane had been too frightened to ask for help from a regular practitioner because the birth hadn't been registered. So she relied on McCulloch's help.'

'And Mr McCulloch died fifteen years ago.'

'That's correct.'

'And was therefore unable to confirm any of this. It was a sudden death?'

'Yes, so his nephew told me.'

'And do you know how he died?'

'I assume it was a heart attack.'

'You need to check the records more carefully, Mr Skair. He died in a road accident.'

'Very unfortunate,' said Ian. 'But people are killed on the roads. I don't see how it relates to Clover's case.'

'Do you not? An experienced driver who knows the area around Murriemuir well suddenly misses a bend and hits a tree. Think about it.'

What was he suggesting? That McCulloch had done it on purpose? Or that someone else had caused the accident. But how?

'And another thing for you to consider, Mr Skair. How does a man who has spent his life using a shotgun to keep down vermin on his farm suddenly manage to kill himself by accident?'

'You think Charles killed himself intentionally?' Guy had suggested the same thing.

'Not necessarily.'

'You think someone else shot him?'

'I'm merely saying that no one asked the question. And no one questioned Sarah Jane too closely about when exactly she left Murriemuir.'

'She told us that McCulloch had driven her to Dundee after Buckland-Kerr threw her out.'

Ming raised an eyebrow at him. '*She* told you that. And the only two people who could confirm her story were dead.'

'You think she was still at Murriemuir when they died?'

'I don't think anything, Mr Skair.'

'Then why am I here?'

'To seek treatment for your leg injury, and...'

'And?'

'And because if anything should happen to me you will know who to look for.'

'Why should anything happen to you?'

'Because I'm a link in the chain of Sonia's history. As are you. But I will leave you to think about that. We should attend to your leg.'

Ian left half an hour later with a jar of ointment and many questions spinning around in his head.

It was almost dark now. Across the water the lights of Dundee twinkled cheerfully like a Christmas display. Ian reached for the jar and massaged some of its contents into his leg. The ointment had a strong but not unpleasant smell; a mixture of mint and eucalyptus. After a few minutes it began to tingle pleasantly, dulling the ache that had started when he was walking back to the car park.

Would he sleep tonight? He probably wouldn't; not because of the pain but because what Ming had suggested left him feeling uneasy. Surely he was wrong. In his head he went over Sonia's account of events and back over what she'd told him on the roof. Was it all a sham, a clever performance? It had seemed genuine at the time. A woman unbalanced by heartbreak at the loss of her child. She had confessed to killing her daughter, after which everyone involved was at pains to reassure her that it had been an accident. But was it? Was it some twisted act to avenge something Charles had done to her? Or because he had loved Clover more than her? Was Clover even her daughter? Ming was right. She could have systematically destroyed any evidence. Had she killed McCulloch and Charlie and then left Murriemuir to create a new identity for herself? But why return? He'd read somewhere that murderers always returned to the scene of their crimes although he had nothing to back up that theory. Then he remembered his background searches on the four staff members. Arkash and Sharon had responded to adverts. Freya had contacted

Ming herself after reading about acupuncture and thinking it was a good fit for her wellness centre. Sonia had written to Freya offering her services after reading the piece in Scotland Today. A full page spread with photos of Murriemuir, including one of the area to be used for forest bathing. Sonia had needed to be there; to know what had been discovered, to cause a diversion and to cover her tracks. She had been very convincing. And now she had been exonerated, would soon be discharged as mentally fit and would no doubt move to somewhere very far away. But Ming was scared. Why? It came to him in a flash. Ming had helped refugees from Hong Kong to settle in Scotland. Had they all been legitimate refugees or had some of them needed new identities? Had he arranged Sonia's new identity and did he think she would give him away?

But there was no way she'd come back and risk all that she'd done to free herself.

Would she?

NEXT IN THE IAN SKAIR SERIES

Book four of the series is now available

The Diva of Dundas farm

Who would want to murder the leading lady?

After a few days at the Dundas Farm Opera Camp almost everyone hates Lucia Pedro Morales in her role as Carmen. She will be murdered on stage. Could she be in danger in real life as well?

Ian and Lottie need to find out before it's too late.

Download your copy here:

https://books2read.com/u/bMYMJA

ACKNOWLEDGMENTS

I would like to thank you so much for reading **Mystery at Murriemuir.** I do hope you enjoyed it.

If you have a few moments to spare a short review would be very much appreciated. Reviews really help me and will help other people who might consider reading my books.

I would also like to thank my editor, Sally Silvester-Wood at *Black Sheep Books*, my cover designer, Anthony O'Brien and all my fellow writers at *Quite Write* who have patiently listened to extracts and offered suggestions.

ABOUT HILARY PUGH

Hilary Pugh has that elusive story telling talent that draws you in and makes you feel you are in the room with her characters.
   Michelle Vernal

UK based author Hilary Pugh has spent her whole life reading and making up stories. She is currently writing a series of crime mysteries set in Scotland and featuring Private Investigator Ian Skair and his dog, Lottie.

Hilary has worked as a professional oboist and piano teacher and more recently as a creative writing tutor for the Workers Educational Association.
   She loves cats and makes excellent meringues.

Visit my website: www.hilarypugh.com

ALSO BY HILARY PUGH

You can also meet Ian Skair in:

Finding Lottie

https://books2read.com/u/4NwDoY

The Laird of Drumlychtoun

https://books2read.com/u/3yaeQp

Postcards from Jamie

https://books2read.com/u/mYGLwd

Bagatelle - The Accompanist - free download included when you join my mailing list. Click the link below:

https://storyoriginapp.com/giveaways/470fd116-75b6-11e9-a014-fb6e89c4fba0

Printed in Great Britain
by Amazon